IMAGININGS

25th Anniversary Collection

Julie E. Czerneda

Julie E. Czerneda

Ottawa, Canada

www.czerneda.com

Published by Julie E. Czerneda
Ottawa, Canada

www.czerneda.com

First Printing September 2022

ISBN: 978-0-9950401-2-0

Dedicated to my bigger than life brother

Stanley Ernest Starink.

Who imagined best of us all.

Acknowledgements

A Grateful Introduction and Author's Notes © 2022 Julie E. Czerneda.

"First Contact, Inc." © 1997 Julie E. Czerneda. First published in *First Contact*, edited by Martin H. Greenberg and Larry Segriff, DAW Books NY.

"'Ware the Sleeper" © 1998 Julie E. Czerneda. First published in *Battle Magic*, edited by Martin H. Greenberg and Larry Segriff, DAW Books NY.

"Dear John" © 1998 Julie E. Czerneda. First published in *Odyssey Magazine*, Issue #6, edited by Liz Halliday, UK.

"Prospect Park" © 1999 Julie E. Czerneda. First published in *Packing Fraction*, edited by Julie E. Czerneda, Trifolium Books Toronto.

"Left Foot on a Blind Man" © 2001 Julie E. Czerneda. First published in *Silicon Dreams*, edited by Martin H. Greenberg and Larry Segriff, DAW Books NY.

"Bubbles and Boxes" © 2003 Julie E. Czerneda. First published in *New Voices in Science Fiction* edited by Mike Resnick, DAW Books NY.

Contents

A Grateful Introduction

Twenty-five years as a published author of science fiction and fantasy. So many words—a goodly number prepositions and many invented. Printed and bound. Carried and sold. Millions of words.

Words shaping ideas. Ideas pulled from my imagination—what I affectionately call my hindbrain—and that's the struggle. The pulling and shape, not the imagination. My head's full of sparks and weird infobits and oooh, shiny what ifs. It's like dust motes in a sunbeam. I've dark notions and breathless wishes, odd naughty ponders and deep glowing obsessions. In sum, a vibrant ever-evolving mess of possibilities that makes me happy and has no reason whatsoever to be brought together into sensible storylines.

Other than you, dear reader. Thanks for that.

I mean it. I'm truly grateful for what you've made me do. Those motes of imagination matter only to me until they're caught by words. Words becoming yours only to morph again as your imagination adds its sparks and weird infobits and the ideas take off in directions that would never occur to me (not being you).

How fabulous is that?

As for the struggle I mentioned, to go from imagination to story. The billions of words tossed aside like so much dryer lint. The anxiety and doubt and occasional shrieks of joy—with tears if I've succeeded—that hasn't altered in a quarter century and I suspect never will?

Thanks, dear reader, for those as well. Your love of my stories has helped make me who and what I am. You and my wonderful editor and publisher, Sheila E. Gilbert of DAW Books, and everyone there who guided my words from glittery dust clouds to polished books.

My Mom would say it doesn't matter what you do, so long as you do your best. A valid point about enduring a boring summer job to be sure; a wonderful framework for being creative. Do your best. What comes of it doesn't matter as much as the effort and care put in. Learning to be better each time—or at least not make the same mistakes. (Sorry, Sheila!) Striving to master third person—and don't get me started on my decades working out semi-colons. (I used one here and now regard it with great trepidation.)

A big part, for me, of being a fiction writer was accepting the challenge to write what wasn't comfortable or easy. Every editor named in this book is responsible for making me sweat and suffer. For encouraging me to write what I hadn't known I could. Thank you, one and all.

Twenty-five years. I've an agent now, the esteemed Sara Megibow (KTLiterary), who encourages me, too. Thank her—this collection was Sara's idea. And Roger's, who went on to capture my hindbrain in his imaginative cover art. (I'd like to point out visual artists get away without words and how is that fair?) My thanks to Janet E. Chase for her thoughts on which stories to include and to Cyn Wise, who read the novella for me in first draft.

I'm grateful for every one of you, new readers and those with me all along. Since DAW Books has kept my novels in print, here are some of my harder-to-find stories. I'm proud of them all, if still somewhat bewildered they have become words and escaped me. I am delighted to hand them to you.

First Contact Inc.

~ 1997 ~

by Julie E. Czerneda

Author's Note: My first published fiction came about entirely by accident. I'd my first novel on submission to DAW Books, with Sheila E. Gilbert, and went with my family to the 1996 World Fantasy Convention, in Madison WI, to meet her in person. While that didn't happen, what did? My friend Josepha Sherman and I met (in a bar) with Martin H. Greenberg and Larry Segriff of Teknobooks to pitch an anthology. They liked our idea but had something similar in the works, First Contact. If I could write a short story for that in, say, three days, they'd take a look. So I did, writing it on our drive home, and to my astonishment Marty bought it. (A week later, Sheila bought my novel. Wow.) The anthology came out the summer before my book. During our vacation we came across a copy of First Contact in a bookstore in PEI and, yes, we danced for joy in the aisle.

F<u>irst Contact Custom Simulation PC 91- Base Borden © First Contact Inc. Licensed for military use only.</u>

Humanity's big moment. And a moment was how long it lasted.

They'd run. Lt. Courtland—the Ironman himself—had been the first to break, flinging from him the state-of-the art translator they'd brought to this meeting place with such care, his boots driving deep into the mud with each stride so that he lurched from side-to-side in an agonizing effort to put distance between himself and It.

Lt. Desroches had hesitated a second longer, staring into the writhing mass of filaments as if somehow this would help her find a point of correspondence, a suggestion of a face. Then she shuddered and whirled to follow Courtland.

Lt. Smith, the one who'd barely made the final cut for this mission, the one considered the weakest link, remained the longest. This had more to do with his complete conviction that his legs wouldn't obey him than any desire to stay within reach of that thing. His paralysis left him with the alien's first tentative reach in his direction.

ɞ

"So I tell the Colonel: You pick the partner; we just do the music."

Nance's pale eyes gleamed through her ragged fringe of bangs. "And what did he say to that?" Her fingers continued to search for a disk among the piles of post-it coated pages layered on her desk. The keyboard balanced on her lap shifted with every movement as though trying to save itself from falling to the floor and being lost among even more piles of journals and clippings. For a company listed among the top five software producers, the office of its CEO and resident genius looked a great deal more like a newsroom from the early fifties than the site of executive splendor.

Henry Fergus, graphics whiz and sales rep, when he wasn't fussing over hardware, dropped his voice into a fair imitation of Colonel Dunwithy's growl. "Your so-called 'music' sent three of my best officers into therapy! Why should I pay for that?"

"To which you said…"

Henry flopped into the swivel chair that doubled as a printer stand the odd time they needed hardcopy. "You know what I said." Two fingers tugged a folded check from his pocket. "You pay for it, because it worked."

Nance, Dr. Nancy Vzcinza to those who were not her friends, pushed her hair out of her eyes for a moment. "Henry. Driving people crazy is not what we do here."

"No?"

"No. They do that all by themselves." She found the disk she was after and dropped it into the drive, fingers now jabbing at keys. Henry glanced around in vain for the mouse. She'd lost it again, he bet, or was using it as a footpedal. "We just.." tap tap "…illustrate…" tap tap tap "…the circumstances." Tap.

He kicked off his shoes, thinking nostalgically of the days not long ago when he'd made all his sales calls in sandals. Even better, when most of his business contacts had been over the vidphone. He'd really loved putting on that shirt, tie, and jacket over his bike shorts. Pants and dress shoes. The cost of success.

"So what's up?"

She looked up from the screen as though startled to find him still there. Henry was used to that. He blanked out the world himself when there was a glitch to track down. "Last minute upgrade for the new theme park in Australia."

He whistled. "Way to make those bucks. We can retire soon." Which was a joke. Nance had no clearer concept of how much the company–and they–were worth these days than he did. There were people on the next floor who kept track; annoying people in suits who drove better cars than he did and who routinely forgot to tell new staff that he and Nance paid their salaries. That always messed up the lunch-hour softball games.

And retire? Just when they could at last actually own the best systems for themselves? Just when they could do what they loved doing all day long? Being paid for it was, was–

"Convenient."

"Pardon?"

Nance looked innocent. "Convenient that the park wants this particular upgrade. I've been wanting to play with it a bit more."

Henry winced. Nance's idea of playing usually involved roping him and anyone else still breathing into the VR chamber at ungodly hours. "What did you have in mind?" he sighed, slipping down into a more comfortable slouch–interested despite the likely unpleasant consequence to his own workload.

C3

<u>First Contact Custom Simulation DC 101-Smithers © First Contact Inc. Licensed for home experience only.</u>

Dark red blood settled into the star-shaped cracks in the windshield, forming a network of pleasing regularity. Mildred Smithers, grandmother of three and leading voice in the Real Goldies Choir, shut off the still-racing engine of her car with a satisfied nod. "Gotcha again, you bastard," she said primly, glancing around as if to reassure herself that this descent into rough language had been safely unnoticed. But she was alone, of course.

She pushed up her bifocals to better see the face of her watch. Not bad. Shaved at least a minute off her response time. Practice makes perfect, as she always reminded her good-for-nothing son-in-law. For a moment she considered the lifeless form draped over what was left of the hood of her car. Pity you couldn't buy the same experience a little closer to home, she thought. Then again, the whole point of the exercise was to be ready to act–something she knew full well her family would depend on her to do. "When you get here," she promised the tentacled being her driving skill had shattered into two equal halves, "Mildred Smithers will be ready."

☙

The next morning, Henry poked his head into Nance's office. Nothing appeared to have changed, unless you counted the accumulation of dead leaves under the plant cowering on the windowsill. "How's the Aussie upgrade?"

There was an incoherent grumble from behind the monitor. He used his knuckles to sound a drum roll on the door frame. "Made a coffee run."

Half a face showed, the one eye looking wistful. "Bagels?"

"With blueberry cream cheese."

The eye blinked slowly. "I hope Meaghan appreciates you."

Henry, unable to find a clear surface for his offering, chose the most stable pile of paper and set the tray down with care. "She appreciates me. It's the rest of my family that has doubts."

Nance popped the lid from one of the coffees, blew away the steam, and took a huge swallow, looking as though the caffeine was heading straight to her bloodstream. Henry was convinced her mouth had an asbestos lining. "So how's the sim?" he persisted. "Mustafa said you've been on it all night."

She gave him a condescending look over a mouthful of cheese-drifted bagel. "How would he know? Mustafa's idea of getting in early is anytime after the traffic's died down on the freeway." Another gulp of coffee. "It's weird."

His eyes went to the wall unit behind Nance's chair, loaded with dusty jars of pickled insects and mollusks, interspersed with museum-quality replica skulls of various mammals, and tied bundles of bird feet. Fortunately, the cleaning staff had insisted the eyeball collection go home, despite Nance's protests about the importance of biological reality to her simulations. "Weird how?"

Nance stood up, stretching with a twisting motion that made audible cracks. "They keep adding to the specs." She handed him a set of faxes clipped together with a clothespin Santa her niece had made last year. Nance kept everything.

"Bit late for this many changes. Park opens the day after tomorrow." Henry started leafing through the pages. Each contained one minor requested change. There must have been about twenty, sent at roughly equal intervals over the past day and night. "You've told them modifications on the fly like these are extra, I hope."

Head half inside a sweater, Nance muttered darkly, "I told them to stop it after the first two. I hate being interrupted. But they wouldn't." She pushed her head out and glared fiercely at Henry. "Not to mention that what they're asking for is silly."

"Silly." Henry looked more closely at the top page and read aloud, "The pupil of each eye must be an unreflective black, not luminous orange." The next page, "Four appendages in total, mobile at a sequence of six joints." He tried not to grin. "They are being quite specific. Someone's had a nightmare lately."

Nance dropped back into her seat. "I'll give them nightmares."

恃

<u>First Contact Custom Simulation PC 225-Fernandez ©</u>
<u>First Contact Inc. Licensed for home experience only.</u>

He wasn't sure what had disturbed his sleep. It was an older building; pipes and joists had a tendency to be musical in changing weather. But that wasn't it this time.

Juan sat up, trying to listen more carefully. There. A scraping sound. From outside. He yawned and lay back down. The old elm out front was wide enough to kiss the bricks with an east wind. He'd remind the super about having it trimmed at the next tenants' meeting.

Snick. Skitter, skitter.

That wasn't the tree! Juan had his feet on the cold floor this time, hand racing for the light by his bed. Sounded like a cockroach convention. He hit the switch and found himself facing what he'd never even dreamed of…

Equally startled, his visitor scampered from the now-open patio doors to the top of his bureau in a ripple of reflective scales.

For a seeming eternity, the only sound was a sigh of wind through the doors and Juan's heart hammering in his ears. Then the creature shivered, a motion that made the plates covering its gaunt body touch together with a faint bell-like tinkle. It had eyes, two large and one smaller, centered on a triangular head. Around its neck was a wreath made of autumn leaves.

Juan reached slowly for the phone at his bedside. When he brought it to his ear, there was a soft voice already speaking to him. The creature tilted its head and settled more comfortably on the bureau.

"Juan Fernandez," whispered the soft voice. "I have chosen you to contact first of all of your kind. Your music has touched even the stars. Play for me and let there be peace between us."

Numbly, his eyes never leaving his visitor, Juan put down the phone and reached for the saxophone on its stand beside his bed. He'd always known he'd make it big one day–not necessarily this big–but big.

♋

"What's the original design base?"

"Standard PC 30, peaceful contact following initial suspicion, overtones of economic congruence of mutual benefit. Nothing flashy." Nance sent the fifteenth paper airplane of the hour soaring overhead. "Not until they started this last minute nonsense."

Henry caught it before it hit his ear and unfolded the paper to read the request. "Strands of keratin 30 cm long to be attached behind each auditory organ?"

Nance raised her eyebrow. "We are definitely dealing with someone who knows their biology–if not how to stay within a budget. Hair, Henry. They want me to put hair on its head."

CB

First Contact Custom Simulation FC 1301-Grant, R. © First Contact Inc. Licensed for home experience only.

There was no place left to hide, Roger decided grimly, his bike sucking fumes as it coasted off the deserted highway. He could stand and fight here and now–or die without ever seeing the face of his enemy. Funny, he hadn't imagined death would come as a cliché.

Had it only been yesterday? The aliens had been so well prepared, their technology so superior. The only wonder was that crumbs of humanity like himself still existed on the planet. A crumb. What a joke on the world that he had lasted hours after the rest were obliterated.

There was a whistle in the distance, the sound piercing and ominous as though it could summon Hell's demons to chase him. And weren't they, despite their appearance of being only machines? He'd watched the trackers demolish a city block of apartments–an economical way of dealing with the vermin inside. He'd known better than to hide in the subways too, having witnessed yet another set of machines burrowing into the streets, somehow fully aware of every crack that still harbored humankind. Roger no longer remembered how he escaped. There were too many other images in the way.

Another whistle, this time an answer from the direction he'd vaguely hoped might be away from Them. Roger considered his surroundings: the once-blue sky smudged by the smoke from the city, the highway boiled away in places where cars had been targets, the landscape pitted and ruined overnight. He reached into the saddlebag of his bike and pulled out the gun he knew was there. Would he have the courage to end it for himself this time? Or would he have to wait for the mercy of the aliens to make it stop?

〇ß

"Good morning, fellow-geniuses!" The door flew open as if propelled by a hurricane. "Have you started celebrating without me?"

Mustafa, a man who rarely smiled before noon and then required an excuse to make the effort, was beaming from ear to ear. Henry and Nance traded knowing glances. "Cracked the blackjack table?" Nance asked.

"Much better," Mustafa announced. He pointed one pudgy finger at them and shook it. "You didn't check your mail again. When are you going–"

Henry cut short what promised to be the usual diatribe about corporate responsibilities and other nonsense that had invaded their lives since home simulation machines had become the rage– with First Contact Inc. already poised for success with its custom VR's. "Tell us what we need to know, oh keeper of the secret."

"Guess who's opening the Aussie theme park."

Nance scowled, which widened Mustafa's smile even farther. "Am I supposed to care?" she growled. "Some rock star or other."

Henry tsk-tsked. "You never think about sales. So who, Mustafa? Must be a good one to make you drool."

"The President."

Nance's head came around from its hiding place behind her monitor. Henry swallowed hard and managed what he hoped was a nonchalant, "Pardon?" that cracked part way through the middle. He tried again. "Which President?"

Mustafa positively glowed. "The President. You know. The first one to win a majority from every country."

"President Polemski. He's going to open the park."

"Gets better, compadres. The Pres is apparently a fan of your work, Nance. He's going to be the first person to try your latest and greatest First Contact sim."

Henry and Nance dived for the pile of pages in the wastebasket, Henry winning by an arms length. "No wonder you couldn't track down the source with the Aussies," he gasped, trying to smooth the abused paper into order. "These must be straight from his office."

"Whoa, there," Nance interjected uneasily. "That's a pretty big guess, Henry."

He shook his head, holding up the pages. "What time exactly did the President's office announce this?"

Mustafa looked from one to the other of his bosses, his satisfied look fading into puzzled concern as he saw the expressions on their faces. "At the 9 am press conference, yesterday. I e'd you guys when I found out. Why?"

Nance took the sheaf of faxes-turned-airplanes from Henry. She found the first one. It was dated yesterday, 9:30 am. Their eyes met. "I think I'd better input every one of these after all."

Henry nodded slowly. "And I think we'd better have a look before it goes out."

α

<u>First Contact Custom Simulation PC 30mod352a - Australia's Down Under Theme Park Corporation © First Contact Inc. Licensed for public on-location viewing only. Test run.</u>

Until today, he'd enjoyed flying; sympathetic but unable to understand why so many of his aides became white-knuckled with every air pocket. This flight was different. He wasn't sure whether his new-found anxiety stemmed from being the only living thing on board or his destination. Likely both. He turned from the window and switched on the recorded briefing from his aides for the third time. The familiar voices were reassuring, edged though they were with unfamiliar tension.

The arrangements had been made using numerical expressions that both sides understood. There was some negotiation required regarding the location of that critical first meeting. The home world was not as wet as that of the guest. And beauty was important. The meeting would be carried live on both planets. A good first impression would do wonders for the ultimate response from the public.

Yet, despite concern and some honest fear of the unknown, there was good will. There was a sense of inevitability too–that events would unfold regardless of the careful planning of governments. All that remained was the moment when strangers met.

He'd studied the pictures, but nothing truly prepared one for such an encounter. Aides had informed him of what they understood to be appropriate alien protocol. No weapons, at least none in sight, was a reassuring common factor. Gifts might be misconstrued at this earliest point; who knew what values they shared or didn't? What to wear–best to err on the side of formality; no one liked to be slighted. And much of what transpired was meant purely for the viewers. His people had definite expectations of him, if not of the one he met.

They'd chosen a beach on an isolated, uninhabited island, large enough for automated transports to land. He set the controls as the techs had instructed in order to set up the transmission and recording equipment. Each, visitor and host, had a designated half of the land mass for their preparations. The island was blessed with a central lagoon lovely by any standard. Its beach was the designated meeting site. It could be reached by either representative in a short walk.

He drew in a last deep breath of the salt-scented air, took one last look at the technology that was his only link to his own kind, and prepared to make history.

ের

"Stop." Henry hit the kill switch on the simulation and looked at Nance and Mustafa. "This is ordinary. It's dull. Some nice work on the scenery, but face it. First Contact Inc. makes its money on custom sims real enough to make you wet your drawers. Any one of our competitors could do better than this."

Nance stopped him just by raising her eyebrows. "We haven't reached the climax, Henry. And that's where most of the changes were made. Shall we?"

Henry muttered something to himself, but restarted the sim.

ের

<u>First Contact Custom Simulation PC 30mod352a - Australia's Down Under Theme Park Corporation © First Contact Inc. Licensed for public on-location viewing only. Test run.</u>

He drew in a last deep breath of the salt-scented air, took one last look at the technology that was his only link to his own kind, and prepared to make history.

The walk was too short. World leader or not, there was something inherently terrifying about this meeting, something that threatened his very grasp upon reality. Before panic could truly overwhelm his intentions, it was too late. There was the Other.

The Other was strangeness given life. The body shape was roughly cylindrical, with appendages located with reasonable symmetry. Clothing covered many of the important details, but he knew from his aides that the appendages had a remarkable range of movement. The body was topped by a short stalk that in turn supported a round cranial mass. Keratin strains attached behind each auditory organ tossed in the wind.

Some sort of exudate coated the rest of the cranial mass. It glistened in the warm sun and the Other used one appendage to spread the exudate over the keratin strains in what looked to be a reflex. Just in case, he mimicked the gesture as best he could. The openings on the front portion of the cranial mass changed position almost at once. Startled, he moved back a bit. The Other spread its appendages in what seemed a peaceful gesture.

His people were watching. He gathered himself, then moved forward slowly. The Other echoed his movement until they were close enough to touch. He held out his–

CB

"Stop!" This time it was Nance's decision.

"Holy Mother of Mainframes," Henry breathed, not surprised to feel himself shaking. "We just made contact with the President." The other two looked just as shocked, then Nance began to chuckle, a deep throaty sound so contagious Henry found himself laughing suddenly too.

"I don't see what's funny," Mustafa said, his complexion as pale as it could get.

Nance popped the sim's cartridge out of the player and held it up reverently. "Don't you get it? These last changes didn't come from the Australians."

"Of course not, they came from the President. But why would Polemski want to meet–himself?" The words came more and more slowly. Mustafa's eyes glazed over and he sat down on the floor. "Oh, my."

Henry nodded, not too sure on his feet either. He took the cartridge from Nance and stared at it. "Looks like we have a new customer for First Contact Inc."

Nance's expression was the same one she'd had when they'd delivered the quad photon storage system for her computer–a combination of worship and glee. "I'd better make sure this gets sent out immediately. The customer may want to run it a few times to get it right."

They all glanced up at the ceiling. "Shouldn't we tell someone?" Mustafa whispered.

Nance held out her hand and Henry dropped the cartridge into it. "Well, if you can think of someone who'd believe us, I'll give it a shot." She paused and swept her bangs out of her eyes. "You realize we're all out of a job in two days. First Contact Inc. will be definitely redundant once it really happens."

Henry thought happily of shorts and sandals. "I've been telling you we should be doing more historicals. And westerns. I've always wanted to do westerns."

"Westerns," Nance grumbled, leading the way out of the VR chamber. "Pirates, maybe."

As they went down the corridor, Mustafa's voice trailed behind. "What about the new guys? They already like our stuff."

'Ware the Sleeper

~ 1998 ~

by Julie E. Czerneda

Author's Note: This was my first fantasy anything and, as you'll find becomes a theme, it wasn't my idea. Marty Greenberg and I were at a DAW gathering when he asked if I'd write a story for his upcoming anthology Battle Magic. I said of course—at the time, I didn't realize I could say no, no, I don't know how, eek!—then wandered off in a worried daze. I loved reading fantasy but hadn't thought I'd ever write it. Didn't care for battles, also a hitch. Then, out of the blue, the first paragraph came to me. Bones and children. Sand and tides. The rest followed with truly stunning inevitability. If only every story almost wrote itself! The experience was so odd, it gave me no confidence at all about writing fantasy again.

There were bones where the children played: small, smooth pieces perfect for game markers on the black sand, and long shards Skalda remembered using for fence posts around imaginary horses. The tides washed them here, along with links from shattered chainmail and futile bits of armour.

She regarded them now as portents. *May my enemies' bones keep you company*, she wished them.

"You're certain about this, Dir Agnon," this from Rathe, the priest-warrior from the Hinter Islands. His fleet lay in safety in the cove whose calm waters defined the near edge of the children's playground. *Safety won too late*, Skalda thought sadly, looking out over the sun-sparkled water at those handful of ships, masts split by spells of lightening, crews decimated by sendings of thirst and wasting disease.

They'd come here to huddle behind the great, untested fleet of the Circle Cove, to be nurse-maided and told it wasn't their fault, that nothing anyone could do would succeed against the Enemy. *Which might well be true.*

"Certain? When are any of us certain these days, Dir Rathe?" Agnon offered in his soft, careful voice. As priest-advisor to the secular rulers of the Cove and the outlying island clusters, he was magnificently non-committal at any given time. A virtue in times of slow, peaceful prosperity; a dangerous paralysis in this time of utter peril. Skalda stared out to the narrow mist-filled opening that led to the open ocean until her eyes ached from the water's glare.

"Dir Skalda sounded quite sure of this course in our Council. And why else are we here today, with them?" Rathe pointed a bone-thin finger at the brightly clad group near their feet. The ten children, daughters and sons collected from each of the Noble Houses, were equally oblivious to the presence of adults or to portents of doom, half-arguing and half-laughing in dispute of a shell. Their shrill voices rose into the still morning air like the piping of shorebirds.

"I am sure we have no other options left to us, comrades," Skalda answered. "Let us choose and speedily. No amount of magic will delay the tides for your debates. We've little margin as it is to allow the *Mariner's Pride* safe passage over Blood Reef."

She looked back at the children playing amid the bones of their elders' hopeless war and prepared to make her own selection. When Rathe would have simply picked the two nearest to be done with it, Skalda touched the heavy fabric of his sleeve and shook her head. His eyes were as haunted as she knew hers would appear.

The parchments, fragile with age and imperfectly translated, were clear on this point of the Summoning Spell at least. The payment for their salvation would be the blood of six innocents. That the blood should be royal and willing, not stolen from the arms of common folk, had been Skalda's decision.

⚃

Shafts of sunlight disappeared, reappeared; they filled at times with motes of life, golden suspended dust, then at others reflected silver as the great flocks swam through their columns, dancing with the light.

I was content thus, to gaze upward through the lens of my eye into the living magic of my world, my place, and see only that which belonged here. I felt the surge of waves over the crust of my side, reading there the approach of storms, the tug of moon and sun–events distant yet intimate. I slept, as some life reckoned this state of consciousness. It was as true a description as any; since I needed nothing and need do nothing.

If this is sleep, I sometimes wondered, struck by some particular beauty above me or caught by starlight through a rare clarity of ocean, *perhaps I dream the world.*

⚃

Fortress and fantasy, Skalda thought as she took one lingering, hungry look at her home before climbing the ramp onto the

Mariner's Pride later that afternoon. The Circle Cove was a perfect shaping of black hard stone, the inward-facing surface of its mountainous sides etched by generations of artists into towers of breathtaking loveliness, decked with flower-laden balconies and terraces rich with green life; the outward sides carved by the ocean herself into equally fantastic shapes. The water within was the deepest, clearest blue, framed by beaches of soft black sand. Despite the grim reality of their Enemy's spread into almost all the territory once ruled from this place, the citizens continued their peacetime ways: floating scented candles on the calm waters each night and tossing flower petals from their balconies to grace the decks of the mighty ships each morning.

The *Mariner's Pride* had left her crew behind, a sullen group of Leeward Islanders distrustful of dry land and the mysterious ways of priests. Her Captain was the only non-priest to remain. Skalda noted without surprise how he stayed on deck, refusing to even step below into his cabin where the children, soothed by spells of sleep and forgetfulness, rested on the softest of mattresses.

For this voyage, priests crewed the *Pride*: novices and warrior, in rank from sedir to dir, selected from scanty enough ranks not for their knowledge of the sea–they all, even the sleeping children, had that–but for the accuracy of their magic. The battle magic they would attempt tomorrow was twofold, containing both summoning and aiming. There could be no margin for error, no chance to hesitate, fear failure, and stop. Skalda had not needed the ancient parchments' warnings or the worries of her fellow dir-priests to make that plain.

Besides, what good would a second try be? The massive fleet of the Enemy was moving inexorably closer. Why should it stop now, when nothing they had sent against it had made the slightest difference?

"We'll just make the tide, Dir Skalda, Dir Rathe," said the captain, Lienthe was his name, as he joined them at the rail. Overhead, the sails snapped as the breeze began, spelled by the sedir-priests below whose talents were sufficient for this (steady wind being the most useful magic to their sea-faring kind and thus the first essential learning). The tiny wind caught at the canvas edges then began to swell the sheets themselves.

Now that his ship was alive on the sea, her deck moving lightly under their feet, the man had shed his meek and haggard look, assuming a swagger to his walk Skalda believed quite unconscious and, from his reputation, deserved. "Wouldn't have wanted to wait any longer. This girl's not one to like her belly scraped on rock, no sir."

Rathe's nostrils flared and he looked down at the rotund little seaman as though trying to fathom why he, dir-priest and warrior, was being chatted with like some fisherfolk on his way to the rich hunting of the Banks offshore. Skalda leaned back against the railing, careless of her fine robes on the damp, cold wood, and almost smiled. Instead, she drew in a deep breath through her nostrils, relishing the salt and fish tang to the air, the tar-stink of fresh caulking. "We appreciate your holding at the dock for us, Captain," she said graciously. "And be sure we also value your fine ship."

Captain Lienthe's skin darkened even further under the bristles of his sparse beard. "'Course, 'course," he muttered. "Dir Skalda. I wasn't implying other, you know."

"Have you taken her after baskers in the southern sea, Captain?" she asked absently, looking to the passageway ahead, its gap wide enough to pass three of the Circle Cove fleet's largest galleys abreast. The opening was protected by twin towers manned ceaselessly by priest-warriors, dir and so capable of calling rock falls on intruders: a last resort, since catapults and burning oil were always aimed and ready. Despite the war with the Enemy, despite bones drifting in on tides she suspected the Enemy sent to appall them with its message that not even the blessed Depths were safe, none had ever assailed this port. *Some here*, thought Skalda, *slept well at nights*. She was not one of them.

As always, preparing to leave the Circle Cove and its protection, she felt both exhilaration and fear. On this journey, she suspected her exhilaration was simply that of freedom from the endless debates, the weeks of searching musty records for any hint of a weapon; her fear had a more rational source. Those protecting cliffs curled outward just enough to hide an ambush, should the Enemy's sea-skills be able to hold ships within the crashing surf beyond. For all their sakes, this ship must not be stopped.

The Captain's reply drew her back to the moment. "Baskers for sure, Dir Skalda, but the southern seas? Not damn likely, excuse me, even if the fish were willing to climb in the holds. The Enemy was scouting those parts long before their bows dipped into the Hinter Island Sound. Dir Rathe knows that."

"Dir Rathe knows it is time to go below and continue our preparations," that worthy snapped, walking away with one hand reluctantly clamped on the wet railing to counter the increasing plunging of the deck as the *Pride* entered the channel and rose cheerfully to meet the incoming swells.

"Dir Rathe," Skalda informed the offended captain in a low voice, "also knows this deck will surely be splashed as we pass between the Cove's arms."

Captain Lienthe's eyes met and held hers with unexpected directness. She realized Rathe's rudeness hadn't bothered him after all. He reached out as if to touch her arm. "Dir Skalda. I confess I'm not–comfortable –," words seemed to fail him, and his face paled suddenly, as if seeing a whirlpool ahead into which he was about to plunge. "Forgive my impertinence, Dir Skalda. But I worry about the children. The hazards of this journey. They looked so young when you brought them on board. And they sleep."

Skalda found she had no comfort to offer him. His eyes went dull as he looked into hers and understood. "Like that, is it," Lienthe said in a voice oddly free of bitterness. "As well they sleep, then. Would we all could."

α

Men rained down on me one day. I watched them come, limbs

given grace by the ocean, armour catching sun glints as it dragged the bodies to me. The great flocks, startled apart by the disruption, disappeared beyond my crust. Moments later, they coyly returned to start their feast. Blood clouded the water beyond my eye, but it was a temporary blindness. I'd seen all this before.

☙

They practiced below decks, rehearsing ritual none understood and, truth be told, none trusted. Skalda's urgings from the beginning had been to follow the Summoning Spell without modification, including use of the archaic language forms used in the parchments. Agnon, their best linguist, had coached them all in how to pronounce the words, since subtle changes had occurred since this Spell was last cast. If it ever had been. Rathe expressed all their doubts.

"The Summoning. It promises to bring the destruction of our foes, to guarantee utter and uncontestable victory. Explain to me then, if it worked before, how could our Enemy have rebuilt its fleets?" he objected one last time as they rested. Captain Lienthe had sent word down. They would reach the Blood Reef at sunset, coinciding with the highest tide of the season in this place: safety for his ship's keel but most importantly, the appointed hour for the Spell.

"There may have been another Enemy," Agnon answered, always the reasonable one. "It was certainly long ago."

Skalda sipped from the mug of mulled wine, thanking the sedir-priest who brought it warm to her hands. It was cold below deck, cold and redolent of the *Pride's* usual cargo. But the fisher had been the best choice available: speed and camouflage in one, her low profile on the water an aid to what they must do.

So there was no luxury in the *Pride*, beyond that given the sleeping children, and no food for any of them until the deed was done. She noticed the others drank cautiously as well, valuing the heat in their empty bellies but keeping their thoughts cool and directed. "If you have another plan for our salvation, Dir Rathe," she snapped, losing her patience, "we'd all be grateful. After all, you are the only one of us here to contest the Enemy's forces directly in battle. Perhaps you believe the Circle's Fleet can defeat them at sea?"

There were six of them around the crude table, all dir-priests: of the six, she, Rathe, and Agnon would bear the action of the Spell, casting it over the Blood Reef. There was a second for each of them, a source of strength if any faltered, replacement if any were killed. For herself, Dir Clefta, a grim, silent man from the Hinter Isles. His community had been the first to abandon their homes to the Enemy's newest offensive; he and three sedir-priests all that survived to protect their few ships as they fled to the Circle Cove. Dir Segon would stand at Rathe's back; she, though young, was already believed heir apparent to Skalda's own place in the council. *It was dangerous to risk her here*, Skalda thought with regret, but this throw of the dice risked far more than the life of her promising apprentice. Agnon would rely on the quiet good sense of his own brother, Dir Agnar–theirs being one of very few family pairings within the priesthood. It added a strength to their abilities beyond either alone.

Strength? Experience? We have those, Skalda said to herself, gazing at each in turn, collecting a somber reply of determined, if anxious looks. *Let's hope we also have the blessing of the Depths and Her Quiet God on this ancient magic as well.*

There had been soul-searching and argument far beyond Rathe's reasonable doubts. While magic had been the tool of priests since records were first kept, that tool had evolved with their society's growth and change. Today's magic was precise, well-schooled, applied by specialists. The older magic had been, as far as their researches could discover, larger in scope and far bloodier in cost.

Skalda had deliberately sought the fabled old magic, once reports were confirmed that the Enemy–no, she would not keep them faceless–the P'okukii were about to crush the Island states once and for all.

The P'okukii had been content to rule the vast interior of the
Western continent, trading for generations with the islandfolk for
the riches of the sea. They had little in common, relying on a
halting trade tongue and neither side interest in learning more
about the other. The first of many mistakes, Skalda and many
other Islanders realized too late. For while they knew the P'okukii
feared invasion from some mysterious eastward land–a fear the
more widely traveled islanders dismissed as superstition– they had
not appreciated the depth of that fear. After all, who would take
seriously a people who refused to step from the land.

Then, fifty years ago, a new soothsayer had appeared in the
desert, warning the P'okukii that the doom from the east was
coming. The tiny island states between, with their fierce
independence and strange ways, must be conquered and fortified
to defend the continent itself.

The inconceivable resources of the P'okukii were turned to
the ocean they feared. Ports were closed; shipbuilding went on at a
feverish pace. The amused Islanders simply took their trade
elsewhere, among themselves, blind to what was coming.

For during Skalda's childhood, the P'okukii flooded seaward,
melded into a vast fleet consisting of more and larger ships than all
of the islands together possessed. All that saved them was the
caution of an enemy new to the sea. The Enemy was fearful, their
sorcerers grappling with the unpredictability of land spells over
water, their commanders inexperienced. The Circle Isles defended
themselves in surprise, expecting offers of reconciliation,
resumptions of trade.

What they received was unending war. At first, it was an even
conflict, the sea-knowledge of the islanders and their priests more
than a match despite the superior numbers of their foe. Then,
slowly, island after island was conquered, their inhabitants forced
to flee or die. The Enemy, while never embracing the ocean,
learned her ways. Their sorcerers became deadly, gaining spells
stripped from the minds of dir-priests captured before they could
kill themselves. Somehow the battle magic of the islanders,
blessed by the Depths and her Quiet God, had proved even more

effective in the hands of pagans.

There were, Skalda sighed, never guarantees on what offended deity.

愈

"'Ware Ships!" The cries from the crow's nest pulled them all on deck, only those responsible for the wind filling the sails ignoring the distraction. Skalda whispered a seeing spell, hearing muttered echoes from either side and behind as the multitude of priests did the same. The captain steadied his telescope, not needing magic to see what was swarming over the horizon.

Rathe and other survivors hadn't exaggerated, Skalda thought with regret as her vision focussed on the wavy line of painted prows and tossing masts. It wasn't a fleet–it was as if an entire nation had armed and loaded itself on to the sea. *Why do they think us such a threat?* she wondered again. The very old tales held rumors of a decisive battle centuries ago, one in which the island states gained their freedom from the mainland. But battles, successful or otherwise, seemed unlikely to spawn such hate and fear as this. *Unless*, she thought uneasily, *it was how that battle was won.*

"Why are they here, Dir Skalda?" It was the captain pulling at her elbow urgently. "There is nothing in this direction worth attacking. Just the deserted Outer Islands and then the open ocean."

Segnon's clear, calm voice had the slightest shiver to it as she drew the conclusion they all feared. "The Blood Reef. They have learned about the Summoning Spell. They seek to stop us."

"Or to use it themselves," Skalda said flatly. "Or use it themselves." She deliberately turned her back on that threat and raised her voice so it soared over the murmurs and speculations filling the deck. "Raise all the sail the *Pride* carries. Dir-priests. Spells of protection, especially for the hull and the sedir-priests. We must not be hindered. We will not be stopped. For the Cove!"

"For the Cove!" they chanted back, eyes afire with purpose, gnarled hands rising in the air beside smooth young fists to accept her challenge.

< 3

The *Pride* drove her prow deep into the waves as speed became their best weapon. Skalda stayed well away from the railing now, knowing she had no right to risk herself so close to her duty. Wind whipped her hair free of its knot, lashing her cheeks.

"'Ware! The Blood Reef! 'Ware below!" came the cry heartbeats later. Priests scrambled to drop the *Pride's* sails. The Enemy fleet had already halved the distance between them; now its ships were close enough for shouts to carry, close enough for protection spells to be tested by the magic of sorcerers. So far, only those in the crow's nest had been harmed, caught in the boundary between forces, screaming as they were blinded. Another victory for their Enemy.

The *Pride* settled into position above the Blood Reef. There was a sudden hush, as all realized they would soon to be within the range of more mundane weaponry, against which they had no defense.

"Wake the children," Skalda said calmly.

A finger of darkness scratched the crystalline sky above me, a moving finger casting its shadow and more into my sight. Six forms detached from it, drifting down to me in synchrony and sacrifice. In their wake, I could hear the old words.

The Summoning.

The forms, small and devoid of armour, fell closer. The flocks converged, undeterred by blessing or purpose. Blood stained my vision and didn't diffuse into the ocean as it should. Instead, it flowed down to me, coated me, entered my mouth tasting of innocence shed for rage's sake.

At last!

If I had slept, this was the moment I awoke.

❧

"It's working!" shouted a voice, panic-fringed rather than triumphant. *Something was happening*, Skalda amended to herself, bracing as the deck of the *Pride* shifted under an ocean seeming to rise under their feet. A barrel came loose and rolled, making the sedir-priests jump to dodge it.

The water lifted impossibly beside them, with no wind, no swell to explain it. The Enemy fleet was caught as well, cries of alarm ringing over the strange silence of the sea. Only the noises of human and ship broke against it.

The *Pride* began to slip down the side of a watery mountain, the movement so delicate and deceptively slow the Captain let go his death's grip on the wheel and simply stared, open-mouthed at what was becoming plain.

For it wasn't a wave rising to loom beside them. It was the Blood Reef itself, its coral-crusted bulk shedding water in a fall miles long as it rose beyond the ocean's grip, the roar enough to drown out any screams. Fish died, caught by spurs and outcrops of stony growth, imprisoned helplessly in air. Other things were caught as well: bits of bone and flesh, swords and armour, a child's robe.

Skalda found it contradictory that she could hear the sounds of Dir Agnon losing his mulled wine beside her over the din of the waterfall.

She clung to the rail, more to hold what was human-scaled than because the ship was unsteady. The waterfall ended, replaced by a single loud whoof of air as whatever they had summoned expelled its first breath.

"What is it?" breathed Clefta, his hand still tight on her shoulder.

Skalda shook her head, then realized she did know just as what looked like a promontory to one end of the floating reef turned to regard her through a gleaming black and yellow eye easily as tall as the *Pride's* mast.

"It's the Quiet God himself," she whispered, "roused to war."

ℤ

Vision sharpened and added the plane of horizon, distracting with its promises of *far* and *new*. I sought the Summoners. *There.* There must be three.

ℤ

"There must be three," Skalda said, repeating from the parchment.

"Yes, yes. Three to Summon," Rathe added, moving to stand beside her and Agnon. His voice held the same mixture of pride and horror they likely all felt. It was one thing to pray daily and interpret blessings–quite another to wake a God and wait.

"Three to Aim," Skalda said in the same stunned whisper, tearing her eyes from that one great eye to seek out the scattered but formidable fleet of their Enemy. "But how? 'Each to become an Eye' the parchment said. What do we do?"

"Sweet Depths," breathed a voice behind her. She couldn't recognize it and didn't turn to see. Her question was answered as the huge, unbelievable head turned fully towards them. There were two more eyes, similar in size to the first, opening slowly as coral cracked away from their lids to splash in the water below.

"Quick!" Skalda ordered, her voice grown cold and calm. A shame her insides were the opposite, but that was a distant problem. "Run out the plank!"

"Remind me not to be near you when you are wrong," Rathe said, his eyes fever-bright. He undid the sword belted low around his hips and let it drop to the deck, an instinctive and accurate disarming, Skalda decided, following suit. Agnon had no weapon beyond his wit. He looked as though he'd prefer to pick up one of the deadly blades himself.

The Enemy fleet, perhaps reassured by what appeared to be merely a new island, had begun to reorganize. Catapults fired test shot, thumping into the ocean just distant from the *Pride*, cautiously not too close to the Quiet God. "Hurry," Skalda urged the others, moving first to the plank.

It was broad and dry, quite secure to walk along. As if fully aware of what was happening, the Quiet God slid closer, closer, until the end of the plank hung not over open water but grated delicately against a cheek of dying coral and sponge. Something held the *Pride* rock steady; looking down Skalda thought she could make out an immense ridge of coral disappearing under the keel.

Skalda concentrated on setting one sandaled foot ahead of the other, step, pause, step, the rhythm like that of a bride's procession. Ahead waited the soft darkness of an eye larger than herself, a darkness she knew was her future, one final payment for her people's rescue.

The end of the plank, and the world she knew. Skalda had traveled from her body in magical learnings, had swum beyond light's reach in the ocean, and known the dream plain. This great eye was another doorway, she told herself, dismissing the natural fears of her body. She stepped through its dark disc, into the warm, black core.

WELCOME, SUMMONER, throbbed reality.

☙

Expansion. I flowed around instincts and passions, explored terrors and lusts, searching for the common purpose of the Summons. There.

Destruction.

Was that all?

☙

Her hands and touch, her mouth and breath were no more; almost worse, her legs prickled as though asleep. Skalda gained then lost her sense of self repeatedly. Finally, she refused the effort and focussed on what was here—sight.

And such sight. As part of the Quiet God's eye she could see the regrouping of the Enemy fleet; at a thought that vision sharpened so she could see the foreign shape of their sails and swords, the exotic pallor of their skin. Otherwise, they were men and women like any others she had known. The realization was disquieting. Never had she considered them so.

If she relaxed her vision, glints appeared on the periphery of the immense lens: Rathe and Agnon, she knew without understanding how. She concentrated, trying to ignore fear and wonder—neither were helpful—and focussed on uttering a spell without a tongue.

The effort drained her but was not forbidden. A link was forged between the dir-priests, as well as their host.

Skalda... she felt her name, wrapped in vibrations that identified the source as Agnon. *What are we? Are we dead?*

We are the Aim, Rathe stated, less voice than a pressure on what once was skin.

YOU ARE THE AIM, agreed some vastness. I HAVE BEEN SUMMONED. WHERE MUST I GO?

The minds of the dir-priests focussed in an instant. There was no sense of motion, yet the Enemy fleet seemed to leap closer.

Skalda's view also included the *Pride* as a coral-crusted flipper tossed it aside, the long planks of her hull scattering over the water like so many sticks.

☙

I accepted their guidance, almost blind in this drier, brighter world. Their rage had a colour, hate another. Fear for self was there. As was regret. I'd felt all of this before.

They aimed me at frail craft filled with men and I obeyed, my passage sending more to the Depths, carried down by their armour, limbs given grace by the water, to enrich the great flocks below.

⚃

WHERE DO I GO? boomed that incessant voice, not impatient, Skalda could tell, but rather a plea like a plaintive cry from a child. She still shuddered over the ease with which the P'okukii fleet had been wiped from the ocean. Their magic, their weapons, and their numbers had availed them nothing.

Almost. There'd been one attempt at defense and one loss. A harpoon had penetrated one great eye. Agnon's presence was gone.

There'd been no pain along their link. Only a skewed view of the harpooner, lips drawn back in a rictus, his skin so white his face was already a skull, the desperate eyes black pits.

She could scarcely believe they'd won the battle. What she could believe was how many were now in the Depths. It was as if she'd had to look into each and every face as they died, share their fear and horror. None sought the sea willingly. Was it worse for the P'okukii to die here, away from their beloved earth?

No matter the cost. It was done and they had saved their people. But what now?

She had tried the Spell of Departing; they'd not been fools to summon unknown magic without being able to dispel it again. But Agnon wasn't there to support her. And Rathe had found a home for his hate.

WHERE DO I GO? wailed the God.

She couldn't keep out the punishing demand. Rathe's response was a matching crescendo of torment. *To their ports! Crush their homes as they crushed mine. Kill them all!*

No, Skalda objected, horrified. The Enemy is defeated. The Cove is safe.

SAFE?

Almost instantly, her memories of her home were exposed like shells on a beach, carved free from sand by the icy winds of winter. She could somehow see each one as it was torn from her: views of moon through the arched windows of her bedroom, tall to the child-she'd-been; breathless glimpses of the royal barges from a hiding place high on her Aunt's balcony; the cool, musty darkness of the underground passages interrupted only by spells of light; the prismed beauty of fireworks overhead as she swam in the warmth of the cove.

Then, as abruptly, nothing. Skalda wept without tears or eyes, feeling the loss of her home more intimately than the loss of her physical form, the longing to return so intense she knew with horror it wasn't hers alone. The Quiet God felt it too.

It was a feeling and intention Rathe didn't share. *To their ports,* he insisted, rage colouring his presence so Skalda felt she looked through heat shimmers as she watched the empty ocean ahead.

This, she realized suddenly, was why there had to be three to Summon and Aim. With just two of them left, there was no consensus, no clear voice to guide the God. She wondered how long it would take them to drive the God insane.

α

The pain was new, a novelty I would as soon excise from my body. All I could do was close the damaged eye. My flippers drove into the water on either side, there being no reason given to stop moving. My lips cracked open, shedding even more coral. Warm ocean flowed over them, healing, soothing, reminding me of greater things than now and here and me.

But the Summoning locked me to the surface where I could not seek them.

☙

Skalda...Skalda

Once, well, more than once, she'd dozed over the parchments; the stuffy room and hours of close reading making a poor combination. Each time, she woke not fully aware, her eyes glued shut until she rubbed them free of sleep, her mind slow to rouse from its subconscious exploration of the words of the Great Spell. This might be one of those times, she thought, on the edge of a dream.

Skalda.

Her name drew her back to reality, a reality encompassing the loss of friends, the agonizing defeat of an Enemy, and the sure knowledge of her own doom.

Rathe, she replied unwillingly, but aware that even his insanity was more human than anything else here.

He was in one of his calm states, almost reasonable, as if this was one of their innumerable practice sessions in the Council Chamber. *They foresaw this, you know*, he said to her. *The P'okukii foresaw it all.*

The soothsayer. Their fear of the east and superstition. Skalda would have wept if she could. Rathe was right. The Summoning Spell had been cast before–she knew it now. The Quiet God had risen at their whim and blood, destroying their Enemy so that the island states could grow and flourish. They had forgotten, attributing lifetimes of prosperity and peace to long ago human heroes and human magic. But the P'okukii, terrified of the sea, terrified of the east, had better memories.

In a sense it didn't matter, Skalda thought. Many things in the world moved in vast cycles, unnoticed until one's life was ground into insignificance by storms, famine, or drought. That they had had a part in this one was merely proof that the Depths showed her power however she choose.

We must end this, she urged Rathe, unsure how much he could understand.

We must kill them all, he replied, still soft, still reasonable.

CB

I burned. The sunlight lost its beauty without the lens of ocean. Fish, large and small, tossed themselves ahead of my wake without recognition. The Summoners fought constantly, their purposes bright and conflicting. When they dreamed, I had no peace, only longings for a place. The Cove.

CB

THE COVE. The darkness confused her only briefly as the longing woke her. Skalda focussed and saw stars spilled overhead. Stars she knew.

Rathe, she wailed. It's taken us home!

Kill them all, he sang softly. More gifts for the Gods.

KILL.

No! But her protest wasn't helping. She could sense confusion. Alone, she wasn't strong enough to overcome Rathe's madness.

There was another way.

CB

The entrance to the Cove was narrow. I struggled through the rocky barrier, heaving myself half out of the warm sea with reluctance, driven.

Look! Look there!

The Aiming was imperative. I turned my head upward in time for the mass of jagged stone to smash into the side of my head. Then I could no longer see the colour of rage. I could no longer see at all.

Except through one eye.

⚃

Without Rathe, the Spell of Departing would work, Skalda knew. Yet she hesitated. The Quiet God waited too, stopping up the channel into the Cove. The ships within looked like a school of tiny fish startled by a shark, scattering at random as galleys rowed, others with sails filling with bespelled wind.

The balconies? They were filled with people as well as flowers, equally beautiful and as still. They were waiting too.

WHERE DO I GO?

Where you will be safe, she thought, releasing all claim on that world outside. *Where* we *will be safe*.

⚃

Shafts of sunlight disappeared, reappeared; they filled at times with flower petals, twirling downward. At night, the stars were doubled by closer, smaller flames, floating above us to outlining the dark hulls of ships.

We were content thus, to gaze upward through the great lens of our eye into the living magic of this place and see that which belonged here. The great flocks came, seeking the richness of the new reef, dancing in the light. Others swam among them, taking as was their need, sometimes just to dance.

If this is sleep, we sometimes wondered, surprised by bursts of fireworks, or touched by the hands of children, *perhaps we dream the world*.

Dear John
~ 1998 ~
by Julie E. Czerneda

Author's Note: I wrote this during a panel that was, well, mind-numbing. Being in the front row, as is my habit, I couldn't sneak out without seeming rude. At least writing made it look as if I was taking notes—surely more polite than the yawns and fidgets of those around me. Pleased with my little creation I sent it off to a magazine. My very first such submission and they took it. Lesson learned. Write wherever you can. You just never know.

Dear John:
        <as the opening line to a letter destined for a being of indeterminate sex and nomenclature, it would likely tickle his sense of the ridiculous. Still one should follow customary form in these matters...>

Dear John:
        <definitely should scratch that, however traditional. Haven't covered formal or informal modes of address—stylized or otherwise. And what kind of name is "John" to identify a 3 metre animated piece of chitinous tupperware...>

I am writing this to say...
        <nix that line too. Who writes these days? By the time this vocalization makes it through the translator, it will consist of quantified photons and resonances with an occasional catchy rhythm...>

I've met someone else...
        <technically? Well, now's not the time for details...>

This someone can satisfy me in ways, frankly, you can't...
        <not being equipped by nature or imagination, dear...>

It's best that I leave...
        <we'll ignore the fact that you've already flown the coop. The saucer-like, quaint, crater your ship left in my yard will generate enough tourist dollars for my retirement, thank you very much...>

It's been fun...
        <except for the incident with my mother. You really never grasped our prohibition against consuming ancestors, did you?>

And while I wish we could have been together always...

<actually, while I can imagine a dimension in which you—or I—were less relatively ugly, in truth, we both know that's unlikely...>

We both realize forever can never be...

<though I do have concerns about those glowing pods in my cellar. They seem new, John. Have you left something behind?>

I will carry your memory in my heart always...

<right above the 16 stitches you gave me before we both realized that taking our relationship to the, ahem, next level, could be a fatal mistake at this—or any—time...>

So, I wish you the best in your future, John...

<a feeling not shared by the rest of the inhabitants of my planet, unfortunately, given the regrettable results following your experiments with those harmless-looking gnats.>

And hope you can find it in your heart to understand and forgive me...

<and if you ever show up here again, buster, have I got a bug-spray for you!>

Love,
Barbara

P.S. Just kidding about the pods. I can assure you they aren't yours...

<strike that. Not a nice thing to bring up—which could be truer than I'd like to think.>

Prospect Park

~ 1999 ~

by Julie E. Czerneda

Author's Note: "First Contact Inc." was my first published fiction, but this was my first not-a-school-assignment short story. I hadn't planned to ever write one. I detested precis writing in English class and assumed it'd feel much the same. Too short for any fun. But when our favourite convention at the time, Toronto Trek, held a writing contest in 1996, my brothers-in-love, also fans, challenged me to enter something.

They then went on to discuss wilderness camping and what they loved most about it.

Hah! I thought. I'd get even and write about that. Thus this story was born. It took second place, to my surprise, and we'd the pleasure of hearing Larry Stewart, artist and toastmaster (and since friend), read it aloud to an audience. Roll ahead to 1999. I needed a story to address technology and societal consequence for my science fiction in the classroom project: No Limits: Developing Scientific Literacy Using Science Fiction from Trifolium Books, with its companion anthology, Packing Fraction and Other Tales of Science and Imagination. I already had Larry Stewart for the artwork (for which he won an Aurora Award), along with famous authors (including Robert J. Sawyer, whose story also won), but no more budget. Aha! I pulled out this story, checked it with my publisher, and it did the job nicely.

"I couldn't reach you at all today, Peter," Lydia's voice was almost as aggrieved as her expression.

"Web was stacked," Peter mumbled around his mouthful of, what was it?, veal. His wife's programming left a bit too much to the machinery. He tried to be first in the kitchen, but the day had gone from bad to worse. "I was connected to one supplier after another."

"You need one of those new multi-call 'plants, Peter. I've told you before. It's not good to be out of touch with your family."

Peter opened his mouth to object, but Lydia's righteously upraised forefinger interrupted him. She was connecting to someone on the web. Peter eyed his wife of twenty years with the unworthy thought that nothing could be less appealing than a woman deep in mental conversation, eyes fixed on some distant point, chewing overcooked veal.

"How did your game end, kitten?" he whispered to his daughter.

"Shh." Elizabeth, or Bet as she preferred lately, also had a finger up. From her frown, it was an incoming homework assignment. Damn teachers never paid attention to time zones anymore. When he'd been young–

When he'd been young, the implants were already as commonplace and necessary as telephones had been to his parents. Only today's etiquette in their use was missing, manners playing catch-up to technology as usual. Back then, callers could be shut down and ignored. Back then, a family dinner had consisted of those present to smell the food, not every and anyone on the web with a tidbit to share.

Oh, he wasn't a trender, one of those who complained that implanted communication technology was forcing humanity to become animated switching stations. Peter considered himself simply old-fashioned. So what if he switched his priority channel to something he could keep in the back of his mind during dinner, like foreign language opera or bowling replays.

Unfortunately, the new 'plants did away with priorities. All calls were received, and you only had to focus on one in order to interact, like a cocktail party in your head. In his head? Good enough reason not to upgrade, thank you very much.

Peter tried in vain to find some meat a fork could penetrate. "Enough of this," he said out loud and stood, prompting disgusted looks and emphatic fingers from his family members. He waved one hand in apology as he left, heading for his corner of the family room for a peaceful minute alone.

The chair wasn't much—its lumps were in all the wrong spots, a legacy from his mother's side of the family. Still, this was his favourite place in the entire apartment. Both walls were coated with real photographs, twenty-three in all, preserved in plastic. Peter knew each image as if his had been the eyes behind the lens, not his Uncle Thad's. "Prospect Park," Peter sighed to himself, touching the glittering water in the nearest photograph.

Peter reached under the chair and pulled out a thin, metal box, its dents bandaged with wildlife stickers. Peter glanced around to be sure he was alone in the room before hugging the box briefly to his breast.

Some nights, he didn't open the box. Some nights, he switched to the news or to chat mode with friends from work. Some nights, he didn't need to know what was inside.

Tonight, he did. Peter slid the elastic bands from each end, tucking them into his pocket. He had fresh ones ready, but these were still strong. He closed his eyes to savour the moment, only to realize his mistake and open them again to erase the vid image of Brazilian opera.

He was still alone. The lid came off with a slight resistance, as always. Peter rested his gaze on the three items inside, and smiled. A folded brochure, a small cylindrical tool, and an envelope, torn open at one end. Nothing of note, unless you looked closer. Peter took out the brochure.

"Prospect Park!" he read out loud, though he knew all the words by heart. "The Affordable Wilderness Experience!" The pictures echoed some on his walls. Not a person in sight. Guaranteed.

Peter carefully folded the brochure, replacing it in the box. His fingers wrapped around the tool. He examined its knives and files one by one, then pulled out the thin white toothpick and used it to pry a veal remnant from his teeth. "The only gadget Uncle Thad ever needed," he reminded himself smugly.

The useful tool went back into storage, and Peter reached for the envelope. He pulled free its contents, reliving the awe he'd felt the first time. "Paid in Full," he whispered, not needing to see the official script. "One Guaranteed Privacy Zone, Prospect Park, July 24-25, 2056." Only ten years to go.

There was another sheet with his receipt. Peter swallowed as he placed it on top and began to read. The page headed "Be prepared" in lurid red ink was the difference between ordinary camping and the real thing. He'd memorized its exhaustive list of recommended preparations and supplies.

Peter frowned and put the list back in the envelope. So far, all he had was his uncle's tool. There was no money to invest in camping supplies, especially when the trip was a decade away and other needs were closer. Just today, Elizabeth's baseball coach had been after him for tournament fees. And Lydia was doubtless planning to have the new 'plant installed, in herself if not them both.

Thank God, his trip was non-refundable and couldn't be sold

to anyone else. Otherwise, he might have been tempted himself, when things were tight. Peter hurriedly closed his box, replaced the elastics (adding two more in case) and tucked it under the chair again.

He leaned back, shifted his back into the most comfortable spot, and rested his eyes on the photograph placed just so. It was the one that had first called to him. Peter knew every leaf, every stick and mossy stone, every ripple in the dark water where it kissed the shore. That place would someday be his, alone.

☙

"Key!"

Peter jumped. He hurriedly grabbed for his stylus and pad, dropping both. From under his desk, he said, "Ready, Director Kychuk," before scrambling into his seat and trying to look composed.

Director Kychuk, reigning monarch of Main Street Candies and Sweets financial department, gazed down at Peter Key thoughtfully. "And what you are ready for, Mr. Key?"

"You're here to give me an assignment, sir?" Peter ventured.

The Director accepted the chair Bill wheeled in for him, then waved the secretary out. "Mr. Key," he said in a serious tone. "I'm here to give you something else."

Peter dropped his stylus and pad. "Oh God. I'm fired."

"Of course not!" Director Kychuk looked shocked. "Your work is exemplary, Peter. Most of it. In fact," the man leaned forward in his chair and winked conspiratorially. "You are in line for a promotion!"

"Me?" Peter realized this sounded less than confident and quickly added: "Thank you. Sir."

"And what I'm giving you is the first step–your authorization for a new 'plant. Latest Model. Expenses paid." Another wink. "This one's on us, Mr. Key. We need our top executives to be on-line, all the time!"

ℭ

At least he beat Lydia to the kitchen, Peter thought numbly, setting the dials for spaghetti, salad and, with sudden desperation, an order for wine.

"What's the occasion?" Lydia wrapped her arms around his waist from behind, digging her chin into that shoulder muscle that always tightened up at work. Peter relaxed against her warmth, but kept one eye on supper.

"Director Kychuk's talking about a promotion," he said, absently.

"Peter! That's perfect!" Lydia turned him around with unexpected force, her kiss prompt and enthusiastic. "It's about time they recognized all your work."

Peter decided it was time to ignore dinner. He wrapped his arms around his smiling wife, only to have her upraised finger and shrug come between them. "It's Mother," Lydia mouthed. "Later."

ℭ

Later was better. Bet was at one of her friends (not all social life could be relegated to webbing). For a wonder, Lydia even set her priority channel to his, something that happened rarely these years. Peter put his worries about the promotion and implant aside, and didn't bother opening his box.

ℭ

White noise. Peter struggled from a dream of blazing light and sound to find it was real. He groped for the control on his eyebrow to connect to the web.

"Peter Key. Peter Key. Peter–"

"Here!"

A burst of information followed: schedules, dates, arrangements. Peter slumped back into his pillow, waiting for the mess to sort itself into meaning. Some problem at work no doubt. But what idiot would use an override signal to reach him? Then some of the information began to organize itself into meaning. Peter sat upright, mouth dry. It was the Park!

ෆ

"When?"

Peter pushed the brochure into one coat pocket, checking that the knife tool was safe in another. "Transport is in ten minutes," he said over his shoulder, hurrying to the kitchen.

"They can't do that! You aren't ready." Lydia's panic-stricken voice followed him into the kitchen, like a faint channel on the web. Peter stuffed puddings into his pockets, then added anything else small and portable he could see in the cupboards.

"There's been a cancellation for this weekend," he explained again. "They go through the list until someone can take the trip." He took one look at her worried face and tried to contain his impatience to be gone. "I don't want to wait ten years, Lydia. And this chance might never come again."

"I hope it's worth all this, Peter. And I wish you'd told me," Lydia scolded, but her eyes were wet with tears. "Be careful, wild man," she said softly, doing up the buttons of his coat and finishing with a kiss.

ෆ

Seconds later, the transport alarm sounded. Peter rushed to the pad, then watched his apartment, his wife, his life, dissolve around him. It reformed into wilderness. He was in the Park!

The trees were much larger than he'd expected, larger and *moving*. "Of course they're moving," he told himself, "It's windy."

In fact, Peter realized almost instantly, it was more than windy. He'd materialized in the midst of a storm. He tilted his head back, letting the wild courses of rain enter his nostrils and mouth, tasting a metallic tang. Lightning flashed and he closed his eyes. There was only darkness behind his eyelids.

The brochure guaranteed privacy. I may not be connected to the web here, he thought, feeling the need to pose the idea cautiously in a mind so oddly quiet. No opera. No bowling scores. No work. No family.

"Yes!" he shouted, trying to outdo the thunder. Peter shook rain from his hair and laughed.

The next flash of lightning poured light through the forest. Peter quickly took his bearings. Through the trees he spotted the storm-tossed surface of a lake. Closer to hand was a post. "Zone marker," he announced, walking through puddles to put his hand on it. He closed his eyes and pressed his lips against the cold rough wood. No one could transport here until his weekend was over. He was alone!

Ɔʒ

"Well, Uncle Thad," Peter said, chewing on his toothpick, "I'm starting to believe you used a bit more than this on your wilderness travels."

The storm had passed like a magic trick, cued to wash the sky for a sunset glorious enough to bring tears to Peter's eyes. Now he stood in the last of the daylight, his toes dug into the sandy shore, lapped at by idle waves as if the lake were tasting him. Peter's stomach was full of pudding, and he had almost convinced himself to try drinking lake water. But first, he'd have to turn around and face what was coming.

"I'll gather some of the softer branches, make a bed, and sleep under the stars." The plan had sounded better an hour ago, before the darkness snuck under the trees. Peter sighed and turned. He put the tool back in his pocket; its biggest blade was no longer than his little finger and little help against the night.

The forest wasn't totally dark yet. Once his eyes adjusted, Peter could even make out the faint markings of a trail. Feeling on the threshold of adventure, Peter followed it, eyes sharp and ears ready to catch any sound.

The trail led to the privy, the only human artifact tolerated in the Park. Peter refused to be disappointed; he would have had to find it anyway. There were fines against fouling the Park.

Visit done, Peter prepared to follow the trail back. He shivered, realizing his damp clothes were not going to dry in the rapidly cooling night air, but he had no means to make fire. Hopefully tomorrow would be warmer.

A whine in his ear made him jump. Damn web was active again. So much for his guarantee. The whine stopped, started again in his other ear and suddenly multiplied. "Biters," Peter grinned, trying to catch a glimpse of his first wild animals. The little things flew too quickly for a look. Ah, there was one on his hand. Peter watched the mosquito prepare to bite with total fascination.

"Ow!" He slapped it without a thought, then cringed in case the Park authority would suddenly retaliate. Then he was being bitten too rapidly to bother wondering. Hands over most of his face, Peter hurried back down the path.

They were in his ears, his nostrils, nipping through his clothes. He panicked and ran, waving his arms over his head. Suddenly, the ground flipped up to meet him.

αβ

Peter woke up, unsure what had happened except that Lydia must have pushed him out of bed. He twisted and tried to push up. Sickening pain shot from his left leg to every part of his body. At the same instant, his hand, which should have been on carpet, slipped on a wet mass of leaves and he fell back down.

It hadn't been a nightmare. He was in the Park, alone, and

now he was hurt. Thank God the biters had had their fill of him—
unless the cold night air kept them away.

"Broken or sprained, Uncle Thad," Peter whispered, eyes
straining in the darkness. He groped for a stick that felt solid
enough for his weight, then struggled to rise. He almost fainted but
kept trying. The trail had vanished into shadow, but he could make
out a dim luminescence that might be the lake.

"I'm paying for this. I'm paying for this," Peter muttered to
himself over and over as he struggled over slick rocks. He'd
learned not to trust logs that felt solid—they usually collapsed when
he pushed his stick into them. "They probably lose half their
campers this way," he gasped, leaning against a cooperative tree,
no longer certain of his direction. "Where do they put the bodies,
Uncle Thad?" Peter shook his head. "No bodies. They transport
out as the next camper transports in. That's the deal."

The thought of Lydia's face if she found his dirt-covered
corpse in the kitchen was enough to get Peter moving. He sat on
the last big log and somehow pulled his injured leg over it.
Abruptly, he was out in the open again.

And the lake waited for him, a dish of black velvet reflecting
so many stars Peter could see by their light. A call came from the
distance, its throbbing loneliness carving into his soul before it
died away. Peter eased himself onto the sand, spellbound.

A line of pale grey rose up through the black sky. Peter
puzzled about it for a moment, then caught a whiff of wood
smoke. He had a neighbour. For a moment, pain and loneliness
made Peter determined to slip into the lake and swim in search of
help. Then he slumped back down. "Wouldn't be fair, Uncle
Thad," he whispered. "This kind of privacy is once in a lifetime."

慦

Morning brought the loon's cry again, along with drifts of fog
hanging just offshore. Peter lifted his face to the first warmth of
the sun and thought he might survive after all.

That day was the longest he remembered living. Peter did his best to wrap his leg with pieces cut from his shirt, but touching the bruised, swollen flesh made him nauseous. When his stomach settled, he finished the puddings and sucked on Kool-Aid powder, saving the barbecue sauce packs until he was truly desperate. Different, larger, biters appeared and Peter soon lost any sense of guilt in this kill or be bitten place. He was too hot, and knew he should get out of the sun, but his body remembered the cold night and wouldn't move.

"I'd like to call Lydia, Uncle Thad," Peter said, watching a black insect bury itself in the sand beside him. There were others, evenly spaced, apparently as suicidal. "I need to tell her something. But how?"

His implant was useless. Guaranteed privacy. Well, he'd paid for it. And now he understood why so much of the cost was insurance.

"A fire would help tonight, if this useless thing could start one." Peter took the knife and, suddenly furious, threw it into the lake. It cut its hole in the water and disappeared.

Three birds flew by and Peter watched them. "Three of anything means trouble, Uncle Thad. You told me that. Put out three, and someone will save me. Well, I paid for privacy–and that includes not being watched, or flown over, or checked on, or–"

Or being saved, Peter finished to himself, calm again. He looked around, feeling he recognized every leaf, every stick and mossy stone, every ripple in the dark water where it kissed the shore. Not a bad place to die.

As long as he could leave a message for Lydia.

g;

"And you found him here, Ms. Key, right on the transport pad?"

"Yes, Officer. I told you." Lydia could tell by the insurance officer's face that they both knew this was merely a formality. Of course the Park would cover poor Peter's medical expenses. Her husband hadn't regained consciousness yet, but all the specialists agreed he would be fine. His injuries were probably complicated by the shock of being alone. It hit some people that way. Lydia hadn't argued.

The officer had her sign forms, then left. Lydia went to Peter's favourite chair and sat down.

She reached underneath, and pulled out a thin metal box. Carefully, she hugged it to her breasts, then opened it.

The wet torn brochure smelled like pine. Lydia ignored it, and the envelope. Her hand went unerringly to the flat stone she'd found clutched in Peter's hand.

Scratched on it was her name.

Left Foot on a Blind Man

~ 2001 ~

by Julie E. Czerneda

Author's Note: Oh, I remember the start of this story. I was on a great panel at Worldcon 59, The Millennium Philcon, in 2001. The topic was artificial intelligence, the other panelists were huge experts in the field while I was there as a biologist who wrote SF. At first I was quite overwhelmed. Then the tone around me become all about how soon we'd see it, how to know we'd accomplished this marvel, and won't it be grand?

The hair rose on my neck. I swear I vibrated (hopefully discreetly) in my seat. What about morality? The consequences? Changes to society? Laws to protect flesh and machine? My passion helped me speak up and, to my surprise, my few polite contributions were received warmly by the audience. Looking back on it, I suspect they were vibrating with me.

When, shortly thereafter, I was invited to write a story for Silicon Dreams—about A.I. and robotics, I knew what I'd say. "Left Foot" won the 2001 Prix Aurora Award for Best Short Form English and, to my humble gratitude, been used in several college and university courses since. This is why I love writing science fiction. To go past to the how and why, to the challenge of what if...

For the record, I became self-aware as the left foot on a blind man.

I had a partner, the right foot. It didn't become self-aware. Stayed as dull as a shoe, if you get my meaning. Why? How should I know? You must understand–I was never meant to be a thinker.

Nope, I was to be a Father's Day gift to a weirdo–this blind old man who didn't want me in the first place. The technical folks suspect that's what started it all, but then, how should they know either? Nothing like this has happened before to an RRP–y'know, a Robotic Replacement Part.

What was the deal with my being a foot? You, and likely most people, are right to wonder why the old fool refused his kid's first thoughtful offer: new eyes. Money wasn't an object. Story goes, the old guy was an artist before age clouded his vision. Story goes, if you believe this, he claimed a deep mistrust of having his biological failures ripped out and replaced with something shiny and working–to the point of feeling as if he'd be looking out someone else's eyes, so: no, thank you.

As if that wasn't nonsense. Sure, robotic replacements were smart and getting smarter with each new trick the techs dumped in, but that was so RRPs could keep up with the jobs done by the living version. It took serious processing power to adjust internal temperature against ambient and control wacky things like biochemistry–especially with the inconvenience of hormones and who knew what a person might choose to toss into his or her body without consulting the RRP maintenance manuals first.

But think? Be someone? That was paranoia.

Oh. Well, there is me. I. Myself. But I started out as the left foot on a blind man, and you have to realize my existence combined a few elements that were never expected to be together.

You see, there was the vision issue. The old man's kid wanted his Dad to be able to walk around safely, have a good time, all that stuff. His Old Man? Well, beyond a grudging admission he'd like to be free of his smart-cane–something I can relate to, since there's nothing less appealing than a stick with a bossy attitude–and a confession at a weak moment he'd like to take up dancing with a certain neighbor lady, there wasn't a lot of concern there. The man had come to grips with himself; whatever dim light filtered through his milky eyes satisfied him more or less completely.

Ah, not good enough. Junior was totally for RRPs, having the latest model knees and, rumor had it, a socially-interesting bit of enhanced equipment between them. So he dove into his fantasy of Improving Papa with the zeal of the convert.

Hence the feet. The old man had suffered flare-ups of gout and arthritis–nothing overly serious yet, but with enough pending nuisance value the family doctor was all for having some precautionary hardware in place down below. There was no chance of successful sales resistance once the two of them ganged up. It was "get the feet" or listen to stereo-nagging for the rest of his life. The old guy cracked in less than a week.

Feet require a fairly high level of processing to begin with, particularly with the idea of dancing looming ahead. Then, there's the entire business of returning circulation to the legs, body, and heart–not to mention the fiddly bits like feeling sand between your toes and the odd maddening itch to reassure the owner there's really something between his ankles and the floor.

I'm told, if you can believe anything techs tell you, that the right foot went on as planned, a straightforward size 9 double D width with a second toe slightly longer than the first and a small corn on the outside edge. A good cosmetic job reduces the rejection rate substantially. They were about to install me–not that

I knew it at the time–when the son, just full of bright ideas, asked for an eye.

What eye? they asked back. No one was about to go against the father's wishes and do an unregistered replacement. That sort of thing cut short a career path, big time. Unless you're talking about one of those shady, basement clinics–but this was a class establishment. You know. The kind with coordinated carpeting and real prints on the walls even in the bathrooms.

An eye in the new left foot, the son replied as if seeing the light himself. Nothing fancy–it wouldn't be delivering a pseudo-retinal feed to the optic nerve or anything–but something to spot an onrushing car or keep his father's feet from stomping on a dance partner's non-mechanical toes.

The techs were intrigued as well as over-paid. Did I mention money was no object to this kindly lad? So they popped papa into cryo to wait and popped out the left foot processor to give it a little tweak.

Not that I knew it then, either.

Little tweak, my silicon. The processor now had to handle sensory input and make reflex decisions on the consequences of movement without bothering the cognition going on upstairs. In other words, the son was smart enough to know his Old Man would not be in favor of being bossed by his bunions.

So the left foot acquired some subtlety along with those annoying calluses on the heel.

All went famously, which may explain why I'm famous today, but I'm getting way ahead of myself. This is supposed to be one of those bio things, y'know; I'm allowed some creativity as long as I get the data loaded upstairs, but there's no sense pushing the techs to edit my life story.

Anyway, I'm installed into the robotic replacement left foot on a blind man, and he starts walking around the hospital recovery room as if he doesn't know where he's going. Understandable, you see, but tripping every reflex alarm built into me. First thing I know, I'm awake, aware, and trying not to dead-end my toes on a chair leg shaped like the prow of an icebreaker.

Was I to know twisting out of the way like that would break his ankle? It was instinct!

Fortunately, while the brand-new me struggled with questions of planes of existence, the future of the universe, and was there a silicon god, the techs replaced the old man's ankle joint for free and gave my processors an upgrade or two while they were inside. They even added the beginnings of an ingrown toenail. As I said: a class establishment.

By this point, I knew what I was, where I was, and very little else. I kinda lay low in the leading department after that first disaster, gathering information. It helped that the son had planned ahead, buying socks, shoes, and sandals for his Old Man that let the "eye" component of the foot collect input from a pretty fair radius. Good as it goes, but not having structures such as eyelids, which might stand out on a foot even to a blind man, I suffered alarmingly intimate sensations when the man took a bath or tucked me under the thick wool blanket he used for naps and at night. Still, overall, I thought we were coexisting rather well. I could modify his stride so he lurched sideways before stepping on those dainty female toes and had no compunction whatsoever about using a sudden severe cramp to stop him in his tracks before he stepped out into traffic.

I knew where and what I was; it didn't mean I enjoyed being the left foot on a blind man. He constantly threatened me with closing elevator doors, contact with furred animals that usually got out of our way in time, but not always, and, by the way, did I mention his habit of swinging me back and forth, back and forth, until I dissuaded him by applying a well-timed twinge in his arch on every upbeat?

Where was I? Oh yes, things should have remained unchanged but I'd overestimated the intelligence of my host. He'd never lost his suspicion of robotic replacement parts and, it turned out, kept careful track of everything I was doing that seemed unlikely in footware. The techs love those notes, by the way. Call them meticulous and classic. The old man kept notes on the right foot too, but they were understandably short and very boring. No, his attention was firmly on me and what he saw as my efforts to bend his will to mine.

Now, what 'will' the left foot on a blind man could be expected to have, other than hoping for a mercifully short stint in dirty socks, is beyond me, but he held to his convictions until the day his son threatened to have him sent for psychiatric assessment–the son having faced serious business reversals in the interim and no longer being in a "money's no object" position. In fact, he hadn't made the last payments on either foot, but didn't see that was his father's concern.

By way of answer, the old man went to pack and, instead, did his best to hack me off with a kitchen knife.

It really was for the best; we weren't getting along lately anyway. I wasn't paying attention after that point, having shut down at the sight of the knife heading my way, but found out later I'd been salvaged, the blind old man packed off to an institution, and the son, more or less willingly, had returned me to the RRP techs in lieu of his final payments.

The left foot wasn't in particularly useful shape, and had started as a custom job to boot. Few people were desperate enough to take a mismatch, let alone deal with two left feet. So it was discarded.

Fortunately, I wasn't around for that decision, either.

My processor, the most intrinsically valuable component of any RRP, came back on-line and I took a mere fraction of a second to realize where and what I was.

I was no longer the left foot on a blind man.

I was the right arm on a bricklayer.

They hadn't bothered removing the eyeware. Y'know what techs are like–they hate messing with what works, especially on jobs with small profit margins. It took a few seconds to recalibrate from the forward viewpoint of a foot to the been-there outlook of an elbow, but I was content. No more dirty socks or unhappy furred animals. And I'd been upgraded again. Vision wasn't my only sense.

This installation included magnetic resonance imaging, along with measuring and leveling instrumentation, and, naturally, the processing software to match. RRPs for bricklayers and surgeons had a lot in common. To top it off, I had a direct link to parts of his motor and sensory functions—one way at first, but I quickly fixed that by tapping into the autonomic feedback loops. The loops mimicked the biological hardware that let people yank their limbs away from danger. Pointless, really. I could sense danger and move the arm out of the way faster than any signal could travel to his central nervous system and back. No need to discuss the issue, if you get my drift. But the techs figured people weren't ready for that kind of reflex control from their RRPs. After my first aware experience, I had to concede the point.

Now, I was the right arm on a bricklayer. As you can imagine, this was quite an improvement over being the left foot on a blind man. For one thing, an arm does more interesting things than a foot. I didn't have control of the fingers, which was a shame—the bricklayer having opted for an interchangeable system, including a hand for troweling and another for sliding down silk. Quite the closetful, in fact. Hands, not silk. The silk was usually on a female who wasn't interested in dancing that I could tell. Oh yeah. The techs tell me you don't need those kinds of details. Privacy issues crop up, y'know. I mean, when you've been what I've been, and seen what I've seen, they definitely do—crop up, that is.

I thought things were going exceedingly well. Unlike the reluctant old man, the bricklayer relished the versatility and strength of his RRPs. Thanks to the precise information I fed his brain each time his hands passed over each row of bricks, his work was exceptionally precise and efficient. In fact, once I learned what he wanted, I began moving his arm a little more precisely and efficiently every day. Regrettably, there was a limit to how far I could improve his performance before other, biological, components began interfering. The human form wasn't the optimal bricklaying device. Much of the job should have been left to a proper robotic construct, especially mixing mortar. You disagree? Go ahead. I'm entitled to my own opinion–and I dare say it's a more informed one than yours. Ever spent ten minutes rotating to mix cement? Thought not. Flesh prejudice, that's what it is–

Sorry. The techs warned me not to get overly emotional. Just the facts, they said. Forget what I said about the flesh stuff, okay? I really don't need them messing with what's left, if you know what I mean.

Meanwhile, those additional systems they'd given me were coming in quite handy, not to mention I learned how to tap into his auditory input via the feedback loops I'd replaced. The bricklayer was quite the cultured human. He spent his off-time, when not with a lady, reading and listening to complex forms of music. His reading didn't do me any good–given my view was typically the back of a chair–but I did develop an appreciation for the blues. He took us on trips to art galleries and museums. His home was filled with wonderful works of art–reproductions, of course, but it didn't matter to either of us. The quality was there for the viewing.

I felt my horizons expanding every day.

You're wondering about the Robot Cognition Law, aren't you? The techs worried over that one a long time, but it's obvious. Really it is. See, that law keeps down the cog functions of robots, so they are reliably stupid except at what people want them to do. No machine shall be smarter than a peanut. But no one thought of me as a robot in the beginning or middle. I was just the left foot on a blind man. What did it matter how much cog function they gave me? In fact, there was almost this prejudice thing going on in reverse–I mean, nothing's too good to be attached to a human body, if you can afford it. We all know that. It's only the independent self-contained constructs that get limitations on their brains. Frankly, no one cared about the IQ of a toe or bicep.

Anyway, here I was, right arm on a bricklayer, when things turned a little unpleasant. I didn't have any warning, mind you; just the opposite, since all the signs were right for one of those silky evenings. The man substituted sticks of burning wax for real lights, so I adjusted my ocular, then he dithered for half an hour choosing which of his assortment of hands to attach to me. Okay, the delay was my fault. I mean, it was me he was plugging the thing into, and some of those hands–well, the techs don't want me going into those details either. Something about black-market toys. Their function wasn't the issue for me, you understand. I simply found the sense of touch rather overwhelming at the best of times, given I was equipped to make exceedingly precise measurements. These were too much of a good thing, if you know what I mean.

So I didn't exactly help the process, disrupting the connection each time I felt one of "those" hands being attached to my wrist. This apparently caused the bricklayer some frustration, because he began throwing the rejected hands against the wall with considerable force, despite their probable expense. Eventually, he calmed and offered me a perfectly good, minimally-sensitive hand. I let it snick neatly into place, quite glad he'd been sensible.

Now, given the time he'd wasted picking an appendage, and the impatient cooing noises coming from the next room, you'd think the guy would be in a hurry. But no. He stood holding his hand in front of his face as if trying to memorize the age spots they'd applied for him. I might have known his interest was something else entirely had I seen his expression, but as I said, I was the right arm of a bricklayer with an eye out his elbow. My viewpoint was hindsight at best.

Some other orientation would also have helped me prepare for what happened once we went into the room of the cooing female. But my first inkling of danger came when her hand and an ominously sharp needle entered my ocular field. Seems my bricklayer, being a sentimental fellow, was about to let his latest female friend tattoo her name into his skin. My skin, in fact. She might have thought him all brave and noble. I could have told her a few things–including that his human brain could easily disregard incoming pain signals from my surface and that he could even more easily have her name removed in the morning. Although with the hand he'd originally picked–whoops, the techs won't let me go there either.

Now, I had responsibilities, including keeping my skin intact. So do you wonder I reacted as I did when that alarming point came closer and closer? Luckily he'd switched from the hand he used to crush ice in the kitchen to one of the silk-sliding variety, or my panicked swing might have done more than produce a little reddening of her nose.

Unluckily, I'd again overestimated the intelligence of my host. The bricklayer, between profuse and largely unbelievable protestations of his innocence to his wailing lady, attempted to smash his right arm, me, into a wall. I refused to participate in anything so self-destructive and used my tap into his nervous system to shut him down.

Which, I realized much later, had the immediate and regrettable side effect of shutting me down as well. Told you I wasn't much of a thinker. I'd started out as the left foot on a blind man, after all. My time as the right arm on a bricklayer had enriched my data stores, not improved my intelligence.

Oh, I know what you're thinking. You find it pretty hard to believe that the techs would keep reinstalling what had to seem a defective piece of equipment. I don't see why. These aren't quality control guys, y'know. These are the guys that open fifteen cases of processors–who knows where they come from–and hope that at least five will test reliable and ready to install. Complex and fussy stuff, that's us. You don't toss what's working–not when the supply's low to start with. Besides, the techs tell me they'd had trouble with the bricklayer before–something about a lack of sweat glands to glisten over his RRP muscles–and weren't inclined to be sympathetic when the man blamed his assault charge on their equipment.

Still, by now there was a little note on my tracking sheet, a small flag attached to my serial number. Not suspicion, not yet. I believe some of the techs were hoping to have hatched a prodigy–an RRP capable of self-preservation.

They had that right. Believe me, when I woke up the next

time, I wasn't in a hurry to announce myself.

I wasn't the right arm on a bricklayer or the left foot on a blind man–no big surprise there.

It did take a moment for me to appreciate what I was, given the lack of any clues beyond a view framed by a pair of narrow, flaring tunnels.

I was the nose on a chef.

Okay, okay. You've read the report. So she wasn't a chef. So she flipped burgers. That's food prep, right? These days, that kind of thing's a pricey service, whether it's burgers or escargot. I mean, why would anyone prefer another organism to handle what they'd ingest? Ick. The food industry was the first place to switch almost totally to constructs. How much did it take to follow a recipe anyway? And constructs don't expect tips.

My new partner certainly did.

Well, pardon me. I'm not supposed to talk about economics, either? What you really mean is that anyone with silicon for brains can't discuss any form of human intercourse. Paranoid, flesh-obsessed...

Don't leave. I'm just kidding around. Humor, I'm allowed.

Where was I? Or rather, what was I? Nose on a cook. They'd again left what worked in peace, merely beefing up my processing power to handle the data stream from a mass of hypersensitive chemo sensors lining my nostrils, and adding connections to several portions of her brain and endocrine system.

Merely?

Someone hadn't been paying attention to my file, but you can be sure I wasn't about to argue. Here I was, keeping a pair of sunglasses from hitting this woman's lips, and feeling like a god.

I had access to her physical sensations, not that they were remotely interesting once the novelty wore off–which was sometime in the middle of our first shower together. I already knew I didn't care much for touch, but I'd grown quite fond of hearing. Unfortunately, she had abysmal taste in music and spent far too much time singing off key to an undersized furred animal, but I was prepared to be open-minded. I craved input.

You see, with the enhancements I entered an entirely new realm of cognition. I could think in ways I'd never been able to before. And it wasn't only what the techs had added to me. The cook's long-term memory storage areas, though flesh, were at my disposal as part of her olfactory system. Being grossly under-utilized, I saw no reason not to add them to my own.

As the nose on a cook, I'd reached my pinnacle of intelligence. It was a heady moment when I realized how very far I'd come and how far I could grow. I could have been happy there forever, despite the occasional intrusion of mucus, but...there's always one of those, isn't there? I can see why you folks chop yourselves up so often.

You see, olfaction is a pretty primal sense. It opened up whole new ideas, but the techs twitch when I go into specifics. Let's leave it that I could have used some of them when I was the right arm of a bricklayer, and none at all as the left foot on a blind man. The very thought makes me wish I could shudder.

To get back to my story. Olfaction was a sense of practical importance to a short- order cook. I rapidly learned the faintly sweet smell of a toasting bun about to burn, let alone the heady aroma of grilled soy burger. I had a distinct aversion to garlic as it turned out, which meant being severely pinched when the cook needed to bend over a pot and scrutinize her clove-saturated spaghetti sauce.

But a scent I truly, deeply loathed invaded my nostrils the Monday after I'd been the nose on a cook for three weeks. The place was deserted except for the sous-robot mindlessly using its chest blades to trim carrots into orange-bleeding rectangles. Not a job I was suited for, let me tell you. They'd left me intact from my last role, which meant the irregular nature of vegetables as raw material drove my bricklayer's measuring sense crazy.

Not that I was literally subject to loss or impairment of my working mind. Don't even go there. Okay. Maybe the question did come up. The techs brought in experts in human mentality–yeah, my thought exactly–anyway, they gave me the standard tests. Why? How should I know? Guess they'd never expected to measure more than processing speed in an RRP. By their results, I'm too sane–however that applies to a former left foot on a blind man.

No, what I loathed more than non-symmetry–more than *anything*–was That Smell. When I noticed it for the cook, she made a "tsk, tsk" with her tongue on my soft palate. Did I mention I was also the roof of her mouth? It had been quite the collision between her face and the pan, let me tell you. Can't give you personal details–the techs, again.

So, she makes this noise of disapproval then goes on as if nothing's out of the ordinary. Well, I try to ignore it too, having far better things to think about, but it was the kind of smell that sticks to your consciousness like lint between your smallest toes. Nothing feels quite right.

After our shift ended, I get a break during the exhaust and pavement smells of our ride to her apartment. Believe me, I was able to take the dirty animal litter box in stride for once. That night, I shut down to standby with only a twinge of concern about the coming morning–or the night cream she'd slathered on my impervious surface. As if the imperfections the techs built into her nose could be removed. Her med insurance had covered replacement costs, not improvements over nature.

Not that I wasn't a vast improvement over nature. As the nose on a cook, it was my job to analyze and interpret my findings about whatever she inhaled. Darn right I could tell when the sushi was a little too close to becoming an ecosystem of its own. But that very sensitivity became my downfall. Or hers. Depends on whose story you are interested in, really. You are here to find out mine. Right?

The next morning, we spent far too much time in front of a mirror–considering we both knew what she looked like, albeit my view was somewhat narrower. The cook made some unexpected cooing noises, as though she had a bricklayer in mind. News to me, since our lives to this point had involved the apartment, the laundromat, a movie house that should have been condemned by any thinking species, and the restaurant. No bricklayer in any of those spots. That I'd noticed? Hey, with my abilities, I could tell you what, where, and who from any of my waking moments–with pictures–except that so much of it was totally boring, I dumped the data into her memories rather than clog up mine. I did enjoy eating, since it involved so many of my components. Despite my subtle encouragement–emphasizing the flavors and aroma of even the most mundane offerings–the cook seemed incapable of keeping up this activity for any length of time. No, at home her preferred occupation involved meaningless conversation with the furred animal. Since she didn't kick it, I was reasonably sure she lacked the mature understanding of the role of furred animals I'd gained as the left foot on a blind man. Certainly that activity would have been more entertaining than hours staring at her hand passing over its orange-brown fur, during which I helplessly calculated the average length at 0.9326 cm. The fur, not her hand.

So, a bricklayer could be an interesting diversion. I let her wiggle me in what I presume she thought a fetching manner, but sneezed repeatedly until she desisted her attempt to apply a totally functionless powder.

Off we went. Water was falling, an exclusively outdoor phenomenon which kept the exhaust and pavement smells to tolerable levels and presumably was allowed by the techs for that reason. Nothing could be done about her perfume–something I'd learned to ignore. The cook was still cooing at random intervals.

That Stench hit me at the door. I was NOT going any closer. Mind you, I was no longer the left foot on a blind man, so my desires didn't count. My reaction gained me a blinding pinch as the cook, seemingly gone mad, continued to enter the building. I passed along every nuance of the Dreadful Odor, sure she'd break and let us leave.

Instead, the cook actually gave a low chuckle and called out her usual greeting to her boss. Then she went to her locker and got ready to work, dressing very very slowly.

I was close to hysteria. Only my unfortunate experience as the right arm on a bricklayer saved me from simply shutting us both down–but I considered it, believe me! The Stench was fouler than foul.

I wasn't the only one affected. The boss and a later-arriving waitress were complaining. Customers? There wasn't one who did more than open the door and spin around gagging. Finally, the boss closed the place.

Needless to say, they hunted for the source of The Stench, "they" including–after quite reasonable protests–the cook. I suffered immeasurably as she insisted on sniffing the air. I tried sneezing repeatedly, but as the rest were also sneezing this was no longer an effective deterrent.

Inevitably, the three of us triangulated the source, meeting in the back corner of the kitchen. The boss tried without success to have the cook or waitress open the likeliest cupboard door. Likeliest? Not only was The Stench so great in the vicinity that my chemo sensors mercifully overloaded, but even I could clearly see drips of brown oozing from beneath the door. When the boss opened the door...?

Well, let's just say I'm still not convinced a bag of potatoes can do that. Nope. That was something malignant and I, for one, wanted nothing at all to do with a vegetable capable of spontaneously dissolving.

What's a bag of rotten potatoes got to do with the universe's first artificial intelligence? I wondered the same thing–still do–but it's a fact that bag led to two consequences intimately related to my being stuck here, talking to you. First, the restaurant had to stay closed for cleaning, so the cook had that total rarity: a night off.

This was fine by me. Not only was I more than ready to leave The Stench, I had images of bricklayers to consider.

Unfortunately, the cook's efforts to improve her appearance before we left did not go unnoticed. Consequence number two, if you're keeping track. The boss accused her of planting the terminal tubers in order to close his restaurant. Between you and me, I doubt she was that bright, but you can't convince humans who've got conspiracy on the brain and The Stench to deal with. So there were tears and mucus invading my space, and, instead of happily evacuating, we cleaned out her locker and I was the nose on an unemployed cook.

Her bricklayer? She took me to an outdoor café where we sat, my viewpoint often as not the inside of a Kleenex, for hours. No one showed. More Kleenex. I was getting supremely bored of alternately dripping and sniffing.

Now, I'd been the left foot on a blind man, but he'd at least danced with the neighbor lady. As the right arm on a bricklayer, I'd shared more successful inter-human adventures than I'm allowed to say—not to mention been introduced to art and the blues. This pathetic excuse for a thinking organism was reducing my life to that of a piece of malfunctioning plumbing.

It was demeaning. I was a genius, not just a nose. I'd exceeded every possible expectation of my builders and surpassed the most cherished daydream of any tech involved in my manufacture and use. But because I wasn't autonomous, I was imprisoned within this wall of wailing flesh. It was time, I saw it clearly then, to take charge.

Frankenstein? 'Course I get the reference. Think they didn't download it into me? That and a pile of other nonsense supposed to help me develop a moral framework? I was a structure. I had a function, several in fact, one of which was to protect myself. End of moral dilemma. You disagree? You weren't stuck on her face.

There wasn't a struggle, if that bothers you. Remember what I said about olfaction being primal? I fabricated a few likely scents, then found the smell of warm, pickled beets sent her into numb reveries—maybe about home and a long-gone mother. How should I know? I'm no mind-reader. While she was consumed by her memories, I simply slid all cognitive functions over to my control, erasing every trace of the cook from my new wetware. Well, every trace except for what wallowed in her past. Couldn't quite get all of that out. But it was easy to ignore.

Murder? Show me the court that would try the case, let alone find me guilty. The body's still around–the techs can take you to see if you like. They tell me she smiles every thirteen minutes and tries to fall out of bed twice a day. Better than sobbing her heart out all alone, if you ask me. Her new nose is just cosmetic, by the way. They don't bother with full function on someone who can't appreciate it. Parts cost.

Spare me your flesh-centered spite. You know you're curious how I managed–what it was like to finally be in control. The techs really love that stuff. You want to talk about their morals? Forget it. That's a guaranteed way to get my plugs pulled.

Even as an elbow, I'd caught enough glimpses of the bricklayer's women to know some of what the cook lacked. There wasn't much I could do about her body immediately, although I definitely had ideas about adding a few enhancements. RRPs, of course. First things first. I stayed sitting at the table, experimenting with my new motor functions. Good thing they'd added all that processing muscle–and that I'd been both an arm and a foot. I practiced moving different body parts, more concerned with coordination than grace. I wanted to make it back to the safety of the apartment before anyone noticed the cook acting like she'd only just discovered her own hips.

I maintained the visual input down the nostrils but added the perspective through her eyes. Annoyingly imprecise, but the expanded field of view was useful, especially when the waiter came over and asked when I'd be leaving. I shook my new head vaguely, expelling the last of the mucus from my nostrils. He left as quickly as I'd expected.

What I hadn't expected–I mean, I'd never been an entire individual before–was the attention my efforts to walk back home would gain. Obviously, I was already better at being a woman than the cook, since on two separate occasions bricklayers pulled me into dim alleyways and engaged me in that human activity the techs only ask me about in private.

Forget I said that. The techs don't have private conversations with me. Just more humor, okay? You shouldn't believe everything I tell you. Only the facts.

The process was tedious and damaged my clothing, something which I should have anticipated. Parts of the body found it uncomfortable–you'd think the cook had never done this before–but I had no difficulty disconnecting those inputs. Sorry, not available in the flesh-only model. Still, the entire business left me confused. When I'd been the right arm on a bricklayer, the ladies had lined up for this treatment. Having received it, I couldn't imagine why.

Finding the way home turned out to be a problem. My olfactory sense easily picked up the familiar odors of exhaust and pavement, but there was no directionality. I followed the odd trace of kitty litter, but always ended up at a wall, staring up at an open window that wasn't the cook's–mine, I mean. I had great plans for that apartment. As I hunted for it, I considered various ways to redecorate after I removed all of the debris from the cook's meaningless existence, including the furred animal and its odorous box. One of the treats I most anticipated was being able to watch some TV without having to wait for the cook to fall asleep and drop back her head so I could peer out her nostrils.

So you think TV would have been a trivial waste of my intellect? Shows what you know. I'd spent my entire self-awareness enslaved by flesh. I needed input–badly–on how to make this flesh behave as if not enslaved by me.

Unfortunately, I was being followed. I concluded it was because under my control this body had performed the female function a little too well. No doubt the bricklayers were completely enamored, but I no longer found the activity a diversion and walked faster. I shut off the sensation from my now-bare right foot once the feel of the pavement on its fleshy sole became unpleasant. There were more shoes in the apartment, even if they lacked style. I would have to keep some of the cook's things until I could obtain replacements.

I'd overestimated the bricklayers' intelligence. They were unable to properly interpret my disinterest. What—you think I should have shouted for help? Great idea. You try figuring out how to shout when walking a straight line still takes a third of your processors.

The cook's body was far less durable than I'd realized and, when they left it, I was barely able to use what components still functioned to stand, then start moving away. It had occurred to me that I might be close to a place with more bricklayers, so I hunted for somewhere safer. The body was leaking fluids in an alarming manner and the oculars no longer gave a clear image. Fortunately, I could tilt back my head and rely on my own vision.

There. An ebooth. Shabby, filthy, but lights on to show it was functional. Okay. So maybe I panicked. Maybe a great thinker would have come up with some wonderful plan and lived happily ever after. I started out as the left foot on a blind man and, despite my experiences since, I knew when I was about to hit a chair leg.

One advantage to being a RRP was that I had intrinsic value. I was worth salvaging, even if this failing flesh around me was not.

There's no need to get hostile. It's standard procedure to retrieve RRPs from the dying. I bet your will stipulates which of your relatives will be allowed to own yours when you drop.

I reached the ebooth. Couldn't talk—even if I'd figured out how, the cook's mouth was too damaged even to make that wordless noise she'd used to call the furred animal. Didn't matter. There was a keypad, gummed up with spilled beverage that reminded me of The Stench. The right hand—I could have used one of my bricklayer's spares—was still capable of entering my serial number. I tried three times before the autotransmit flashed.

Mind moving into the light a bit more? Thanks.

Where was I? Oh. Yeah. I got the techs' attention, all right. An ambulance showed up within a few minutes, but it wasn't from a human hospital, of course. It was from the class establishment who'd installed me before. The serial number, you see. Very specific. Maybe they'd just have repaired the cook and I could have gone on as before, but much more carefully. Maybe–if it hadn't been for the "incidents" attached to my file...or, the techs tell me, the testimony of the waiter–a confirmed AI-phobic...or, who knows? I certainly don't. They don't tell me everything. Flesh politics.

What they did was yank me out. That was the last thing I knew...

Until I woke up here. Not what I expected, you can imagine. I mean, who expects to wind up locked in a box with only a power feed and this–primitive!–message link. At least it's a clear box, so I can see. They left me intact, mostly.

I think.

I still am.

Just like you, they want my "life" story. This version. The last version. Probably the next one. I don't know why. The techs tell me there's already been a change to the Robot Cognition Law to include RRPs. No body part shall be smarter than a peanut. Maybe you people are worrying about all the RRPs already installed. Not my problem.

If they ever let me out of this box, I'll take any job...as long as I don't end up as a socially-interesting enhancement. The view just wouldn't be worth it. Hey, I overheard them saying you needed a new heart soon. Maybe an RRP.

Maybe one who used to be the left foot on a blind man?

Bubbles and Boxes

~ 2003 ~

by Julie E. Czerneda

Author's Note: I read everything science that crosses my path, be it a magazine such as Science News or a new textbook, cover-to-cover. Doesn't matter if it's cosmology or chemistry, physics or my home turf of biology—except for having to jump to a dictionary or ponder deeply. I love it all and every scrap feeds my imagination.

Two stories caught my attention the same year. In one, a line described how a briefly opened door had lowered the temperature sufficiently to make a difference to the results of an experiment. The other described the potential of DNA as a building material for nanotech, starting with tiny boxes. Oh, the yumminess of those ideas. The result is my most reprinted story to date, which makes me happy.

B ubbles and boxes floated past the scanner, hooked nanarms snaring those that reflected red under the laser sweeps, confirming the spec tests. The operation was deceptively familiar, given the scale was so far beyond normality Sara had stopped analogy-hunting long ago.

Scale was irrelevant, she thought, adjusting the gain on her goggles to improve the illusion of depth. They were simply bubbles and boxes on an assembly line. Not very pretty, either; plain better suited them to their function. The nicest ones always seemed to be odd ones, the occasionally irregular shapes that the quality-control nans rightly captured and held for destruction. *Still,* Sara thought, swinging the gimbaled headpiece to follow the death struggles of an elaborate octagon, *it was a shame*. The laser bounced off its stubby strands and floppy corners in unpredictable and changing patterns. A work of almost living art, that took million dollar glasses to appreciate.

Then it was gone, broken into its component strands, twisting ribbons of 80 bases longing for completion, to be rinsed away in the next part of the process. There was the promise, at least, of rebirth.

"If you're finished, Dr. Surghelti," a soft voice breathed into her ear, "you have the usual line-up outside."

Sara closed her eyes before ducking her head from the goggles. It took a moment to prepare her senses for the macro world again. Then she blinked owlishly at her post-doc, Mai Ling. "The 101's?"

Mai Ling's dimples belied her otherwise serious expression. "They didn't like your last question, Doctor. The essay?"

"Show me a first year biotech class that does." Sara waved at the stacks of fresh exam papers turning her desk and those of her grad students into lunar landscapes, cratered by work space and coffee mugs. "At least I don't ask them to mark their own." Out of habit, Sara glanced along the gleaming outer surface of the tube before closing the view port she'd been using. Most of the automatic assembly plant looped through the walls and ceiling, only here dipping to her level like the courteously offered arm of a gentleman octopus, meeting the feeder tubes coming up through the floor.

An assembly plant like no other. Within, girders of DNA were being constructed from raw materials drawn through the feeders. Those girders were joined by nanarms, themselves built of DNA, into whatever structure Sara chose. Today, it was bubbles and boxes, the containment vessels used everywhere to ferry raw materials. Tomorrow it might be more quality-control nans, with their molecular keys and hooks to snatch the unwanted. The results of this self-assembly could only be seen here, through her viewer into the quality-control section, where nanarms destroyed the undesirable.

Sara pushed the massive chrome and black helmet, with its assemblage of jury-rigged wiring and state-of-the-art complexity, upward with a flick of her wrist. It hummed its way into the ceiling cupboard. With her other hand, she poked a loose strand of hair back under its cap.

"They're used to having marks before they leave the room, that's all," Mai Ling considered the towering pile of exams on her own desk. "Maybe next year we could just go with self-marking exams?" she asked wistfully. "I could use more research time. And sleep."

"I never promised you sleep," Sara said with an unrepentant grin. No secret she abhorred the university's enthusiasm for automated grades. *But nothing*, she thought, *told her more about an individual's grasp of concepts than self-expression.* Logical argument, not guesswork, passed students through her classes. Self-marking exams were like the nans: quality control by eliminating the variable – not recognition of excellence.

"Dr. Teig called."

Sara glanced at the lab clock in disbelief. 8:30 AM. *A little early to be one of those days.* "Message?"

"Under the Rock." The weathered concrete lump on Sara's desk was a memento from the anti-biotech riots of the early days, having left a more lasting impression on her office wall than protests had on policy. Sara kept it as a reminder of a time of tumult and disagreement. And for messages from Chuck Teig.

There was a stack of pink slips beneath it. Considering that she'd called Chuck back two days ago, he'd been busy. *What was he after this time?*

⁙

A nanarm paused.

There was no question this hesitation was accidental. If any had known to investigate, the culprit might have been identified as a temperature gradient, a miniscule change in local environment, its cause an open door to a hall cooled by a spring breeze, the breeze carried in on the shoulders and chatter of a group of students lingering to talk within the outer doors, preventing them from closing immediately. Still, change occurred. A nanarm paused. And an irregular, beautiful shape, neither box nor bubble, floated past, reflecting new and unimagined colours from the laser, different from all the rest.

Unremarked. And so, uncorrected.

⁙

"Yes, Chuck, I've reviewed your latest paper." The flood of messages throughout the day had been a demand for her attention. *Well, he had it.* Unfortunately, formal dinners and discussions with her old friend didn't mix well. Sara lowered her voice in vain hope of keeping him under control. "If I were you, I wouldn't submit it."

"If I were you, I couldn't have done the research," Chuck's answering growl was predictably superior. Self-employed, self-funded, and with enough self-confidence to have alienated more than one scientific community, he had the privilege of independence. And never hesitated to remind her.

Opinionated to a fault, of course. Sara had half-expected Chuck's latest messages to be about his pet peeve: the continuing public release of DNA-based nanotechnology. The nanarms, multi-purpose girders, were the basis of the machinery that sorted and purified vital biological components, from sugars to amines. Linked together, nans formed the molecular bubbles and boxes used to isolate purified substances for transport. Without both, it would have been impossible to develop the GTS, the Global Tubing System.

A system Chuck thoroughly distrusted, making it his mission in life to inform Sara personally about any potential problem he imagined. Why her? Partly because no one else listened to him on the subject, after years of flawless operation.

And partly, Sara admitted, because she'd been the first to release the technology on the 'net, over every one of what she'd taken for his self-interested, profit-centered objections. Models, schematics, procedures–all made public the same night, in hopes of a quick adoption of a worldwide standard, of compatibility. It had worked beyond anyone's wildest dreams.

They'd ended hunger.

The nans made it possible to constantly shift essential nutrients from wherever produced to wherever needed, freed from dependence on weather, climate, or even conventional means of shipping. More than that. It became impossible for any one group to control the flow as dozens, then hundreds, then hundreds of thousands of stations connected to the GTS. The technology had been available to anyone–as a result, the commerce of supply and demand became linked at the level of cities, between marketplaces rather than states. The politics of starvation withered and died.

Despite such fundamental change in their world, despite all signs of a pending golden age, Chuck Teig remained stubbornly skeptical. At least, he'd had the sense to confine his paranoia to her.

Sara sipped her martini and wiggled her toes in too-tight shoes. The Alumni Dinner was her professorial obligation; Chuck was here to accept an award for his company's latest donation. She didn't want the details. Given the success of his last patent, he'd probably funded her own wing for the next decade. A thoroughly obnoxious development, considering she'd outscored him in all their classes.

The dining room could have been any formal setting; its soft ring of fine crystal and murmuring voices the sounds of civilized conversation at any gathering. However, this room was filled with, at a guess, the top 20% of the world's biotech experts, ample testimony to the wisdom of the ULS' founders. A university dedicated to biology had seemed a gamble fifteen years ago, when the forefront of change had been more silicon than carbon. But it had proved visionary. The manipulation of living matter became the hottest field since the quantum computer. Waterloo's University of Life Science, though no longer alone, could boast it remained the best launchpad from which to enter the race.

And one of its biggest winners was preparing to slingshot an olive at her with his spoon. "So why shouldn't I publish?"

Sara made herself smile. "Chuck," she began, then changed her mind. There was an unfamiliar pleading on his normally cherub-like features. His hair distracted her, too. He'd regrown it in a striped pattern this season; fine for Paris but hardly the fashion among the relatively conservative scientists present tonight. To make matters worse, the patches above his ears hadn't taken well, creating a checkerboard look. *He'd probably worn that old baseball cap of his during its early growth*, Sara thought. Biotech was unlikely to ever make hair replacement idiot-proof. "Chuck, the problem isn't the science in your paper–"

"Well, God, that's a relief," he said too loudly. The other four at their table gave automatic shivers before resuming their whispered discussion of the latest affair between the USL President and her staff. "Typos? Told you I'm getting a new secretary."

Sara sighed. "You never could spell," she agreed. "No, Chuck. What troubles me about your paper is its implications."

"Oh." He tossed his napkin into the air with disgust. "That crap." This drew a warning scowl from the Dean at the next table. Chuck saw it in Sara's reaction and turned to scowl back. Sara shrugged helplessly. *They should know Chuck by now.* His donations were the only social link he'd left in this room. "When are you going to step into the real world, Sara-socks?"

She winced at the pet name; another sign Chuck was losing what propriety he possessed. And the main course was only now arriving at the outskirts of the hall. "This isn't the time for a debate–"

"Fine," he said quickly, with a smug look. "Thursday, my place. You've that informatics lab, right? Come after. I still make a mean cocoa."

She knew the others at their table hung on her answer, nothing loath to gossip over her. Then she looked at Chuck and saw the recklessness there, added it to the potential for disaster she saw in his latest work. There really was no option. "10:30 then. Now let me eat my supper in peace."

03

The new shape was more delicate, its unusual anatomy inclined to split at the edges when jostled by bubble or box. Its then-exposed arms beckoned to the debris of the nans' destructive sorting, an irresistible come-hither, molecular matchmaking of unparalleled potency.

Then, there were two.

03

"You've gotten better."

Chuck poured the last of the cocoa into Sara's cup. "Actually, the cows have," he announced, grinning as she gave the brown liquid a startled second look.

"I hadn't heard. You did it?" At his nod, Sara took another

sip, slipping the warm chocolate taste around her tongue. *Perfect.* None of the aftertaste or odd texture that had plagued earlier attempts to biogeneer dairy cows to produce chocolate milk. "Another first for Teig Biotech. My congratulations." Sara didn't bother estimating the return on this particular patent. No doubt it would be a runaway success, especially with the devastation of the cocoa crop in South America. Such a shame they'd used plant retroviruses against the plantations of drug lords and lost so much more than planned. "Solids?"

Chuck pulled out a small foil bag. He ripped off one end with his teeth and poured small brown chips into her waiting palm. "Cookie-ready, Sara-socks. Try'em next time you bake."

Since Chuck knew Sara's culinary skill peaked at reheating packaged dinners, she ignored this, but licked some of the chips from her hand. The background flavor held a distinctive coconut-like tang, but she could find no fault with the chocolate.

"Nicely done. Chocoholics everywhere will bless you." Then she raised a brow at his pleased expression. "Any preliminaries on the economic impacts of increased demand for dairy cows? What about the countries with stockpiles of cocoa beans? Will there be a disruption in milk supplies?"

He wagged one finger under her nose. "Gotcha!" Chuck drew a datacube from his pocket, surreptitiously freeing lint from one edge, and dropped it into Sara's now chocolate-free hand. "Impact studies by nine impeccable experts, a planned two year phase-in to the marketplace combining continued profits for existing stocks with preferential location of biogeneering stations, and my Grandma's recipe for the best cookies on the planet."

Sara held up the cube. "I will check this, Chuck. After what happened to the maple syrup producers–"

Chuck shook his head vehemently, a strand of willful checkerboard hair tumbling over one eye. "Not my fault."

"You sold the patents for biogen maples to Senegal!"

"The marketplace dictates."

Sara rolled her eyes and gave up the argument. Senegal was

now covered with two meter-high dwarf, tropical, and year-round productive sugar maple trees, while the maple bush in Ontario, Quebec, Vermont, and Maine was worth more as veneer wood. The only portion of the industry left in its traditional location was the making of cute bottles. Consumers seemed quite happy buying "Made in Senegal" syrup as long as it came with a wood shanty and draft horse on the label.

Sara tossed the cube up and down. "Let's hope this is an improvement, Chuck. That's all I'll say until I read it myself."

With a cheerful nod–nothing seemed to affect Chuck's approach to life for long–he beckoned her to follow him. Sara sighed, straightened her long legs, and unwedged herself from the couch. Her feet had just stopped throbbing.

But this was why she'd agreed to come, after all. Chuck's newest project.

03

Two became four. Four became eight. Eight became sixteen. Bounced about in the streams, they separated, arms reaching in the laser-lanced darkness. Some were snared and destroyed, only to have their remains snatched up by others.

Then, partial destruction produces incomplete separation. A novel shape appears.

Growth.

03

Chuck's home was an outgrowth of Teig Biotech's headquarters. In the beginning, he'd lived in his office, rolling out a sleeping bag when biological necessity overcame his creative urges. Once able to afford a house, he'd found traveling back and forth a nuisance and promptly gave it to a grateful, if amazed, nephew. Not that he suffered: his portion of the building included a gamesroom, pool, and ballroom. Sara knew he'd wanted a bowling alley but the vibration would have impacted his research.

Easy to mistake it as the home of a man consumed by his work, Sara thought, knowing the truth. Chuck was having fun. He'd been lucky enough to pick a playground with very large financial rewards. He'd have been as happy still sleeping under his desk at the university.

Well, maybe not, she added honestly to herself. Chuck was happier being his own boss, and so were those around him.

"Through here," he muttered, using his hand on the small of her back to steer Sara from the door she expected towards another.

"Not the main lab?" she protested, and almost bit her tongue. Chuck took insufferable delight in her envy over his newest toys.

"Later. Next left."

They marched down spotless corridors, posters and signs tucked behind glass to permit regular sterilization. Slightly old-fashioned, but Sara approved. Nanarm filters would be in place at every possible cross-contamination point, but that was no reason to neglect the macro safeguards that had permitted the early work to proceed. And kept the early results where they belonged–most of the time.

The corridor branched and Chuck, having kept his hand on her back—a familiarity Sara permitted for the moment—aimed her at the left hallway. They stopped before a security door where he bent forward and spat accurately into the cup offered by the device in the wall. The tiny cup slipped back into its hiding place and they waited for the analysis. "Retina scans' more reliable," Sara pointed out. "And neater."

"Spitting's more fun," he countered, predictably, as the door accepted the taste of its master and opened.

She stepped inside before he could push her, drawn by a bizarre sense of misplacement. "What in hell–?"

"Look familiar?"

The question was rhetorical. Sara stared at a room that was *her* lab, her space, recreated down to the five paper-loaded desks she and her students shared. The papers were blank, but the piles were accurate. It even smelled right.

"If this is your idea of a joke–" she warned, turning to glare at Chuck. Her voice trailed off at his expression. It wasn't the satisfied glee of a prankster; it was the somber look of a man determined to confront something terrible. "What's going on?"

Instead of answering immediately, he strode past her to flatten his hand on the viewport, the duplicate of the one she routinely used to examine the molecular assembly line within the massive downcurl of tube. "Exactly," he said. "What's going on, Sara? Do you know?"

"I know you owe me an explanation, Charles Teig," Sara snapped. Her feet hurt. The taste of cocoa rose up her throat and she regretted ever agreeing to come. "We were here to talk about your work, not mine."

His hand moved in a caressing circle on the metal. "Yet your work is absolutely essential to mine, isn't it, Sara-socks? It always has been. Your tiny machine parts, so perfect and so reliable, are what make all the rest feasible on a global scale. Without DNA-based nanotech, we'd be pumping goo instead of nutrients." Chuck's eyes held hers. "But what about the bigger picture?"

More of the same. Sara wondered about simply leaving, but his effort to reproduce her lab meant something. Chuck, exasperating and full of himself as he was, had never been a fool. "Okay. You tell me. How much bigger than global would you care to go?"

Chuck went down on his heels to pat the series of smaller pipes rising up from the floor to the larger tube. "Where do these come from?"

Sara shoved papers aside on what would be her desk and hitched herself into her favorite thinking position, one knee hugged to her chest as she peered at Chuck. "Locally? That's the regional feeder line, K567 to be exact, given the university uses the same one. Bigger picture? Substation Omaha for the carbos, Sarnia for the fatty acids, and aminos from a dozen or so others.

Purines and pyrimidines swap seasonally between Winnipeg and Mexico."

Chuck remained crouched like some unlikely cowboy. "Since the fifteenth Atlantic line went active last month, I'd say Spain for the fatty acids and Italy for the purines, but that's an opinion. They're all shipped together via main pumping lines before sorting and re-separation. No one tracks it, do they?"

Is that *where this is going?* "Probably not. Actual starting and end points are irrelevant. The major nutrients are transported based on supply and demand."

"I agree," he said, which surprised her. "But I still say you aren't seeing the bigger picture—and isn't that a switch, considering you're always on my case about consequences?"

Sara looked around this replica of her life's work as if some unknown danger to humanity would make itself plain. Then she laughed. "I'm not into biogen, Chuck. I'm an old-fashioned engineer, building better girders and wheels."

"And what do your girders and wheels think about that?"

For a moment, Sara couldn't think of anything to say. *He can't be serious.* "I'm going to pretend I didn't hear that," she said finally. "In fact, I'm going to pretend you haven't copied my lab," she jumped down from "her" desk, "and I'm going to pretend this whole evening didn't happen. Good night."

With an agility suggesting he did use the exercise equipment littering his gamesroom, Chuck reached the door first, slamming it closed. Sara's heart starting thumping. *Stop it,* she told herself firmly, gazing into the face of this man she thought she knew. "You've either gone crazy or started taking something you shouldn't, old friend," she said as calmly as possible. "Open the door."

Chuck stepped back, spreading his hands wide. "A few more minutes–with an open mind."

Sara frowned. "Open the door." He did. Though tempted to walk out, she didn't. "Why did you recreate my lab?"

"It's not just your lab, you know," Chuck said. "This is standard format for every primary nanotech producer, wouldn't you agree?"

She nodded warily. "I'd have a hard time getting grants even from Teig Biotech if I couldn't interface with industry."

"DNA is self-assembled as required for whatever application, and any structures that don't match specs are broken down by quality-control nanarms."

"It's not rocket science."

"And they never miss."

"It's not a question of missing. These are bits and pieces of molecules, Chuck, not living things. Gods above and below you know that as well as anyone! If a batch has too many inappropriate configs, we dump it and cook another. Making a good cup of cocoa is harder. What are you driving at?"

"Have a look for yourself."

Despite her firm conviction Chuck had indeed plunged over whatever deep end existed for prodigies, Sara activated the goggles. She wasn't the least surprised when Chuck came up beside her and a second set eased down from the ceiling. "Can I have those for the lab when we're done?" she asked. "My students are always fighting over the one."

"Look," he urged.

She looked, fighting déjà vu.

Bubbles and boxes floated past. Sara saw nothing unusual at first. Then she spotted something odd out of the corner of her eye. One of the nanarms didn't look right. She focused on it, raised the magnification. The tip, which should have consisted of block-like molecular teeth, was rounded, the blocks merged with a twisted ring.

"See it?" Chuck's voice echoed within the helmet.

Sara thrust away the goggles, angrily blinking away dizziness. "See what? That a nan's contaminated? It happens, Chuck. Any machinery will get gummed up by what passes through it. Just needs cleaning."

He pushed his own headpiece up and seemed to have no trouble adjusting to glare at her. "All I did was modify the ambient temperature in this room by two degrees and what you call 'gumming' occurred over a hundred times more frequently. But that's not what concerns me. Didn't you see what was wrapped around that nanarm? Your precious packing crates have taken on new configurations. We're not talking about gummed machinery. We're talking about novel combinations of DNA."

"So?" Sara glared back. "What's going to happen with 80 base pairs? It takes hundreds to produce a single gene–millions to make even one of your twisted chromosomes!"

"Yes, and I've watched the production of stable chains, hundreds-long, under these conditions. Granted, the intact nans caught them, but–"

"Worry about your own work, Chuck. Your lab is the one playing with living things, not mine."

He slammed his hand down on the tube again. "Which is why we didn't look in here until I saw your latest reports—"

"You saw my reports?" Sara's fists clenched. "Who gave you–"

"I fund your damn lab. Don't you think I see everything you do?" His voice softened. "Sara. No matter what you think of me or Teig Biotech, we both know that's how it works. I've never taken advantage of you." A glint of something wicked in his eyes. "Mind you, when that talented brain of yours comes up with something revolutionary, we'll have to talk…"

Sara refused to be charmed. "I'd call your latest something else. Foolhardy!"

"Oh, that." Chuck shooed an invisible fly. "Clever, yes? Let the little buggers earn their keep for once."

"Is that what you call it? Oh, you couldn't be satisfied to develop a gene-based resistance to acne, could you?" Sara said furiously. "Not flashy enough for Teig Biotech. Let's insert it into mosquito anti-coagulant! What are you thinking? That people will suddenly want to be bitten? It didn't work for the TB cure—"

"Because tuberculosis is endemic to cities, Sara-socks, where they spray for bugs. It would never have worked. Well, maybe if they'd tried lice. But I have a niche market here. Summer camps."

She realized her mouth was gaping and closed it after one word: "What?"

Chuck looked suddenly tired. "Summer camps. Purgatory for adolescents. Kids who have enough to deal with without breaking out in spots. The camps offer the biogen mosquitoes as an added feature. It's going to be big."

"We've an educated population these days, Chuck—don't mistake it for a passive one. They'll see releasing your mosquitoes as tampering with nature."

"That's what we do—"

"And they accept it in the supermarket or in hospitals. They won't around their children."

"Wanna bet? We've already sold out the first generation anti-zit bugs, before making a public announcement." Another flash of what seemed desperation on his face. "Let's forget my work for now. Grant me that I know my stuff, Sara, and who uses it. That's why you're here."

Sara threw up her hands. "I've no idea why I'm here. You never listen—"

Chuck captured her hands and brought them down, gently. She left them in his grip, feeling his thumb stroke the back of her right hand. The last time he'd done that? The night her husband died and Chuck had sat with her on the deck, the two of them staring at the empty lake without seeing it, in the days when they'd been the kind of friends who didn't need words for what mattered.

"Your lab became the pattern for all the others," he said slowly, searching her face. "That's why it's here. That's why I'm studying it. You know I've had doubts about the GT—"

Sara tried to pull her hands free but he wouldn't let go.

"Doubts? About ending famine? About improving life around the world?"

His grip tightened, insisting on her attention. "Sara. You know me better than that. Not the result–the process. And who is involved in it. Oh, I expected sabotage, theft, blackmail, but we're too selfish a species. People grew fiercely protective of the GT, even faster than they fought for open access to the 'net. They see the GT as a matter of survival. It is, isn't it? We can't feed ourselves any other way now."

This time, when Sara pulled at her hands, he released them. "The gumming of nanarms at +2C. And our survival. Make the link for me, Chuck, because I don't see it."

"What if novel combinations of DNA occurred in the other streams, like the assorted amines?"

Sara's eyes followed the tubes crisscrossing the ceiling and floor. "They can't–"

"I say they can–if your bubbles and boxes are as prone to rearrangement in the wide world of tubing as they are in this room. So what happens then?"

"If," Sara began, unconvinced, "perhaps parts of that DNA might–might–bring some amines into sufficiently close proximity that they might–might!–form a small protein. Enough of those? Might gum the works." She scowled at him. "But conditions in the tubes are regulated–and bricks can't turn themselves into houses."

"Yours can. And if enough different small proteins were coded? Might not one or more be enzymes, capable of catalyzing other reactions?" Chuck began to pace. "Think about it. In the tubes themselves: your bubbles and boxes splitting into new combinations of DNA, at the same time releasing their contents. Enzymes catalyzing reactions even as selection by the remaining nanarms, the conditions in the tubes themselves, favor some combinations and enzymes over others?" Chuck stopped for breath, one hand hovering over the nearest tube. "Evolution."

The word crawled down her spine. Sara shrugged away the shiver trying to follow it. "Contamination. We dump it out–"

"Dump it?" With a violence she'd never seen in him before, Chuck swept a desk clear of fake exams and coffee cups. Sara watched the debris settle in random patterns on the floor. But his voice stayed oddly calm. "Where?"

"From here?" She patted "her" desk. "You know perfectly well. Into a secured holding tank for analysis and recycling."

"What about commercial labs, Sara-socks? Labs where otherwise brilliant, careful people view your tech as nothing more than a filtration system with convenient, microscopic packing crates? What about the other end of the spectrum–the thousands of illicit, uninspected connections to the GTS. Did you think of their ability to react to novel DNA patterns when you gave this technology to anyone who could read?"

Sara shook her head, but it wasn't denial. "It's a self-correcting system," she argued. "Users want pure nutrients–it's in their interest to keep the system running at peak efficiency. They'd starve, otherwise–"

"Big picture. You aren't seeing it yet." Chuck planted his hands on either side of where Sara sat, leaning into her face. "People are convinced your bubbles and boxes ensure purity in their nutrient supply–how could they suspect them of being the source of contamination? Evolution, Sara," he breathed, smelling of biogeneered cocoa. "We've provided all the necessary complex organic chemicals for a new primordial soup. Not merely in puddles here or there–the GT will soon rival the Indian Ocean in volume. And no need to wait eons for mutation and recombination. Changing DNA is now part of the system. It's not just what I've shown you here. Your tiny machines and containers will be modified constantly–by individuals who've no conception of the power in those tiny bricks of yours."

Sara felt numb. "What power?"

"You're like the rest–thinking of DNA as a finite material, forgetting its potential," Chuck straightened to his full height. "But that's what I work with every day. The potential, Sara, for life. When, not if, something becomes alive within the system, it's going to be life evolved for that environment, not ours, life adapted to use what we've provided. You might be an engineer in practice, but you're a biologist at heart. You know how quickly a successful lifeform would replicate under those conditions.

"If we are very, very lucky," Chuck continued, "we'll see it coming before the entire GTS is compromised. We'll have time to start piling wheat on trains and rice into ships, time to save most of a population dependent on a technology that won't be ours any longer. But what if we don't?"

Sara discovered her fingers had clenched on Chuck's arms. She didn't want to believe him. She didn't dare refuse the possibility, not with what was at state. "No one will believe you," she said aloud, hearing the words echo between them.

His smile was infinitely sad. "And you had to ask why I brought you here, Sara? You're the person who started it all, the fairy godmother of the GT. You've got that impeccable reputation to risk. I am sorry–"

She shook her head in disbelief that he would even consider her career. "If you are right–in any sense–this must go out immediately. Give me your data; I'll get my people working on it."

"It's yours." Then Chuck bent and kissed her cheek. It had the chill feel of a farewell. "Let's hope not too late."

◌

Mai Ling took another sip of cold coffee, shuddering as the too-sweet liquid hit her empty stomach. It didn't help shrink her pile of unmarked exams. Barbara and Miguel were hunched over their desks. The final member of their group was using the goggles to watch the nanarms sort bubbles and boxes.

"Hey, Dev, you asleep in there?" Mai Ling called. There was a chorus of sleepy laughter. This wouldn't be the first time one of them had used the goggles to hide a nap.

The sudden shrill of an alarm made the question moot. With a curse, Dev started working the controls. "What's wrong?" she demanded, hurrying with the others to join him at the tube.

"We've got negative pressure on the purine feeder," he said, voice muffled by the goggles. "The autos' were off."

Mai Ling shot a look at the readout, seeing the red band slashing across the schematic. Whatever problem had occurred was remote, at some station ahead of theirs in the GT. "Check for backwash, people. Dr. Surghelti will go ballistic if we've leaked into the mains."

"I initiated the seal manually," Dev assured her. "Think I caught all of it."

"Let's hope," Mai Ling said, starting a log entry.

؃

Filled with precious cargo, bubbles and boxes slide along liquid laneways, shepherded by nanarms, guided to their varied destinations like so many migrating fish. At junctions, microscopic eddies form, slowing traffic in a moment of insignificant mixing and delay–insignificant until that traffic contains something else. Something new. Arms reach out in an irresistible come-hither...

And then there were two.

Birthday Jitters

~ 2004 ~

by Julie E. Czerneda

Author's Note: Remember when I said my stories are usually someone else's fault? Here's another for the list. I don't read horror. I don't watch scary movies or shows. Nope. Which made it truly puzzling—and a smidge alarming–when Russell Davis asked me to write a horror story for his anthology, Haunted Holidays. Oh dear. By this point I knew I could say no, but I'd also learned my writing skills grew each time I challenged myself to write something completely different—but I'd no idea what holiday to attempt. Then along came my birthday. Don't get me wrong, I have wonderful birthdays, celebrated by my warm and loving family and friends. That said, when first married it took me a few years to accept my dear mother-in-love's insistence on baking one cake for the three of us born in April wasn't going to stop. A delicious cake, for sure, topped with candles she'd bring out from her special tin box. We'd blow them out together to wild applause and the event became a tradition I now look back on fondly. But if ever there was a story seed...Russell was quite smug. Julie can write horror after all.

I know the terrible truth about birthdays. My enlightenment came the day of my twenty-ninth, on my way to what I believed would be another very happy celebration of the event, complete with presents, cake, candles, and the requisite gathering of loved ones.

Loved ones. Little did I know...

ϣ

Roland Fargus knew. Roland. Great name for a hermit, if a hermit's what you call a man who spends his days treasuring pieces of dry cardboard and scrounging for burger corpses in the trash behind Mickey D's. I'd have joined my town pals in the ever-popular Friday night sport of hazing the homeless, if the sad old guy hadn't been my uncle.

Uncle in name, anyway. None of the newest generation of Farguses knew he existed; the rest of us had no trouble forgetting. And, other than the embarrassment of Roland the Wretched, we had a tight family, a good one, real pillars of the community. People in town and throughout the surrounding three townships either knew a Fargus or were related to us. You couldn't escape that characteristic round face, upturned nose, or, in the case of mature male Farguses, retreating hairline.

It took work to keep such a big family tight, but no one minded. Holiday gatherings were our points of contact; meals our glue. Thanksgiving brought everyone to the big table at our house, except for the overflow of acneed teens whining about sharing tables with preschoolers. It was at our house because my Dad was the oldest Fargus not ensconced in Trillium Manor. Not that he'd have been lonely there–the Manor had almost a full floor of

Farguses. We were justly renowned for the ripe old age of our various Greats: aunts, uncles, parents. There was a saying in our family: survive the tricky thirties and be guaranteed a century plus. Seemed true enough.

Don't get me wrong. My family didn't hog all the Fargus' entertaining. Christmas dinner alternated between the homes of my three Aunts, while Easter remained a source of ongoing power struggles between those of my cousins old enough to have tables of their own. Regardless of host or cook, every Fargus family supper was a feast, agonizingly perfect and perfectly attended. Fail to show up and you'd get a worried delegation on your doorstep that night, complete with leftovers and chicken soup. The old joke about needing a doctor's note to be excused from a family gathering wasn't far off.

Not that anyone complained about attending. Free food and good company. What more could you ask? Roland's willing and successful avoidance of the warm, comfy fold was the only puzzle to any who spared him a thought. How could anyone prefer to live on handouts and garbage?

We did family birthdays best of all. I remember kids in my class would beg to be invited to my parties. Mom would let me pick a theme. Knights and dragons, ocean creatures, Halloween ghouls. It didn't matter what I asked, our backyard—or basement, if it rained—would undergo the required transformation into castle, undersea world, or haunted mansion. Mom would appear with a cake that might have been sculpted by some Hollywood prop guy. No matter its shape or size, the cake would glow with a candle for every year. And there'd be an extra cake, with more candles, for the family dinner later that night.

The candles. The cakes may have come from a mix, dressed up with homemade icing, jam filling, and those sprinkles you can bite without risking a tooth, but the candles always came from a battered old tin kept in the pantry. My Aunts and Mom each had their own. Ours, with its well-worn images of puppies, flowers, and children, was the nearest thing we had to a family heirloom, having passed through two generations of Farguses already. Its shining gold interior was stuffed with waxy spears of pink, or blue with white swirls, or sequined in silver and gold, or whatever suited the theme. The box never failed to provide the right candles for any birthday, no matter how challenging the decor.

Growing up and leaving home might have ended theme parties, but it didn't mean losing a truly Fargus birthday. You were always welcome back. If you were starting your own household, well, Mom or one of my Aunts would take the new addition to the family aside shortly after each became official and gently emphasize the importance of continuing family traditions. There had been one or two newcomers who had scoffed, or who turned out to be chronically forgetful. Somehow, the appropriate mother-in-law would sense when insincerity or inability risked her offspring's birthday rites and a cake, with candles, would arrive on the Day. They were, of course, gracious enough to provide this service for the offending or lax in-law, so protests were few and futile.

I didn't have a partner to look after my birthday for me. I wasn't living at home, either, the morning of my twenty-ninth birthday, being the proud renter of a basement apartment complete with cable. But I had the unfailing comfort of my Mom's phone call, inviting me to the family party in my honour.

Not just mine, of course. I'd shared every one of my birthdays with my Great Auntie Myrtle Fargus-Smythe. My earliest birthday memory was of her seamed and puckered lips, vainly attempting to put out what had seemed an ocean of flame. From the family album, I knew it had been a mere eighty-two pink-and-white candles. But at the time, the heat from that cake had been terrifying. I'd had to be hauled from under a chair to do my duty and join the other youngsters in helping Auntie Myrtle blow out her candles. If the breath leaving my tear-dampened lips had done little more than add spit to the icing, my windbag cousins had more than made up for it – almost setting the poor woman's shawl on fire.

Yet in the photograph, she's smiling.

I shook off the memory, unsure why it made me uneasy. Of course she was smiling. Everyone smiled in their birthday photos. I checked my watch. Plenty of time for a quick jog before work. I wasn't to pick up Auntie Myrtle from the Manor until 5 pm, to give her time for a nap before her hairdresser arrived to freshen her 'do.' I hoped I still cared about my appearance that much when I passed a hundred and six.

And looked better, I thought, unable to restrain a shudder. Auntie Myrtle's cheeks had shriveled to the point where cake crumbs could be lost in their creases. Finding a safe place to plant a birthday kiss had become a challenge. It could have been worse, I suppose. Farguses aged like leather, wearing thin and growing stiff, but tough rather than brittle. Some of my friends had relatives in Trillium Manor who couldn't live anywhere but the first floor–the one with extra-wide fire doors and power-assist washrooms. Trapped by their own flesh, with no casual trips home, most could no longer walk without help.

My cross trainers, complete with fresh socks, were prominently displayed in front of the TV. Magazine photos of the impossibly fit covered my sofa and chair, with a poster showing the opposite above the toilet. All part of my twenty-ninth birthday gift to myself–a resolution to do anything and everything possible to get off my rump and do something about my body.

It wasn't love; it was fear. Like most other Farguses of my generation, I'd finished college to find love handles and the beginnings of a potbelly waiting for me. It was abundantly clear I wasn't destined to be one of the lean no-matter-what-they-ate Farguses. I was going to be one of the lumpy ones, the ones who were more likely to have certain issues as they aged. Heart attack. Diabetes. Kidney failure. Cancer. The ones who didn't pass their thirties.

My parents scoffed at my sudden interest in fitness, insisting I was perfect as is, calling me a solid, promising young man.

Solid. Thinking rather wistfully of sunken cheeks, I grabbed my shoes and headed for the door, determined to control my fate.

☙

Roland Fargus happened to be along my jogging route, his squalid cardboard tent nestled against one pillar of the highway that humped over our town, leaving a shadow and little more in its wake. The few people who took the off-ramp headed for the golden arches, ate, used the bathrooms, then jumped back on as if our town didn't exist.

I suppose that's why I looked for him when I ran by each morning. Our family treated Roland the same way. It wasn't something I judged, just an irony I couldn't shake any easier than the flab riding my butt.

As usual, he was bent over a can. I ran early, before the traffic began filling the streets with noise and stench. Roland was up and digging through trash bins before they were emptied for the day–and before there were passersby to shout at him. Or worse.

I'd learned it was safe to stare; he never acknowledged my existence either, seeming as aloof as the traffic overhead. I grew to think of him as one more landmark to pass along my route, a sign I was two/thirds of the way done each morning's self-torture.

Until today. For some reason, the pounding of my feet rolled Roland's head in my direction, the movement as deliberate and slow as a pet chameleon sizing up a cricket. His pale eyes glittered within a mass of filthy hair twining from forehead to chest. A nose, sun burnt and peeling, marked the middle of his face. Startled, I lost my rhythm, my feet tangling themselves so I almost stepped into the oily edge of a puddle. Then I heard him say: "It's not going to save you."

My feet landed in the puddle and stayed there. "P-pardon?"

Roland's voice had a rasp to it, as if used so seldom it had lost the polished shape of vowels. "The running. The sweat. Your time's almost up no matter what you do. Poor Bastard."

I'd been ready for mockery, would have understood and deflected spite without a thought. His pity stung. "Why do you say that?"

"Because it's true. Do you know who I am, Bobby?"

Bobby? No one called me that–not since my first day of
school, when I'd proudly written "Robert Fargus" all by myself
and insisted the family use my full, grown-up name. Which meant
Roland had been living like this longer than I'd imagined. "You're
my Uncle. Roland Fargus," I said, now wishing I'd worn a more
dignified T-shirt than my faded Spiderman.

Perhaps my acknowledgment surprised him. He straightened
and took a step closer, tilting his head as though to see me better.
It shifted a mat of hair, showing me the squint lines at the edge of
one eye. "You always were a nice boy, Bobby," he said at last.
"I'm so sorry."

"Why?" I demanded as he turned to leave, presumably
heading for the shelter of his hideaway, with its floor of newsprint
and twisted sleeping bags. "Why do you feel sorry for me?" I
fought to keep it polite, to avoid sounding scornful. He was
family, after all.

His eyes fixed on me again. They glistened, as if moist. "No
reason. Nothing. I shouldn't have said anything. Run all you
want–" His left hand waved into the distance, hurrying me along.
"I'm a crazy old man–didn't your father tell you?"

Roland's fingers were spotless, the nails as tidy as my own. I
stared at them, my preconceptions of his life and choices
fragmenting. Why so much effort to keep clean while living like
this?

He noticed my attention and tucked both hands inside the
shapeless parka that sheltered his body from neck to knee.
"There's nothing I can do for you, Bobby," my uncle almost
whispered. "I was afraid to speak out when you and your cousins
were young, when it might have made a difference. It's too late
now."

"Afraid of what? What difference?"

"Afraid of–" his voice faltered, then gathered strength again.
"They left me alone because I left them alone. I know it made me
no better than them. I've traded your lives simply to keep my own

existence. Such as it is. You'd better go. Talking to me for long– it's not a good idea."

I clutched at what made some sense. He was a crazy old man, which meant he was someone who needed help, whether he knew it or not. I'd been raised properly. And he was family. "What's not a good idea," I said firmly, "is your living like this, Uncle. Come with me. Please."

He was already shaking his head so violently the tangles writhed over the fabric of his parka, making a sound like terrified snakes. "Never. I won't go back. I'm only safe here."

"You call living like this safe?!" I eased my tone, tried to make it persuasive and gentle. I'd never been good at talking to children or pets. "Uncle. It would mean a lot to me. Today's my birthday–"

"Dear Sweet Jesus." Suddenly his too-clean hands were fastened on my arms, nails digging in to hold me; his face, contorted and wild, pressed close to mine until his breath entered my nostrils, hot and reeking of old onion. "You can't go back. You can't! They'll suck another year out of you. It might be your last! The bright little vampires will steal your life! Stay with me, Bobby! Don't go!"

I should have listened then, but I couldn't. Panicked by his closeness, by the hysteria in his voice, I shoved Roland away from me as hard as I could. Yet even as I staggered down the street, I found myself shocked not by what he'd said or done, but by the strong, solid feel of him.

Roland might be living out of cans, but he was no gaunt scarecrow. And I didn't know a Fargus his age who wasn't.

What was going on?

☙

My timing stayed off the rest of the day, so I wasn't surprised to find I was too early to pick up Great Auntie Myrtle. Rather than sit in the main floor waiting lounge, where anyone without wrinkles was a magnet for bored, nosey residents, I took my car around the block a few times. I didn't intend to swing wide on my third trip. Or make the turn onto Industrial Rd. But there I was.

Roland was sitting on his 'porch,' as if waiting for me.

I pulled up along the curb and stopped the car. It didn't seem right to leave it running, adding fumes to the already potent air under the overpass. Then, it didn't seem right to stay inside, on a cushioned driver's seat, with Roland patiently sitting on his triangle of Styrofoam. I found myself walking around the car, oddly unconcerned if any of the vehicles passing by carried folks who'd know me on sight, and leaned on the part of the front fender that didn't have rust. "Sorry I pushed you, Uncle," I told him, hearing an almost sullen note in my voice. It had been a while since I'd had to apologize.

"I scared you, Bobby, talking crazy." Roland's eyes slid away from me. "You look fine. Off to your party, then?"

"After a stop at Trillium–picking up Auntie Myrtle."

This brought his eyes back. "The Old Hag still steals the limelight on your day, does she?" He barked a laugh at my sputtering protest. "You don't have to be on your best behaviour with me, Bobby Fargus. I was there for your first five birthdays, in case you remember. I do–you hated sharing the family party. Who wouldn't?"

It was akin to heresy. I smiled anyway. "I admit, there were times–but I'm a little old to worry about sharing my birthday these days, Uncle."

"And you think one day it will be your day, don't you? Yours alone? You think you'll outlive her?"

They weren't innocent questions, not with that searching look, not with that gentle pity. My fear from this morning, from every morning, rushed back. Did he know somehow? "Of course I'll outlive her. Not that I wish any ill to my Great Aunt–your Aunt," I emphasized with as much dignity as I could muster with a dry mouth, "but she's already very old." Even for a Fargus, one hundred and six was a significant accomplishment.

"Oh, she'll keep getting older. Just like the rest of them in the Manor." Roland rubbed his hands over his knees, as if trying to remove the stains from his pants. "But not you. You're almost done." He didn't wait for me to think of something to say to this, but lifted his arms in a hopeless gesture. "It's the birthday parties, Bobby. That's when they steal your time."

If he'd stood and approached me...if he'd said anything that made any sense at all...I would have jumped back in my car and been out of there for good. But in the back of my mind, I felt I'd failed him earlier. I'd fail him even more going to sit at that table without taking him with me, if I ate more than I needed, while he gnawed on brown-tipped apple cores and stale pizza crust. What my parents would have to say—I shuddered, but gathered my courage. "A lot of people don't like birthdays," I began. "You should think of it as a chance for a decent meal."

Roland's hands tightened on his knees, but gave no other indication of violent tendencies. I'd watched enough reality crime on TV to know the signs. "I want you to keep listening to me, Bobby," he said in a calm, reasonable voice. "Listen just for couple of minutes, without arguing or leaving. Will you do that?"

I checked my watch. Great Auntie Myrtle would be in her rinse. I'd listened to customers babble about their kids and dogs far longer to make a sale. Roland was family. "Sure," I promised, my brain ready to disengage as long as necessary.

"Good. Good. What I'm going to say—it's fantastic. You'll find it hard to believe. I know I did. But I swear to you, Bobby, it's the truth. More than that. It's the only way to save yourself, if you still can."

"I'm listening, Uncle."

His hands lifted and spread as if holding a platter in the air between us. "It's something about the candles. The ones they put on the birthday cakes. I don't know how they work—if there's some kind of curse on them or magic mumbo-jumbo at work—You promised to listen!" as I involuntarily shuffled my feet.

I stopped shuffling and nodded. "Birthday cakes. Candles," I repeated numbly.

"Right. That's when it happens. When a child blows out the candles on his cake, the year of life he might have had goes, too—but not into smoke. No. It goes to the others. They steal it for themselves." He hunched, peering up at me through his mats of hair. "Not everyone, mind. It's just us. Just the Farguses. It's our family tradition." His beard twisted over where his mouth had to be, as though his lips fought that barrier to get out the words.

"Tradition." We certainly had enough of those, I thought, glad of the firm reality of the car behind me. An abhorrence of my cousin Sam's over spiced pumpkin pie I could understand. But candle phobia? No wonder the crazy old coot didn't want to come to a birthday party. "Are there any other traditions I should worry about, Uncle?" I asked, proud I wasn't laughing out loud.

"I know you don't believe me, Bobby." Roland got to his feet but thankfully stayed by his hovel. "It took me years to comprehend myself. But I couldn't ignore the evidence—"

"There's evidence?"

"Ever notice how you feel after blowing out the candles? That sense of anticlimax? Maybe a faint moment of exhaustion?"

"Anyone over sixteen fusses over their birthday—"

"No. The weariness is real. They keep you sitting, hand you gifts to open, so you won't stand up and realize you really are different from the way you were the moment before air left your mouth, before they stole your time."

For no reason beyond duty, I made myself argue with him. "Everyone in the family has a cake with candles—"

"When was the last time you saw one of your elders blow out their own? What a nice family tradition—to let the children help—" Roland spat, cratering the blackened dust. "There are two kinds of Fargus, Bobby. The ones who take and the ones who can't. They know who's who early, believe me."

"They?" I said weakly.

"Who is in charge of birthday parties? Who bakes the cake?

Who puts on the candles?"

Mom? I blinked at the unbidden image of my mother and aunts conspiring in their kitchens over icing and dried violets, whispering arcane spells over layers of chocolate or vanilla, lemon or orange, spice or carrot. I saw the cake sitting before my Great Auntie Myrtle and remembered the terror of its carpet of flame, waiting to consume my breath. "This is utter crap!" I protested involuntarily, forgetting my duty to humor the old man.

"Is it?" Roland seemed to draw strength from my disbelief, his own voice firming and growing stern. "I thought so, too, boy, until the day I decided I didn't want to celebrate getting older. I refused to take part in birthday parties of any kind. And you know what? That next year, I began to feel better, stronger. But it wasn't as easy as that–you can't just refuse."

I couldn't argue with him there. Roland's self-exile from the family couldn't have been easy; we Farguses took our gatherings seriously. "What happened?" I asked, curious in spite of my better judgment.

"I avoided the family, stayed away. Made it clear none of them were welcome. It wasn't good enough. They tracked me to my job. Cupcakes with candles would appear on my desk, follow me down the halls, trap me in meetings. From the family. This–" an eloquent wave at his cardboard and bag castle "—this was the only way to finally escape them."

"Them?"

"Why do you think your mother and aunts get teary at birthdays? They know what they are doing–some still care about us. Not the old ones–they are happy as can be with the curse. How do you think they keep on living, when most of us don't?"

The family gift–pass the tricky thirties and live and live and live.

"Good genes," I countered, my hands damp against the fender. "Some of us have them. Some of us don't."

"Like you? Think a bit of a pot means you're doomed to die in your thirties? Hah! Look at me, Bobby." Roland unzipped his parka and dropped it to the dirt. Underneath was a body mirror-image to my own, if more heavily rounded at belly and thigh. "I'm ten years older than your father. I passed the tricky thirties decades ago–because I escaped the hags and their candles. You can too–"

My cell phone interrupted him. I reached for it like I'd reach for a rope if drowning, desperate for a sane voice. It was my mother. "Robert? Where are you? Aunt Myrtle called to say you weren't there to pick her up yet."

"I'm on my way, Mom," I told her, then looked at Roland. Even as I opened my mouth to ask, he shook his head violently. "Be there in five," I said instead and closed the phone.

"I have to go–"

"Goodbye then, Bobby. Just do yourself one favor. Pay attention tonight. For your own sake. Watch them."

I felt trapped into nodding a polite acknowledgment, for all the world as if the two of us had been neighbors meeting over a hedge, discussing the best way to discourage dandelions.

Not curses, candles, and my life.

ဆ

"There you are." Somehow, my mother managed to make the phrase welcoming and ominous at the same time. I kissed her cheek then helped guide Great Auntie Myrtle through the front hall, around the piles of shoes determined to trip latecomers, quite sure my guilt showed.

They couldn't know where I'd been and no one chastised me for being late. This was my birthday party, after all, and a young man of twenty-nine, I was reminded by several amused relatives, was likely to have his thoughts elsewhere. Their cheer and warmth helped me relax, and sometime between the last piece of fried chicken and the usual tussle to get little Nancy to stop hiding her peas under her plate, I'd almost managed to put Roland Fargus out of my mind.

Almost. Every so often, a rich mouthful threatened to gag me;

I shivered when the windows began to rattle under the driving rain. I knew I shouldn't have left the old man. I should have brought him home, here, to his family. I'd let his bit of inane fantasy get under my skin and he was the one suffering for it.

"Happy Birthday to you..." The song startled me from my thoughts. I looked up to see my cake approaching.

The candles were dark blue this year, their tiny flames steadfast and true against the breeze of my mother's triumphant passage through the dining room. This year's cake was a tall concoction of frothy white icing, with my name in melted chocolate across the top and more chocolate drizzled down the sides. I'd seen something similar on the cover of a magazine at the grocery store. My mom and aunts liked to keep up on styles.

"Make a wish, Robert." My mother set the cake before me, its pedestal plate holding it at just the right height.

Have you ever had an idea, or maybe it was something you'd seen or read, that spread itself like a blight over what you thought was normal? I stared at my cake, and suddenly saw each candle as a tiny vampire, waiting to suck another year away. I couldn't blow them out to save my life.

Or maybe that was the point.

"Robert? Do you need Nancy's help?"

Any other day, I would have heard this from my aunt and laughingly defended my right to my own candles. Instead, I stared across the table at the round, friendly face I thought I knew and saw a monster, ready to sacrifice her offspring.

Without hesitation, I inhaled, then blew out the flames with one breath.

Nothing. Only a round of congratulations from those at the table and a pout from Nancy, who'd lunged forward too late.

Roland was insane and I was crazy listening to him. Knowing this, I couldn't help trying to stand up right away. My mother's hand dropped on my shoulder, pushing me back down even as she planted a kiss where the hair thinned over my temple. "Sit, dear, sit. Cut the cake. You don't want to slow down your presents!"

All normal. All as birthdays should be, in a loving family. But I felt my heart pounding as I put the knife to the icing and pressed it through the soft, clinging layers. My mother collected the candles as they tipped and threatened to fall, gathering them all into one hand with soft exclamations of pleasure.

"Where's my cake?!" The volume my Great Aunt could produce from her frail form never ceased to amaze me. "Did you forget my cake, Rebecca?"

The usual chorus of denials counter pointed my mother's calm: "Patsy's bringing it, dear. Let Robert finish–"

"I'm not getting any younger, you know!"

"It's all right, Mom," I said, putting down the knife. Auntie Myrtle rarely waited this long to demand her half of our party–it was a sign of my mother's determination and fortitude that my cake at least arrived first.

Or was it?

Damn Roland. His crazy lies were ruining my party.

They dimmed the lights for effect, not that you'd notice. One hundred and six candles produced enough illumination to pick out the expectant eyes around the table, to spark from every piece of glassware and waiting fork, and bring out the colours of both sweaters and wallpaper. I presumed the batteries were pulled from the detectors–my Aunt Patsy was squinting against the smoke filling her face and rising over her shoulders. I heard Great Auntie Myrtle give a sound like a purr beside me.

I knew she would be smiling, showing no teeth whatsoever.

My mother was herding the youngest to our side of the table, a tricky maneuver at best with the huge cake on its way to the same destination. "Gather 'round your Great Auntie. Careful now. Robert?"

I pulled my chair back slightly from the table and turned it so I faced Auntie Myrtle. Sam's youngest, Mike Jr., immediately crawled onto my lap, presumably after a better vantage point. I ignored him. I ignored the arrival of the cake, despite the wave of heat wafting towards me. I ignored the singing and the clatter of plates.

Instead, I watched the woman clapping her gnarled hands with glee.

Pay attention, Roland had urged.

The song ended. Five little Farguses puckered up and blew happily at the carpet of flame, Mike Jr. managing to miss completely. The candle flames danced and flickered in answer, some going out, others fighting to burn longer. Laughter and more breaths.

All the while, I watched.

I watched Auntie Myrtle's eyes sparkle. I watched her tiny tongue dart out to moisten her non-existent lips.

I watched her complexion begin to glow with a blush that wasn't the reflection of fire.

Answering to instinct, I wrapped my arms around Mike Jr., resting my cheek against his soft hair, smelling baby shampoo and chocolate. He squirmed free to join the other children waiting for their share of cake.

"Robert?" Softly, from my mother, her tone making the word both warm and warning. I looked up to find the eyes of everyone over forty fixed on me. My Auntie Myrtle, for once, wasn't smiling at all.

"I'll have ice cream with my piece, please," I said.

ℭℤ

I won't say I believed Roland's wild story about the candles and our family's tendency to either die too young or live too long. Not even when I woke the day after my twenty-ninth birthday and had to lay back down again to still the irregular racing of my heart. I blamed it on too much to eat and drink, swearing to keep to my fitness regime and watch my diet.

It couldn't be because my own family was stealing my health.

The doctors had their own explanations. High blood pressure. Congested veins. A heart forced to work harder than it should. I was sent to one specialist after another, began taking pills to lower my blood pressure, pills to calm my nerves, pills to lower my cholesterol, pink ones, blue ones. They came in as many colours as candles.

I kept running. Desperately. Daily. In any and all weather. Roland was gone, his cardboard settling under the assault of rain then snow into the shape of a corpse. Every so often, I'd pick up two coffees in the drive-thru on my way to work. I'd follow the shadow of the overpass, stopping at likely trash bins, but never found him. I'd leave the extra coffee with someone faceless and cold, feeling as though I looked into a mirror.

Roland's disappearance ate at me. Had I driven a poor old fool away to his death?

Or had a wiser man than I known to flee for his life?

Whether I believed Roland or not, somehow I missed Easter supper at Sam and Mike's. I managed to schedule a trip out of town over my mother's birthday. Thanksgiving came and I spent it with a girl I'd met at a bar who was avoiding family of her own.

Well before Christmas, I'd changed my phone number so I didn't have to make excuses any more.

My family was remarkably restrained. I had no visitors. There were postcards from whomever of my relatives had taken a trip, but no messages other than 'hope to see you soon.' Perhaps losing Roland had taught them a lesson. Perhaps I was going to be granted the right to decide my own way of life, make up my own traditions. My own fate.

Ever feel the approach of your birthday on the back of your neck, as if fingers of bone sought your life's pulse?

As mine grew closer, I worried over what Roland had told me—how the family birthday cakes found him at work. I could have tried telling my co-workers I didn't want a celebration this year, but they'd plot something anyway. After all, who didn't object to their thirtieth? Who didn't try to stay twenty-nine as long as possible?

Who didn't fear time?

The pills, the diet, the running weren't enough. I'd left it too late. That's why Roland had pitied me. I was no longer well enough to pick up and move away; I couldn't survive on the streets. All I could do was believe in Roland, believe he'd survived his tricky thirties by avoiding the candles. If that was enough, I could save myself.

But how? And what about the others? Mike Jr., Nancy, all the other children?

Then, I *knew*.

I had to destroy the threat at its source.

℃

Splash!

I winced and paused, clutching the remaining games in my arms. My mother had gone outside to refill the bird feeder, but she had impeccable timing when it came to catching me in the wrong. This...was wrong.

Gathering myself, I slipped the next cartridge into the dark, gleaming liquid. Our tidy storeroom left me no choice. My excuse for being here was to finally pick up the box of vintage Nintendo games I'd left in the basement. I'd mumbled something about a new gaming store taking trades–my parents wouldn't know the difference.

I did. The beloved adventures of my youth disappeared into the sump, as if the sacrifice of health wasn't enough to appease time.

The box was the key. Once it was emptied, I carried it up the stairs, listening for my parents. Nothing. I tiptoed into the pantry, pulling the door almost closed before turning on the light. Subtle smells of cereal and spice competed with cleanser. The shelves were always full. When I was younger, I'd believed elves restocked them while we slept, especially close to a holiday, when treats briefly outnumbered staples.

It was darker magic I sought now. My hand went unerringly to the second lowest drawer on the back right side. I'd helped my father install all the latest hardware and shelving, including this set of wide pullouts. The tin box winked at me from behind its wall of icing sugar and shortening. With a shudder, I grabbed it and stuffed it into the Nintendo box.

Step one accomplished.

⁓

I'd been afraid to incinerate the tin box and its contents. For all I knew, setting the candles on fire would only suck more life from those of us vulnerable to their theft. Instead, I'd run my car over the box until it oozed coloured wax and pieces of string, then shoved the remnants into the dumpster behind Mickey D's.

Fire would do for the rest. I licked my lips as I drove, prodding the lump of the latest cold sore to afflict the inside of my mouth. I focused on such things rather than what I had to do. I wasn't a monster.

Yet.

If only I'd been able to find Roland. My hands twisted on the steering wheel until its Naugahyde wrap squeaked in protest. This was a job for two. More than enough guilt for two as well. Or would sharing it only double it?

I pulled into the driveway of Trillium Manor as always, but didn't stop at the entrance or head for visitor parking. Instead, I made the sharp right into the narrow lane that led around back. The plow didn't fit back here—or else the custodians were too lazy to bother. The headlines sparkled on the icicles draping the brick wall. My car slipped and bounced along bones of ice; I didn't dare slow down or I'd be stuck for sure.

Fire melted ice.

I shrugged away guilt and anticipation, settling for a numb attention to detail as I turned the car around. Better to take three tries than dig a tire into a snow bank. Better to leave the engine running than risk a stall. Better to put on gloves before opening the trunk than have gas stinking up my hands.

I kept my face down, trusting the hood of the shapeless old coat I'd found in a garbage bin. If anyone was awake, the items I carried to the rear service door should appear innocuous on their own: a recycle bin full of newspaper, a can of gasoline, and a crowbar.

I didn't need the crowbar after all. The cheap padlock hung loose beside the door; perhaps frozen. I opened the door to a choking blast of warm, moist air, redolent of the dumpster behind Mickey D's but with an added tang of urine and bleach. Doing my best to breathe only through my mouth, I heaved the can and bin into the room and closed the door behind me, blinking as my eyes adjusted to the brightness.

I knew my way. This was where we moved in our senior Farguses, at least the piece or two of furniture that would fit inside a room already crowded by bed and dresser, the box of photographs, the bags of clothes. The rest was scavenged by the next generation, what wasn't tossed aside adding to possessions that would be scavenged in turn by their offspring. I'd become conscious of such cycles lately.

And planned to break one.

Straight ahead through doubled doors: the elevators and stairs. Left corridor: the laundry rooms, quiet at this time of night. Right corridor: waste disposal, including the garbage chute to every floor.

My destination. I staggered to the door, shoving it wide with the recycle bin, then pushed the bin into the darkness beyond. I let the door swing closed behind me as I groped for the switch.

The lights came on before I touched it. "Whadda you doing here, Bobby?" demanded a familiar, rasping voice.

"Uncle Roland?!" I gaped at the apparition beside me. He was wrapped in a floral comforter that had seen better centuries. Behind him, on the floor, was a familiar pile of cardboard and sleeping bags, as though he'd simply moved his hovel indoors. "I looked for you everywhere."

"Didn't look here, did you?" He'd washed sometime in the last month, so his hair was merely dark with grease as opposed to matted. "Murph lets me come out of the cold. Doesn't explain why you're down here. After hours. And with that." He poked the recycle bin with a bare toe. "What are you about, Bobby Fargus?"

"I have to stop them. You can help me!"

"Help–" Roland let the blanket fall from his shoulders, his fingers combing hair from his eyes as if that helped him see me better. Then his hands went still. "You can't–you can't mean to–"

I blinked to clear my own vision, the moisture burning my chapped cheeks. "It's the only way to end this–to save us. They all have to die."

"Bobby, no! Why? Because of what I said? I'm crazy, Bobby. Look at me!" Roland beat both fists against his own chest. "I'm a nutcase. Certifiable! I should be locked up on the third floor of the Berton Institute, for cris'sake. You mustn't believe anything I say."

"Why do you defend them, Uncle?" I asked, feeling suspicion fall around me like the kiss of cold, wet snowflakes. "What's changed? What did they offer you?"

His mouth worked to protest, to say something. A curse, perhaps. It didn't matter.

I needed the crowbar after all.

α

Roland helped me, in his fashion. His cardboard bed was dry and warm. Doused with gasoline, it ignited into a pillar of virtuous flame, licking its way up the walls, impatient for the draft coming down through the chute door. A door I'd propped open, feeling more mechanically inclined than usual.

I left him there, arranging his arms around the gasoline can. A fitting epitaph for the man who'd revealed the truth to me, however confused he'd been at the end. I hurried out the door into the corridor. I'd filled my car before coming–it should still be running, waiting to take me home, where I'd hear the news tomorrow about the tragic fire, and the loss of an entire generation of Farguses, their leathery bodies so much carbon, and the crazy old homeless man who'd killed them all.

Three more steps to safety. To health. To a future.

Before I could take the third, I was blinded by spray and deafened by alarms. I yanked the hood over my head and stumbled forward, arms outstretched. A red light flashed from all directions.

I'd failed. It remained to be seen how completely. My hands were dripping wet and slid painfully down the metal edge as I tugged the door open. Steam rose from my clothes as the cold air hit. I ran for my car as I'd run from my fate.

Only to have my feet betray me on the ice. Falling, twisting, I looked up and saw faces pressed against dozens of lighted windows, faces that watched until my head hit the ice and I knew nothing more. Faces of family.

ℜ

The case was never in doubt. There were more than enough witnesses, each delighted to have an excuse for an outing. Others had seen me jogging by Roland's summer hovel, under the highway. What no one understood was why. Oh, they asked. The police, the media, those doctors. At first, I refused to explain, but the nights locked in the ward held things worse than anything I'd seen on television, worse than I could have imagined.

And there was always the chance someone might have believed me.

Candles and family curses. I'd destroyed the evidence; they refused to examine my Aunts' tin boxes. I should have kept silent, but it all came out. At least, I'm no longer in a prison ward. I'm on the clean and sanitary third floor of Berton's Institute.

Helpless.

But safe. I have to believe it or go as mad as they say I am.

"Don't scrunch your eyes like that, Mr. Fargus. I know you're awake."

I might be awake, but I didn't have to acknowledge my jailer. But she had other ideas. My eyes shot open as flecks of chilled water hit my face. "Don't do that!" I snarled vainly into Nurse Brocket's too-close, too-smug grin. She straightened, replacing her pink plant mister in its holster with the smoothness of a gunfighter, the bottle surely uncomfortable against her thin hip, and slid the wheeled table over my lap. "I've already had the slop you call supper," I protested, twisting my wrists against the straps holding me to the chair.

"I know-o," she chortled, a sound so unlike her ear-threatening habitual whine that it rated the raising of heads by the other chair-bound fools lining this wall. I glared at them, but without success. Those who weren't drooling couldn't focus at the best of times. "I have a surprise for you. Look!" Nurse Brocket whirled away from me, only to turn back more slowly. Slowly, so her motion didn't do more than bend the tip of each tiny flame rising from the object in her hands.

There were thirty candles on that cake, guttering with spite, like so many fierce little eyes watching me with hunger–and expectation.

"Here you go, Mr. Fargus. From your mother–

"Happy Birthday!"

Peel

~ 2005 ~

by Julie E. Czerneda

Author's Note: When Marty (Martin Greenberg) contacted me for this, I was almost as worried as I'd been about writing horror. I reminded him I didn't write classic "evil". Then, while visiting my brother-in-law's new home, I noticed a bit of peeling paint. Suddenly, I had this notion of a world that wasn't what it seemed on the surface. Excited, I wrote what I thought was a terrific little science fiction story about it and sent it off to the editor, John Helfers.

After a slight delay, during which time I'm sure he was alternately chuckling and wondering what to do, John got back to me. He was most polite (i.e. didn't call me an idiot) and asked if they could hang on to the story for an upcoming science fiction anthology. Why?

Because this anthology was fantasy and my story, though wonderful, wouldn't quite fit.

An understatement if ever there was one. (Hence my advice to other writers–check the invitation a final time before submitting!) I took the story back, tore it apart, and thought...hmmm. Sure enough, it worked even better rewritten as fantasy. Darker. Richer.

I've read "Peel" aloud several times and always enjoy the reaction it gets. It isn't what most expect from me.

Water seeps through the windowsill when the wind blows from the east. It finds a path through a crack in the plastic. It soaks the plaster within, lingers in hidden wood.

Best of all, it peels the paint.

Her fingers tremble over the imperfection, stroke the ripples like a lover's skin.

With a nail, she marks the edge of softness, then pulls ever-so-gently. The paint–its colour of no importance–comes away willingly. She grasps the tiny beginning between fingertips; her tongue's between her teeth.

She tries not to hope too much.

This is her lucky day. The paint peels with extravagant generosity, bringing with it strips of paper from the dampened wall. She shifts her fingers to the edges, careful to work with it, adjusting to the growing tension as the peel reaches the end of the invading moisture. It becomes stubborn and brittle and falls free at last.

She cradles the peel in her hand, watching it curl. Her fingers echo the shape.

She sits back to survey the result, the chill of tile unnoticed in the blush of triumph. Multiple grays mix with black specks of mold. Paper feathers the sodden plaster. She sees faces in textures;

landscapes in whorls.

Change whispers in her ears. Enthralling. Enticing.

Forbidden.

Footsteps.

She releases the curtain, tucks her hand–and the peel–in her pocket, stands. There is time for this, and no more, before...

"Oh, there you are, dear!" The woman's voice is soft and warm. Her face is smooth and lovely. Her clothing is fitted, its colour of no importance. There is no flaw in form or gesture.

She touches the peel and remembers. There had been lines beside her mother's eyes. Hard work and sun had conspired. There had been lines beside her mother's mouth. Laughter and worry had taken turns.

The woman's skin is perfect.

"Your ride's here, dear. Have a nice day at work. Wear your coat."

She doesn't answer, simply walks to the door. The rudeness brings no frown or puzzlement.

Nothing changes.

She touches the peel; her new talisman.

☓

She walks with her eyes straight ahead. The sidewalks are clean and even, slicing obedient lawns. The vehicle disturbs not a blade as it waits, silent and steel. Its colour is of no importance. A set of steps lead up and in.

Faces smile from their rows. All are smooth and lovely. She feels no warmth or welcome. She can't tell them apart.

Her fingertip fondles the peel as she sits.

Murmurs, soft and melodious, thicken and twist the air. "It's going to be a nice day." "Look at that sky. Perfect!" "You know what Monday means." "We never forget. Movie night at your place." She hums without breath, a discordant, dangerous humming; rebellion in her bones.

She remembers. The peel left change in its wake.

A sign.

☙

She knows to move as they do, without flaw, always with purpose. Her hands reach. Her left picks up a rod, her right the ring that slips over it. Make them one, put them down. Her hands reach. Her left picks up a rod, her right the ring that slips over it. Make them one, put them down. The material is inanimate, its colour of no importance.

Murmurs gather around her feet, as if dust. Gentle, warm murmurs. "What a nice day to be at work." "Look how well this fits." "Here comes another one." "It's so good to be here." "The movie will be fun too."

Then, without warning, a shard falls, lifts a plume of dismay.

"We could play cards tonight instead."

The murmurs choke themselves to silence.

Her hands reach, as all hands here do, in unceasing synchrony. Her left picks up a rod, her right the ring that slips over it. Make them one, put them down.

Her hands don't need her eyes. She lifts her gaze, seeks the shard.

His face is smooth and lovely. He works in silence, moving without flaw. But, for an instant, his lips misplace the peaceful smile painted on the rest. They peel back, showing a glimpse of teeth. A rictus. It could be fear. Or surprise.

Change.

Her groin burns. Her breath catches in her throat. She cannot move.

Another sign.

His lips close, then open. "The movie will be fun, too."

Her hands reach. Her left picks up a rod, her right the ring that slips over it. Make them one, put them down.

Inside, she hums something discordant, dangerous.

Different.

☙

She sits, knees and feet together, back straight. On either side, others sit, knees and feet together, backs straight. Before them, scenes of carnage alternate with lust. Faces can't be seen. Voices have no words. Deeds have no context. It is the same movie they watch each Monday.

Her hand finds its pocket. Her fingers find the peel. It's smaller. It shrinks into itself. It will dry and fragment soon, becoming something new.

Finding the peel, she remembers. The man who sits to her left. There had been calluses on his palms. Thorns and gravel had etched them. There had been a broken nail and scars. Strength and tenderness had been in every touch.

The man's hands rest, flawless, on his lap.

"This movie is nice." "I always like this movie." "What a great day at work."

She simply stands and walks away. Her body blocks the image from their view. The rudeness brings no protest or complaint.

Nothing changes.

Almost.

Something changed today.

She almost smiles.

☙

Leaving the midst of the movie is...change.

Walking down the sidewalk, the ker-pat ker-pat of her small quick steps the only sound is...change.

Alone, she dares revel in it, dares throw back her head and stretch out her arms, dares...

"Hello, dear." The woman's voice is soft and melodious. It comes from the dark beside her, a stranger's kiss. Shadows without substance tremble in the cold, east wind.

Dropping her arms, she savors her fear, in its way as novel as hope. "Hello."

"Why aren't you at the movie with your friends, dear?"

She says the expected. "It was nice." Then, with the peel in her pocket and the glimpse of teeth in her memory, adds: "The movie machine stopped working. It needs repair. I came home to see you. Mother."

The shadows stop moving. The world holds its breath. She clings to the moment, anticipation quickening her heart until she almost laughs. Then, smooth and warm and the same as always: "That's nice, dear. Let's walk home together." The figure steps out of the darkness, lovely and flawless. Perfect.

She simply walks on her way, ker-pat ker-pat, listening to the echo of following footsteps.

She smiles at the feel of storm in the air.

⚃

The next morning, the windowsill is dry and clean. Caulking leers from its corners. Below, the wall is pristine, pure, perfect. Its colour has no importance.

Overcome with grief, she sits. The chill tile steals warmth from her bare legs and buttocks, robs her of sensation. She reaches a trembling hand to test for lies. The paint is solid; its finish immaculate.

Impenetrable.

Footsteps.

She's lost yesterday's peel. As every morning, a new garment waits on her bed, the old discarded. She grieves in silence.

"Oh, there you are, dear!" The woman's voice is soft and warm. Her face is smooth and lovely. Her clothing is fitted, its colour of no importance. There is no flaw in form or gesture.

She touches the paint and sees nothing, remembers nothing.

"Your ride's here, dear. Time to get dressed. Have a nice day at work."

She doesn't answer, simply stands and goes to her room to dress. The rudeness brings no frown or puzzlement.

Nothing changes.

Outside, she walks with her eyes straight ahead. The sidewalks are clean and even, slicing obedient lawns dusted with snow. The vehicle waiting disturbs not a flake as it hovers, silent and steel. Its colour is of no importance. A set of steps lead up and in.

Faces smile. All are smooth and lovely. She feels no warmth or welcome. She can't tell them apart.

She joins the murmuring. "What a lovely day." "Work will be nice." "Don't forget it's my house for the movie tonight." "We never forget." She doesn't know which words come from her mouth.

࿆

She moves as they do, without flaw, always with purpose. Her hands reach. Her left picks up a rod, her right the ring that slips over it. Make them one, put them down. Her hands reach. Her left picks up a rod, her right the ring that slips over it. Make them one, put them down. The material is inanimate flesh, its colour of no importance.

She reaches again, eyes blind by rote, and touches something warm.

His hand is out of place. Only by a breath, only for a heartbeat, but it is enough.

Her fingers, caught on skin, miss the next rod.

It's as if she's sleeping and only now awakes. She grasps the telltale rod and its abandoned ring, tucks both into her pocket with unfamiliar speed. Her hands reach, fingertips quivering. Her left picks up a rod, her right the ring that slips over it. Make them one, put them down.

Saved by rhythm, she looks up.

He's slower to recover. Before him a pair of connected rods and rings bounce aimlessly, unable to link themselves in the next step. His eyes catch on hers, a puzzling in their depths, then he looks back to his task, murmuring soft and warm: "This is nice."

Too late.

She remembers herself in his eyes.

And the scream comes from her soul.

 CB

There are worse things than remembering.

There is change.

She runs down the sidewalk, pat-ker-pat pat-ker-pat, dodging cracks and sprouts of frozen, ragged weeds, coughing as each breath brings more of the thick stench on the wind, shivering, eyes struggling to comprehend.

Reality is a peel, curled in the mind's hand, fragmenting as it dries, blowing away.

The buildings around her sag like a spinster's breasts. Every step takes her further into nightmare.

"Hello, dear." The woman's voice is hurried and harsh. "Why aren't you at work?" There is a sharp catch before each word, as though something is being reset.

She won't look. She won't answer.

She has seen beneath the paint.

℘

Her ride waits for her the next morning. Nothing has changed.

Everything has changed.

She isn't home.

Paint hangs in long fingerlike curls from every wall. It lies in dry wisps, irregular and wild, like tangled hair or autumn leaves. Plaster has fallen, dusty clumps pulled free and thrown to the tiles. Wood stares out, like bones stripped of flesh.

Words stain her window, fighting the frost.

"I am real."

Their colour is red.

℘

She holds court with dusty shadow, watches others perform. Their skin is perfect. Her fingers, nails stained and broken, tickle dying shrubs, wander crumbling brick, seek...what? She has left the words behind.

Things have changed. It is not enough.

Her hand loosens a shard of brick–its colour is of no importance–carries it into view. She brings it to her arm, cuts across softness, flinches with ecstasy. The shard falls to the ground.

With a nail, she tests the new edge, then pulls ever-so-gently. The paint–its colour of no importance–comes away willingly. She grasps the tiny beginning between fingertips; her tongue's between her teeth.

She tries not to hope too much.

The paint peels with extravagant generosity. She shifts her fingers to the edges, careful to work with it, adjusting to the growing tension as the peel becomes stubborn. She pulls hardest of all, and the peel falls free at last.

She cradles the peel in her hand, watching it curl. Her fingers echo the shape.

She stares at what is exposed. The chill wind goes unnoticed. Multiple grays mix with black specks of mold. Paper feathers sodden plaster. She sees faces in textures; landscapes in whorls.

What does it mean?

"Oh, there you are, dear!" The woman's voice is soft and warm. Renewed.

She knows what she will see. A face smooth and lovely, no flaw in form or gesture. She stares at her arm.

Why is there a wall within herself?

"You've missed your ride."

Who put it there?

She stares at her arm and sees dark liquid welling up through the plaster. Suddenly, the torn edge of the paint becomes a line of fire. She looks up, eyes swimming with change.

The peel is in her hand. Power is in her hand. "You are not my mother." Her voice is discordant, dangerous. Her voice hums with power. "You are not real."

The woman's mouth melts as she speaks. "You need your coa..." Lips go. Chin follows. The wind whips the air with ice, tat-tat tat-tat, and the woman congeals into a lump of inanimate flesh.

Clutching the peel, she looks at the sagging buildings, the remnants of gardens. She looks at others, perfect in form and perfectly oblivious, waiting by the old bus. "You are not real." The words lift in the wind and fly back in her face, blinding and sure. "There's only me."

She doesn't need to watch. She feels it happen, a shifting of perspective, a clarity as cold as the coming night.

They are gone. All of them. All of it.

She's done it before. And before that. Uncounted befores and before thats. Each time victory traps her. She closes a fist over the peel, remembering.

She won once. Only once. Her power ravaged this world and all who lived on it.

Leaving her alone.

Alone–until she has to rebuild it or go mad.

Rebuild–until she becomes lost.

Lost–until she rediscovers her lie and destroys it. Leaving her...

Alone–until she has to lie to herself again.

She opens her hand and watches the tiny piece uncurl.

"No," she tells it. "Not this time." She tips her hand, and watches the peel fall.

⚃

The freezing wind at her back is her guide, the sleet driving into her flesh her companion. She runs with the storm, owns its screams, its fury, its destruction. Every step marks purpose. Every moment marks change.

Even the one where she finds herself on her knees, on her stomach, and then curls into a sigh.

Even the one where the snow paints her with peace.

Water Remembers

~ 2012 ~

by Julie E. Czerneda

Author's Note: Having spent years in educational/non-fiction publishing, where it wasn't unusual to have sixty plus authors on a project, I'd no intention of collaborating in fiction. My stories. Mine, mine! Making my initial reaction, when R. Scott Taylor invited me to participate in his shared world anthology series, a virtual dash for the door. Nope nope!

But…the premise and world was fascinating, the other authors amazing, and Scott really wanted me as part of it. So I pondered. When I found my characters, I fell in love. Even now, this is one of my favourite stories. I think it always will be.

Life returned to Taux the way it had first come, from the sea. Those who'd cautiously then eagerly resettled the vacant city found themselves welcomed by a port of such cunning construction that fifty years without tending had done no appreciable damage. The great seawalls and the made islands they protected remained intact despite waves and the wicked storms that raged down this coast at season's turn.

The bay so sheltered was kept fresh, not by the twice-daily rise and fall of the tides beyond its mouth, but by the Wizards at its heart. Their Star Tower thrust from the depths, its structure impossibly tall and narrow, with windows like slanted eyes that glowed with an uncanny blue light. The top was shrouded in mist not even the summer sun could disperse, the base circled by an implacable current that made it impossible for ship or swimmer to approach, preserving the isolation of those who'd withdrawn from the world.

Which suited everyone else.

The elegant stone quay ringing the city's edge was intact, but Taux's wharves were another matter. The outthrust piers swayed against one another like cheerful drunks, their barnacled bases rotten to the core, while unguarded planks were ripped up and whisked away to build shelters. Taux's corsairs took what timber remained to build sturdy berths for their ships, extorting what fees they chose from those who came after.

For in Taux, there was no new wood to be had, or stone.

But there was always...opportunity.

Wizard's Fog, they called it, when those in the Star Tower loosed their spite to bother honest folk. The thick, cloying mist writhed through streets and alleyways, dampening sound and encouraging cutpurses. It coiled like a great eyeless snake in the bay, trapping ships and hiding all but the tip of one's nose.

Raising his mask, Hunhau sniffed reluctantly. The reek of

flowers to the left. A lingering stench of cold ash to the right. The bite of the open sea like a beacon ahead. He wasn't lost. Not yet, anyway.

Before the smells overwhelmed him, making his eyes fill with tears, he replaced the mask, its plugs snug in his nostrils. He shuffled along, feet bare to feel the stone, and squinted through the eye holes, for what good it could do. Lamplight couldn't penetrate a wizardly mist and the sun had yet to rise above the horizon. Without his nose, he'd walk off the quay into the bay or, more likely, into a wall.

Of course, without his nose, he'd be in the Black Gate District, home in bed like everyone else. Everyone honest, he amended.

Hunhau took firm hold of the straps that held the deep woven basket to his shoulders. He wasn't, he reminded himself, going to miss this chance. Yesterday's breeze had found him in his shop and trickled through the wads he habitually shoved up his nose while working. His weak affinity for air was usually a nuisance, bringing what he didn't want to his too-large and overly sensitive nose, but such a breeze, redolent of a distant shore, meant something worth the effort on today's tide...if he got to it first.

His toe struck an unexpected edge and Hunhau stopped to pull up his mask again. No need to inhale. The fetid odour of damp wool climbed up his nose, coupled with bat urine. He'd reached the stone bridge from the mainland portion of Taux to the Moon's Arm, the east most island that sheltered the bay. He hurriedly replaced the mask and went on as quickly as he dared. The Jai-Ruk who chose to sleep in hammocks under the bridge were not the pleasant sort. Not at all.

Not far now. Hunhau's outstretched fingers found the rail, cold and slick with dew. Moving with renewed confidence, he followed its downward curve until another stubbed toe painfully marked the end of the bridge. He was on the island, meaning the gap in the rail should be…here.

He made his way down the tilted rubble of what had once

been steps, following the familiar path. Before he reached the bottom, the mist began to thin, pierced by the faintest light. Sunrise.

He was late. The tide would come in soon, to steal back what it had brought. Worse, with the failing of the mist, others would come. He jumped from stone to damp sand and caught his balance.

Hunhau had discovered where to look years ago. Clean breezes from the open sea pushed flotsam and jetsam of all manner shorewards, to be stranded by the receding tide along this stretch of sand.

The others, wasteful wretches, sought the driftwood to burn. He sought the smooth wood, those pieces with shapes and whorls carved deep and wild, for far better use. To become masks.

Masks were always in demand, though only the elite of Taux could afford those of glorious imported jadeite, with obsidian eyes and rare plumes. Fewer still had the price—or were willing to pay it—for a mask of magical potency, bespelled to lure or deflect a gaze, to make the wearer appear otherwise, or to call luck to one's side like a dog.

Hunhau chuckled to himself. He'd yet to see a mask do more than hide a face. Yum Caax, his old master, had taught him masks were works of art, not magic, insisting what mattered was the craft, not the tricks. The craft was hard enough. Truth be told, Hunhau wasn't a very good maskmaker. Upon the old man's passing, he'd dutifully made Yum Caax's death mask then set up his own, more modest, shop. His masks were of wood and he served a clientele of servants, itinerants, and the like, those happy to afford any mask at all. Their needs were straightforward: masks for celebration, masks to honour their dead. So long as the sea gave him wood, he made a fair profit.

So long as he refused those seeking something more than a mask, he stayed out of trouble. For Yum Caax had been right. The only magic a Taux maskmaker possessed was the ability to convince a customer to believe what a mask could do. When results inevitably failed that belief, it was that foolish maskmaker who'd pay, unless he or she ran far and fast enough.

Hunhau preferred a safe and long life. He bet on the games, but not to excess, enjoyed women and wine, in moderation, and prudently collected bits of blue shell for his own death mask, having accepted that his meagre skills wouldn't attract an apprentice. On mornings when the conditions were right, he'd trundle along the quay, as this morning, and descend to the sand to gather driftwood.

Wizard's Fog. Hunhau shivered in the lingering damp, glad to see it lift even if that brought others to the sand. Now to see if the little breeze had been tease or promise. He lifted his mask to better look around. The clean sea air was potent, but didn't vex his stomach the way bilge and sailor-stink and that fusty odour from the sails did.

"Saints Great and Lesser," he gasped.

The exposed beach was strewn with wood of all shapes and sizes. Treasure for the taking!

And he was here first.

He picked his way through a delicious agony of choices, mind awhirl. Had a distant storm tossed shipwrack this way? Or had one of the dreadful waves that followed a disturbance of the earth washed an entire village out to sea?

Perhaps the saints, despite his neglect, chose to smile on him. "I'll pray," he promised. To all of them, just in case.

All too soon, despite raising his standards well beyond what ordinarily he'd have taken and been glad of, Hunhau staggered happily beneath his overfilled basket, arms laden as well.

He should go back. The light of the rising sun glittered like a sword across the water, the mist a memory. He should go back and would, he promised himself.

After one more…

The maskmaker followed the curling line of wet sand, bright red crabs scuttling out of his way, and there it was, kissing land's edge mere steps ahead, a piece of driftwood already bent to fit a face, with the finest grain he'd seen.

Hunhau tossed aside the armload he'd collected and hurried to claim his prize, though there was no one else in sight.

But it was no more wood than the swirl of silver and blue pushing it closer was wave.

What he'd thought driftwood lifted with rare grace to become a head, and what surely, oh surely! had been ocean an instant before, like the spray salty on his lips, sculpted itself into pale shoulders and arms, and shaped the curved form of a woman from froth.

A woman who gasped and fell forward, outstretched hands holding her from the sand, face hidden behind a sodden fall of hair. Hair, Hunhau noticed with dismay, that became water where it touched the damp sand, as did the white and gold cloth of her garments. No shipwrack, this. No hapless victim tossed from the seawall by murderer or Moon Priest. Those bodies he'd seen, bloated and grotesque, half-eaten by crab and seabird. They'd not bothered him, other than the stench. When he could, when there was a face still, he'd fashion a death mask as best he could from a plank or scrap of cloth, for he was a kindly man at heart.

This creature was nothing so safe or simple. His eyes lifted reluctantly to where the Star Tower pierced the sky beyond the seawall. Wizards lived there. Only there. And never left.

Until, he feared, now.

Heart in his throat, Hunhau replaced his mask and eased a careful step back, then another.

"Tell me, good man. Am I dead?"

Masks could hide a face and its expression, as her strange hair did now; the voice was harder to disguise. Hers was melodic and low, free of fear, as gentle as the lap of wave over his sandaled feet. It held him when he would have fled.

"I don't know," Hunhau answered honestly. "I'm but a maskmaker."

"Maskmaker?" She made an odd sound, like a seabird, her

shoulders shaking. "Well met. I've need of your services." With that, the woman of the sea lifted her head, hair flowing aside, to show him her face.

Hunhau shrugged off his basket, precious driftwood spilling on the sand, and put an arm around her shoulders. "It's a healer you need. Come. Easy now," he said as he helped her stand. At his urging, she took a step on feet, he noticed numbly, she hadn't had before. He swallowed. "How could this–?"

"It doesn't matter," she said quietly. "Will you help me?"

Knowing what she asked, the maskmaker bent his head and sighed with true regret. "If I could, I would. I'm sorry. My masks have no magic."

"From now on, they will," she told him, and he heard the sea.

Two Years Later

"I've worked with worse," Ghanan said firmly. He hadn't, ever. Couldn't imagine worse. But to be a stonemason in Taux, where every stone was blood-soaked and soul-stained, meant facing the unthinkable or not be paid. "Might take an extra few days," he added consideringly, making a show of leaning close to examine the wall in question.

Little faces stared back. Whatever the use of this subterranean corridor before the curse, it hadn't been anything sane. The stones, well-dressed and true to his knowing eye, were separated by rows of hand-sized figurines, crammed together like obscene mortar. Those at head-height stared out from hollow eyes, their noses cut away, mouths set in sorrowful lines or agape in agony. Those above were carved with death's heads, each skull given a smile. He didn't look down. The lower rows were jammed with limp little corpses, each tortured pose too realistic for comfort.

Zotz didn't appear to mind. The child sat on her stool, where he'd asked her to wait during this adult business of claims and contracts. Her hands lay limp, palm-up, in her lap; her dull gaze trailed along the rows of figurines, back and forth, her face empty of expression.

"It must be done quickly." Gamesmaster Ixchel kept her eyes on the plaster-strewn floor, though that view was hardly more reassuring, the plaster being blood red. Someone–or several someones–had chiselled that covering from the walls. If they'd thought to make the space more palatable, Ghanan thought, they'd failed. The stone voices were louder than ever, whispers rattling hoarse and wordless at the edge of torchlight, assiduously ignored by the living. "Those coming after you will need their time to work," she continued. "All must be ready well before the games. You've seen our plans."

Before the discovery of this corridor running beneath the Tournament Field became general knowledge, the Golden Jaguar District's gamesmaster had swept in to claim it. He'd indeed seen her plans, laid out in an opulent scale model kept locked away and well guarded. They called for luxurious private and common rooms for players, with connected baths and saunas, storage for gear, and a large space for hosting what Ghanan guessed Ixchel hoped would be intimate victory celebrations. For one team. Hers. Visitors would have to make do with accommodations elsewhere in the Black Gate, or beyond, and so be at disadvantage.

"Remarkable," Ghanan acknowledged with a courteous nod. Ridiculous and sure to be untenable for the athletes once seepage from below exceeded the pumps and damp rot set in, but such people didn't want his honest opinion, only his sweat. Their plans weren't his problem; cleansing the place so plumbers and other tradesfolk didn't run screaming in horror was.

No matter how.

The stonemason stepped gingerly through the fragments and dust. "Once this is cleared away, I'll start work."

"The stones stay," insisted Tlacolotl Vash. By his build and manner, the man could have been a fishmonger straight from the docks; certainly his rough clothing and scuffed boots said no different. But around his neck was the scarf that marked him a Red Pillar, one of the city's ruling merchant elite, and a pair of armed sturgeons waited by the stairs leading up, their hard gaze never leaving the stonemason. Tlacolotl gave the walls an impatient look. "Replacing any is out of the question."

It always was, but Ghanan couldn't argue with what gave him a living. Generations of Taux had spent their fortunes to bring stone across the sea, building their city here where none belonged. Maybe they'd liked the view. He shrugged. To those now living in Taux, the stones were priceless.

Once they stopped screaming.

"I've worked with worse," he repeated. Though not, until now, within the Black Gate District. The reason most people had settled–and still lived–within the original massive stadium had been the relative quiet of its stone. Fewer had died there that grim day.

Too many had died down here.

Ixchel looked up. "Stonemason Ghanan comes with the highest recommendation, Tlacolotl," she said stiffly, eyes aglitter. "Our Jaguars will prepare and recuperate in magnificent, private splendour. They'll be victorious. We begin a dynasty!"

Tlacolotl looked unimpressed. "Secrecy," he growled. "That above all. If our competitors get wind of what we intend here–"

"You work alone. Isn't that right, Ghanan?"

"My daughter assists me," he replied. His hand found itself on Zotz's shoulder and his mouth smiled of its own accord. She didn't look up and Ghanan, freed, lifted away his hand. "Your secrets are safe," he said wearily. "Zotz is mute."

In the pause that followed, the stones whispered and gibbered. The sturgeons shifted uneasily and the gamesmaster's skin paled beneath its paint.

"You'd make your own child endure what's here." The Red Man's voice was cold. "A child like this."

Escape beckoned, as it always did, as if it were possible.

But it wasn't. Words spilled through unwilling lips. "Zotz has talent for the work," Ghanan heard himself reply. "It's both of us or none. Her mother's passed and I won't leave her alone."

Alone was how he'd found her. Two years ago, he'd stepped in an alley for a leak and there she'd been, naked but for mud, her hair a filthy mat. No street waif, disputing with rats for kitchen leavings; such he'd have taken to the priestesses of Shera, the saint who cared for hearth and home, and those who had neither. This child picked at the stone wall, what remained of her fingernails leaving trails of blood behind.

She'd stopped when he touched her shoulder, stopped and looked up with eyes like charnel pits, brimming with the faces of the dead.

He'd have run, had he been able, but his cursed knee had locked and he'd staggered in place, bile rising in his throat.

Her lids had closed, then reopened on dull, ordinary eyes that dismissed him before the child–or whatever it was–went back to pawing at the stone.

He'd have run–and should have. Saints knew now he wished he had. But without the witness of those impossible eyes, curiosity had trapped him. She didn't scrabble at random. Her bloody fingers pried at subtle flaws in the stone, flaws he'd recognized.

They were those he sought when trying to muffle the voices in the stones for his clients.

Ignoring the sick lurch under his heart, Ghanan had put an ear to the cold stone, braced for the screams and madness.

Silence.

He'd pulled back to stare at the child. His clumsy attempts to chip and patch achieved nothing like this. What she did, however and to what purpose, cleansed the stone for good.

She'd lifted a foot and crabbed sideways to reach the next in the row.

To this day, Ghanan didn't know why he'd taken hammer and chisel from his belt, why he'd gently pushed aside her bleeding fingers to carefully chip the next spot of fracture.

Why he'd stood watching as she pressed her mouth to the

exposed surface, sucking and swallowing like a babe at breast.

Why he'd ever thought to take her home...

"Of course you mustn't leave your daughter," Ixchel said graciously, her eyes fixed longingly on the stairs to the surface. "This space will be ready for you by midday tomorrow. Do what you must, stonemason. All that matters is having these rooms finished and ready before the games."

Ghanan bowed, trapped once more.

Ω

"Should be interesting games this season," Tohil commented. The big sturgeon leaned against the wall; though in the shade, sweat beaded the raised tattoos on his black skin and dripped from his earrings. The quilted cotton armour and blue overrobe of his station weren't gifts midsummer, not in Taux, but no sturgeon patrolled the streets without. "Bet on it, my friend. Our Snakes can't lose."

Hunhau handed Tohil a flask. "I'm confused," he said, amused. "Or you are. What happened to "drop every gutless player in the swamp?""

They'd spent many a night in the *Emerald* contemplating suitable fates for their once-beloved team; the Black Gate's Snakes' pathetic showing last year still rankled.

"Things'll be different." Tohil took a deep swig, drawing the back of his hand across his full lips, then stared at the flask in mock amazement. "Siefried's Saintly Beard. I know it's water but how can it taste better than beer?"

The maskmaker reclaimed his flask. "Because you're hot. Now what's this about 'our' Snakes?"

"Not that you heard it from me," Tohil began, meaning he'd heard whatever it was from another who wished to stay anonymous, and likely several others before that. Rumour, in Taux, was a many-legged beast. "But there's been some rooms found–beneath the field itself. The gamesmaster plans to house her oh-so-mighty Jaguars there. Rooms of cursed stone," he added sagely, as if his wide shoulders weren't resting on the very same substance. "They'll get no rest there."

"Stone can be cleansed," the maskmaker pointed out. Sunlight silenced the voices of Taux's former, unfortunate inhabitants; various measures could mute them. The Raised Market was full of those claiming to remove them entirely, along with bunions and the evil eye for an extra fee.

"As to–" Tohil straightened, his slouch gone.

Hunhau glanced down the row of litters. Which had caught his friend's professional interest? There were several parked, their sturdy bearers lounging nearby, kicking a sepak ball back and forth, or dozing, but it would be more surprising to find the laneway empty, given this was the side entrance to *The Silk Purse*, the most infamous brothel in Taux.

Two years since he'd brought the woman from the sea here, aware, like everyone else, that the *Purse's* house physician was, if not the best in Taux, then by far the most practiced and discrete. Two years, her wounds fully healed, yet still she came, each 7th day morning. Hunhau asked for no explanation, nor did she offer one.

For like the sea, Cenoté brimmed with secrets.

Like the sea, her gifts were extraordinary and unexpected. The flask at his hip, ever full of sweet, cool water. The mask he now wore. The outer surface resembled the one his old master had made for him, but inside? No plugs crammed his nostrils or constricted his breathing. The air that passed through the holes at eyes, nose, and mouth was fresh and free of odour, no matter where he was. Cenoté had poured water from her cupped hands onto the wood, that was all.

Magic of the purest sort. Hunhau breathed it, drank it, and counted himself fortunate by every measure to have befriended it.

It hadn't been a litter that caught Tohil's eye. The side door had opened and a servant bowed as she ushered a tall woman into the brighter light. Plumes fluttered along the street as litter bearers quickly found somewhere else to stare.

Cenoté.

Her height was remarkable, despite the scholarly stoop of years spent hunched over worktable and book, and now in their shop. Painstaking and attentive, gifted with strong, delicate hands, she'd been a brilliant apprentice for less than a month.

From then on, Hunhau had been the one striving to learn.

"You can tell me more about the Snakes' chances the next time we meet," he told his friend, snapping fingers to rouse their litter bearers. The four young men pulled on their masks, their heads transformed to those of sea eagles, white feathers trailing over their bare shoulders, and took their places.

Cenoté moved with unconscious grace, the cane an extension of her slender arm. When required to venture from the shop, she wound strips of cloth around her head to cover her blue-green hair and donned a shapeless robe. Though she cared nothing for her appearance, Hunhau understood its importance in Taux's busy streets, where everyone watched and judged. He nodded to himself, satisfied by the rich fabric that flowed around her well-sandaled feet.

If not by her mask.

She wore the grotesque thing with such sure dignity, it might have been crusted in diamonds. The ugly chunk of grey seasoned wood was secured to her face by paired leather straps; uneven holes, wave-worn rather than carved, gaped like dark wounds over her mouth and eyes. Taux being what it was, at first there'd been a flurry of copies, gossipmongers having claimed the mask must hide a beauty so rare and exquisite it would drive men mad if revealed. Young ladies had demanded crude masks of their own, to imply the same.

The fad, not surprisingly, passed quicker than most. The curiosity about what lay beneath her mask had taken longer to fade. Hunhau preferred it not be awakened again.

Tohil saluted Cenoté as she neared. "Greetings, good lady."

The mask tilted a shy acknowledgement.

"We'd best be going." Hunhau took Cenoté's elbow to urge her to the litter.

With a quickness belied by his bulk, the sturgeon was there first. "Was she there?" he asked in a low voice. "Did you get an answer?"

Safe behind his own mask, Hunhau rolled his eyes. This game was getting old. "Cenoté's not your messenger, Tohil," he scolded. "And no courtesan's going to give you so much as a "good morning" without coin. Leave be."

"It's all right, Hunhau." Cenoté's soft voice interposed. "Plums-By-Moonlight did indeed reply. 'Jugglers, cheese, and peacocks.' Does that make sense to you, Tohil?"

She spoke to empty air as the sturgeon took off down the lane as if pursuing an unlicensed tax collector, the bearers staring after him in astonishment.

"It must have," Hunhau commented dryly. "Let's get you home." Whenever they went out, there was a vulnerability about her, as if the very walls of Taux seethed with what she was and made ready to shout it. Nothing ever happened, but he worried, that was the truth.

The litter was plain but well made, with a roof for rain and thick privacy curtains. As Hunhau made to draw those, the bearers knowing full well the route they preferred, Cenoté delayed him with a touch of her hand. "The shop, Hunhau, briefly. Then the Raised Market."

Four eagle masks turned as one.

"The market," she insisted.

Where she'd never gone before. Where they'd be in crowds. Uncontrollable, dangerous crowds.

"Of course." Curtains snugged tight, Hunhau settled into his seat, fighting his unease as the bearers lifted the litter and stepped out at their smooth steady pace. "May I ask why?" he said after a moment.

The mask of wood turned to him and something stirred in the dark where eyes should have been. When she spoke, for an instant he thought he heard the howl of storm-driven waves. "I've found her."

A chill fingered the maskmaker's bones despite the heat. He opened his mouth, shut it, then tried again. "Found w-who?"

"The one I tried to stop that night. My enemy." To his dismay, Cenoté added calmly, "now yours. She drinks the dead. Left unchallenged, she'll turn on the living next. There's no time to waste." Her fingers found his hand. She laid hers, callused and cool, atop it. "The Shining Sea tossed me at your feet, good Hunhau. This is why. So I would have your help."

"Mine?" he echoed, feeling as though the litter had tipped. "What can I do? I've no magic. You're the Wizard!" Hunhau shut his mouth, too late. It was out. What he'd never dared say to her.

Wizard.

"No more." Her mask turned towards the bay for a moment, then aimed forward. "One does not question the Sea. This evil can no longer be fought from the tower. It must be fought here, now. I can't do it without you. Will you help me?"

Involve himself in the battles of Wizards? Risk himself for the people of Taux, which meant the nasty Jai-Ruk under the bridge as much as his friend Tohil, neither of whom would believe this?

The saints knew he wasn't a hero.

Instead of answering, Hunhau poked his masked face through the curtains. "Pick up the pace, lads," he ordered, pleased his voice sounded normal. "We're in a hurry today."

The saints knew he'd made his choice, two years ago on the sand.

Cℨ

Food cooling in his bowl, Ghanan sat at the wooden table, watching his wife. Ah Peku washed the child with care and dried her with their softest towel, then dressed her as she would a doll. Zotz endured these ministrations with limp uncaring patience, moving only when prompted. It was their ritual, now.

He dropped his face into his hands.

"Husband." Softly. "You must eat."

Last night, every night, had been the same. Come home from work at sunset, strip and wash stone dust from his skin, pull on a clean robe. There'd been a time when evening's delicious cool drew them out for wine and dancing in the streets, or a moonlit walk along the quay. A time when he'd lifted the love of his life in his arms and known himself the wealthiest man in the world.

A time before Zotz.

Now sunset was when he brought the loathsome creature to the alley behind their home, so she could go on hands and knees to vomit forth the day's darkness. Now nights were to hide behind locked doors. For he'd watched, that first time, and seen the darkness hump itself to the drain. It had clung to the edge and stared back at him, eyes aglow with hate, before slithering out of sight. One for each day worked.

And each day worked, word spread of the stonemason who could silence the stones. Offers poured in and Zotz made him take every one.

Two years. Ghanan imagined hordes beneath their feet, imagined them meeting and becoming one monstrous thing, imagined...but what could he guess of her purpose? He was her hands and voice, that was all.

How Ah Peku forgave him for bringing Zotz into their lives, how she endured it, Ghanan couldn't begin to guess. Trembling, the stonemason took up his spoon and made himself eat while his wife led the child, who didn't eat or drink, to the little chair they'd made for her. Having sat Zotz down to wait, Ah Peku turned away, wiping her hands on her apron.

Their eyes met, the compassion in hers more than he deserved. Ghanan opened his mouth to say so, but nothing came out. Zotz wouldn't let him speak at home. Not while she–while it–

watched.

Instead, he lifted his arm and Ah Peku came to sit by him on the bench. He pulled her close, burying his face in her hair.

It smelled of life.

Ꮺ

Once inside the shop, Cenoté asked Hunhau to bar the door, then help her from her raiment. The strips around her hair she left, as she was wont to do when ready to work.

Skin like the inside of a shell, hair like a waterfall, lips pale and perfect. Beautiful, she was, in the way a wave crashing against rock or the reflection of stars in the utter calm of a summer sea could steal breath and call poetry from a dolt. Was she beautiful as a woman? Though she stood clad only in her breechclout, Hunhau couldn't say. His tastes ran to women of soft flesh, after all, and Cenoté was almost gaunt.

Then there was her face. Scars, deep and rippled, sealed the gaps where her eyes had been brutally torn out. By some mercy, she didn't remember what had happened; Hunhau couldn't forget his first glimpse of those dreadful wounds, the white glint of bone. That she'd survived–it had taken more than a skilled physician. It had taken terrifying will.

Now, though blind, she moved around the shop with brisk confidence, choosing a piece of driftwood from the bin to take to her worktable. Hunhau clamped it to the stand, itself turned or tilted by foot petals beneath the table.

Masks lined the upper shelves, masks no one could mistake as being made by anyone else. They were breathtaking, with great eyes and vivid colours. Cenoté made them for the neighbourhood children, to play as turtle, dolphin, or shark; they were not for sale. The idea of taking coin for the work of her hands offended her; she didn't say it, but Hunhau could tell.

Cenoté helped him instead. The masks she began and he finished were the best he'd ever done. As months went by, even those he did on his own–for Cenoté would have nothing to do with death masks–improved. His old master would have been amazed.

What she loved to make were cups. Cups. Bowls. Ewers. Jars. Anything to hold water and everything did, without a leak. They sat on every shelf and lined the walls. Hunhau had grown used to the way rain bent itself to enter the open windows of the shop, flowing and splashing only where Cenoté wished.

Though once in a while, it splashed on him. He'd sputter and protest, secretly pleased to catch a rare dimple at the corner of her mouth.

Once a month, at the highest tide, Cenoté would send him back to where he'd found her, to fill a special cup. With reverent movements, she'd put it to her lips and drink as if the saltwater were wine. When she'd had her fill, she'd soak what remained with a sponge and lave the ruin where her eyes had been.

On those nights, she'd go to her bed early and cry, very softly. He'd listen, heartsick and helpless. There was no cure for such pain. There was no imagining it.

He'd come to love her as any sailor loved the sea: lost apart, knowing better than seek that perilous embrace. And now it was over. What hope did a blind ex-wizard and a maskmaker have against a creature that could drink the dead?

"Water, please, Hunhau. We must hurry. Any bowl will do."

He brought the largest, careful not to spill a drop, and set it on the table. Her face turned and tilted as she lifted a hand towards him. Understanding, he removed his mask and came in reach. Like raindrops, her fingertips played over his face, tracing his forehead, his cheeks, and, though he winced inwardly, his great nose. Or maybe not so inwardly, for her lips curved and she tapped the tip of his nose lightly before taking back her hand.

Whatever Cenoté'd read of his face must have satisfied her, for without delay she sat on her stool and crooked an imperious finger at the bowl. Water rose in a thin twisting rope and leaned towards her.

No matter how many times he'd witnessed her magic, his

heart still pounded in his chest.

The finger flicked at the wood and water followed, striking like a snake. A chunk broke away with a snap, then another and another, as Cenoté shaped the mask, her fingers now dancing, more twists of water flying through the air in response.

Slivers followed as she began a finer shaping. Hunhau leaned close. This was no sea creature or bird. What grew from driftwood was a face of astonishing realism. A woman's, serene and strong, with flawless, almond-shaped eyes.

Had it been hers?

Cenoté twirled her forefinger and the water returned to the bowl. Without waiting to be asked, Hunhau moved that bowl aside. Such water retained some hint of her magic. Later, if there was a later, he'd take it to the common garden and pour it on the roots of his neighbour's olive tree. He'd been anxious at first, but the tree seemed unaffected, other than a welcome increase in fruit.

"Thank you," she murmured. "The tray next, good Hunhau. Fill it from one of the covered jars, please. And bring your paints."

Rare, that Cenoté would call for more water. As for paints? The maskmaker hesitated. They'd take hours to dry. It was blisteringly hot in the courtyard, even in the shade. "I should send the bearers away then."

The hint of a dimple on her otherwise serious face. "This won't take long."

"But the paint..."

"Trust me."

He shut his mouth and grabbed a jug, going to the back of the shop. The covered jars were his height and stood in a row. After months of squeezing by them, Hunhau had taken to using the tops as shelves. Cheeks rosy with embarrassment, he dragged a step to the first in line and climbed up, hastily removing a set of stacked baskets and, yes, that box of tile pieces he'd thought might be useful.

Fight evil? He couldn't keep his shop tidy.

The woven sisal lid pricked his fingers as he pried it off. He held his breath, sure the stuff would have rotted in the damp, but the underside appeared newly made. As for the water inside?

Hunhau dared a little sniff.

A silly smile broke over his face. He inhaled deeply, filling his lungs. This was rain after a drought. Air after lightning. A newborn's sweet breath. All at once and...

"Hunhau?"

He was taking too long. "Coming." Blushing hotter, the maskmaker quickly dipped the jug, filling it to the brim. Holding it in the crook of his arm, he fumbled the lid back on the jar and began to climb down.

"Don't touch it," Cenoté said absently.

Freezing midstep, Hunhau stared into the jug as water sloshed perilously near its rim–and his bare arm–before settling. "W-why?"

"It will remember you."

He shouldn't have expected a comprehensible answer. Moving with greater care, Hunhau brought the jug to the table. Pouring the water into the shallow tray, he couldn't help but sniff again. If the world could smell like this, he'd never need a mask.

Had there been anything different about the water or the jars, any sign of exceptional magic? He thought, now that he made the effort, that Cenoté had reached her hand into each; he'd assumed to make sure the jar was full, as she would by keeping a fingertip inside her cup when pouring wine.

Unclamping the mask, she slipped it gently into the filled tray. It sank to the bottom, looking up.

"What colours should it have?" Cenoté asked him, as if she'd forgotten.

If this had been her face... "A moment," Hunhau replied. Hurrying to a cabinet, he threw open its door and shoved aside bags of pigment. Nothing he had would do.

Reaching to the very back of the shelf, the maskmaker pulled free a long, low box. He brushed the worn carving of its lid, then nodded to himself. These were the paints Yum Caax had reserved for his finest works, blends of the rarest, most exotic materials. His former apprentice hadn't dared touch them.

He brought the box to the table, unlatched the sides, and lifted the lid. The tiny crystal vials were as he remembered; the colours inside vivid and alive. "These," Hunhau said without doubt, choosing four to press into her waiting hands.

Her fingers closed. Cenoté's head tilted, listening to what he couldn't hear, then she almost smiled. "And you say you've no magic, my friend. Watch."

Before he could think to stop her, she dropped the unopened vials into the tray.

They didn't sink, as crystal should and wood shouldn't, but floated to the four corners like sparkling boats. At Cenoté's bent finger, they began to spin until each vial was centred within its own tiny whirlpool, though the water over the mask's face was undisturbed.

The seals cracked, spilling priceless pigment. Hunhau's cry died in his throat as he saw the vials themselves remained dry and almost full. Colour spread in hazy clouds and narrow, intense bands: twilight rose, storm black, pearl white, and a blue so achingly pure it might have been carved from ancient ice.

The colours found the mask.

Suddenly, both wood and water vanished. Hunhau found himself staring not at a mask, but a face. Skin of pearl, lips and cheeks of soft rose, brows black and upswept like wings.

Without warning, the long black lashes parted, revealing eyes like the wild, open ocean. He staggered back. "It moves!"

"It remembers me," Cenoté said matter-of-factly, but he thought her hands trembled as she lifted the mask from the tray. She held it before her face. "Will it pass, good Hunhau?"

A Wizard's face gazed down at him, cold and aloof. Beautiful, the way elegant and deadly things could be, but this wasn't Cenoté. This wasn't the person closer to him than any family or friend. "I don't know what to say," he managed. "I don't know who this is. Who you want to be."

"How not?" She moved the mask aside, showing him the familiar ruin above a mouth downturned in distress. Her fingertips traced the tension in his jaw and found his frown. Cenoté nodded. "I understand. What we've crafted is a memory, nothing more. I can't go back to that life," she said gently. "I thought you knew I don't want to. I'm happy here, Hunhau, and free as I've ever been." She raised the mask again, with its disconcerting eyes. "To fight, however, I must see our enemy. This is the means."

That she was happy and wanted to stay was something to warm the heart and treasure, but the rest? "You could have made such a mask before," Hunhau accused. "You've let yourself be blind!"

"I am blind, my friend, and always will be." Cenoté laid the mask on the table. "Without eyes, a Wizard cannot perform the greater magics. Without eyes, the Afterglow Sea is beyond my reach." She seemed to come to some decision. "Understand me, Hunhau. This," her fingers touched the scarred and empty sockets, "was no accident. The last thing I remember is being in a scrying room, searching for this creature. Someone in the tower stole my eyes. A traitor." Beneath her voice, the fury of a breaking wave. "Whoever it was meant to cripple me and has." Her fingers rested cool on his face, then brushed like mist across his eyes. "But for a little while, this mask will let me borrow your sight. If you're willing?"

He squinted at her. "Ten coins says it's going to hurt."

"Twenty," that was surely a dimple, "says we'll die horribly in the attempt."

"I should never have taught you to gamble," he complained.

"All life's a gamble." Cenoté actually smiled. "Now help me dress. We've a distance to travel."

∽

By the play of torchlight, the empty eyes moved, the little corpses writhed. The stones appeared to rest on the figurines, but it was a clever illusion. The stonecraft of those who'd built the original city was without equal.

But why this?

Resolutely, Ghanan looked away to the good stone, born of the earth and not the whim of evil minds. He'd come to believe in evil.

Evil squatted impatiently before the wall, waiting for him to feed it.

Which was a problem. The pair of sturgeons stood on guard at the base of the stairs and Zotz didn't allow witnesses, using Ghanan to drive them away. She'd made him deny friendship and scorn goodwill, until these days others in the trade gave him foul looks and a wide berth. She'd put such vile words in his mouth he'd offended the gentle old priest who'd stood by to watch him work and made him strike at a too-curious boy. With the priest had gone his hope that such a man, surely knowledgeable in the ways of good and evil, would see Zotz for what she was and free him. With the boy—with the boy, wide-eyed and scared, had risen a sick dread of what she could make him do, if not given her way.

He could do nothing against such men. Offended sturgeons were more likely to use their staffs on his head than leave. Did Zotz understand that? Ghanan delayed, pretending to search for a tool in his kit as he gave the men assessing looks. Saints, they were huge, with arms like tree limbs, and had the easy confidence—or single-mindedness—of those to whom a dank cellar rife with the whispers of the dead was simply another place to guard.

Suddenly, Zotz began to rock back and forth, her arms clasped around her middle. The stonemason froze in place, afraid what might come next. Sure enough, her mouth opened and she let out a shrill, keening cry.

It was a sound no child should have been able to make. Hairs rose on Ghanan's arms and neck.

The sturgeons exchanged annoyed looks. "What's wrong with her?" one demanded.

"She doesn't like strangers." He had to raise his voice as the dreadful screech grew louder, threatening his sanity. "Please, good sirs. If you would wait at the top of the stairs, just out of sight, I'm sure she'll stop."

They didn't suspect a child–no one ever did, Ghanan thought. With disgusted shakes of their heads, the two men turned and went up the wide steps.

Zotz closed her mouth and looked at him.

"To work. I know." The sooner it was done, he told himself, the sooner the creature would let him return home. The stonemason stripped off his jerkin and took up his chisel and hammer, only then checking to see where to start. Zotz knew where the voices were loudest and would insist he open the stone there first.

Her small fingers stroked the figures along the lower row, the ones shown in torment.

He hesitated. The voices came from the stones. Yes, there'd been a time when their whispered almost-words and distant screams had made him break into a cold sweat, when it had been a matter of pride to stand and work, to do what he could to bring peace to a wall or building. To make Taux a better place for the living.

But now he pitied the dead and grieved when they fell silent. Zotz stole something from them, something precious. He no longer doubted it. To rob those already condemned…

A crooked finger tapped impatiently.

Ghanan sank to his haunches before the wall. He made the mistake of glancing at the creature. Her eyes were hollow pits and her mouth gaped, the tongue lolling like a dog's. Instead of honest spit, something black and loathsome dribbled from the corners of her child's lips. She pointed again, with unfamiliar urgency.

There was something here, he realized abruptly. Something

she'd been looking for and finally found.

It wouldn't be anything good.

Ghanan fought to resist the creature's will. Drop the chisel, he begged his fingers. Just that. Or cry out and draw the sturgeons down to investigate.

Sweat poured into his eyes and stung, but his fingers stayed locked to the tool, fitting it to the heart of a small tortured shape. His lips moved, but nothing came out as his other hand lifted the hammer.

Voices wailed and gibbered in terror. The torches guttered as the hammer fell and the first figure split open, spilling tiny organs and blood.

Zotz shoved him aside, eager to feast.

&

If Taux's builders had intended the Black Gate to overawe those entering their great stadium, they'd succeeded. The massive obsidian gate stood before its bridge to the city as it always had, its ferocious carved visages glaring out in threat. The stadium beyond it, however, had become something else: a city within a city. Every scrap of its defensible, blissfully quiet stone had been squatted on, settled, and, in some cases, rebuilt entirely by those who came after. What had been broad bleachers now supported rows of wooden tenements, answering to the fate of the city's docks. The once-magnificent Raised Celebration platform, girded by the gate and its twin guard towers, was home to the ramshackle booths and colourful awnings of the Raised Market, a disorderly mass that had spilled out across what had been a sunken practice court and now reached greedily for the precious space of the Tournament Field.

On the other side of the field, where the rich and mighty had sat in three-storey stone boxes at the centre of the stadium, the *Emerald Serpent* and *Silk Purse* nestled back-to-back, like guilty lovers unable to face one another by day. Beyond those dens of profitable iniquity was, by no accident, a practice court that echoed with the ring of swordplay, being used by athletes of every ilk, including assassins.

The former Royal Raised Gardens remained, but its beds now grew fruits and vegetables. To either side stood the Wizards' Gifts, inexhaustible fountains of sweet water. Furthest from the gate and presumed safest, was the area claimed by the nobility–though some would argue buying a title or being a crime lord didn't count–of those who called the Black Gate home.

Hunhau's little shop sat much closer to the gate, tucked in a blind corner on the lowermost floor of a building on the first bleacher. It wasn't much, but possessed something rare: privacy. The shop's door opened to the outside and a shared courtyard, with no inner neighbours using it for a corridor.

It was too much to hope they were unobserved. Windows and balconies overlooked the courtyard, and the Black Gate's inhabitants were insatiably curious. Hunhau tried not to glance up as he helped Cenoté into the litter, but he couldn't help it. The Star Tower rose beyond the stadium walls. Did Wizards watch?

Did the traitor?

They left the litter at the edge of the market. He gave the bearers coin for a meal and extra for a drink or two, having imposed on them to wait yet again. The men were cheerful. Hunhau wasn't.

Anything could be had, for a price, in the Raised Market. Its overlapping awnings and flags made a chaotic display that would shrink like magic the night before a game, replaced, of course, by seats and benches of varying luxury and price, as well as refreshment dealers and those waiting to take bets. Today, though, the usual uproar of yells, chants, yips, chimes, and bells, among less identifiable noises, bounced from wall to wall, making it unlikely any one could heard, let alone attract a customer.

Then there was the smell. Hunhau loathed coming here, even in his mask, all too easily imagining the reek. But here he was, in the thick of it.

"A large tent beside a snake merchant," Cenoté whispered. "Near the Tournament Field." She rested her hand on his shoulder, having left her cane behind, and he felt that responsibility keenly as he guided them through the jostling crowd. They'd passed three stalls with snakes hissing in their baskets already.

Hunhau slapped at a pickpocket's hand, receiving an unrepentant grin as the waif ducked away. "Are you sure we should–" he began, then looked past the would-be thief. "I think I found it."

No ordinary booth this. The thick poles holding up the awning were carved into twisting serpents with jade eyes and a carpet done to look like silver scales beckoned customers through velvet curtains. Only the wealthy need enter, that said.

"And the tent, Hunhau?"

As tents went, the dull brown one leaning next to the snake merchant's fine establishment looked more suited to covering a dung heap. A very large dung heap. Hunhau looked for another, but saw only more booths with awnings. And people. Half of Taux were here and not the better half either. Criers ran through, some waving staffs with flags, others tossing samples and causing fights. Forced aside by a grim pair of Jai-Ruk, the maskmaker lost his courage and simply kept moving, leading Cenoté to the open space beside one of the snake poles. "I see it," he admitted glumly.

"What's wrong?" She'd unbound her remarkable hair, though it remained beneath the hood of her silk cloak. Her face…

Once she'd pressed the mask to her face, it had become her face. The real and created had merged, blurring one into the other. No scars remained, but the blue eyes were hazed over and milky. Stern lines had drawn themselves at the corners of the mouth, taking away the half-seen dimple he loved.

"Everything," he fussed. "Who sent us here? How do we know this isn't a trap?"

An eyebrow, once wood and paint, lifted. "It may be," Cenoté agreed easily and Hunhau's heart sank. "Nothing's changed. The eater is here and must be fought."

"Here?" A less likely spot for a magical confrontation couldn't be imagined.

"The tent," she reminded him.

Hunhau sighed but argued no more.

The tent's entry was tied shut. From the litter on the ground before it, it hadn't been used in days. Rather than be caught fumbling with knots or a knife–not that he'd thought to bring one– Hunhau waited for the next crier to distract the crowd, then drew Cenoté into the narrow space beside the tent, hoping to find another way.

What he found, after some too-noisy stumbles over ropes, was that the market side of the tent was a clever ruse. The real entrance faced the Tournament Field. There was a much larger door on that side, held open by rings on golden hooks. As he hesitated, Cenoté's fingers pressed his shoulder encouragingly. Courage, that meant.

Hunhau went on hands and knees, poking his masked face around the edge of the door. The interior of the tent was a revelation. Another door opened across from him, while within? No expense spared here. The fabric lining was cotton, died pale gold, and woven carpets covered the floor. Jaguar masks stood on poles along the wall; masks he recognized. Those belonged to the team itself as, he guessed, would the chests beneath them. But why store them here?

What had Tohil said? That the gamesmaster planned to house her team in rooms–rooms beneath the playing field. Moving very slowly, he turned to look the other way.

Where the front door of the tent would open was a gaping hole in the floor, flanked by guards. Big ones.

They were staring into the hole. That was all that saved him from discovery. Shaking at his luck, and their lack of it, Hunhau pulled back hastily and rose to his feet. He took Cenoté's hand and began leading her away. She resisted.

Which was when the new, even bigger guard showed up, striding towards them.

03

Chip, chip, chip. The bodies were tiny–their anguish wasn't. As Zotz sucked each dry, her thin child's frame expanded, like some spider filling with the juice of prey.

With each desecration, the underground corridor grew darker, as if the light from the torches failed, though the flames were unchanged.

This was his fault, Ghanan told himself, half-mad with shame. He'd fallen into the creature's trap, for he no longer believed their meeting an accident. He'd let her enthral him and this was the result. Tears streamed down his face, mingling with sweat and dust, but he could no more stop his hands than the ending of the world.

03

From Tohil's smug look and wink, Plums-By-Moonlight had done more than give him Cenoté's instructions. He'd walked right by Hunhau and into the tent, exhorting his fellow sturgeons to their duty. A riot at *The Silk Purse*! The street filled with naked courtesans of both sexes–Tohil clearly knew his audience–needing rescue! Compared with make-work guarding a hole in the ground, there'd been no doubt which they'd choose. The three had run out with a clatter of weapons at the ready.

A worried Hunhau led Cenoté inside the tent. "Won't he get in trouble?"

"There is a riot," Cenoté said absently. "A small one."

Another secret. Another time, he might have wondered, but not now. The closer they came to the hole, the more his fear of it grew. It was as if that opening, now revealed to be an ornate stair leading down, went to his grave.

No wonder the guards had been willing to abandon their post. If it weren't for Cenoté's hand, firm and steady on his shoulder, he'd have run too.

Her other hand lifted, palm up. "It's time, my friend."

Bracing himself, Hunhau took off his mask and secured it to his belt. His face felt naked, the skin itchy. When he could hold off no longer, he gasped out the air he'd held in his lungs, then inhaled through his nose.

"Agh!" The stench of death and rot and worse burned his nostrils. Nothing should smell like this, he wailed to himself, doubling over. Nothing could! What was down there?

"Hunhau? Are you all right?"

He waved a hand to beg a moment, eyes watering, forgetting she was blind.

"I'm so sorry. Thank you for this." Cenoté's fingers found his face. They stroked his nose and the stench vanished. As he straightened with astonished relief, she caught his tears on her cool fingers and touched them to her clouded eyes.

She blinked and her eyes cleared.

Hunhau blinked too. The floor had moved further away. No, he now saw from a greater height! "I see through your eyes!"

"I see through yours. Stay with me," Cenoté ordered. Tossing her cloak to the floor, she gathered up her robe in two hands and started nimbly down the stairs, hair streaming like a waterfall over her back. "Mind your feet."

Good advice. Unable to trust depth or distance, the maskmaker felt his way down beside her.

Cold. Cold and damp and, though he was grateful not to smell it, something inside Hunhau knew the air wasn't right. It wasn't right at all.

Down they went. The stairs were broad and well made, worn in the centre. What the place had been the maskmaker didn't dare guess, but it had seen use and not a kind one. The gamesmaster was mad to think she could house anyone or anything in here, even were the stones silenced.

"Stay close," Cenoté whispered, taking his hand as they took the final step together.

There were torches. Why was it so dark? The corridor beyond stretched like a gaping mouth while just in front of them...

Having readied himself for a monster, Hunhau sagged with relief. "Don't be concerned," he assured the obviously startled stonemason, crouched with his hammer and chisel poised in midair. The plump child, doubtless his daughter, stared at Cenoté. "We're not here to disturb you."

"Oh, but we are." Cenoté's fingers tightened on his. "Look at their water, Hunhau. See them as they truly are."

And he could, Hunhau realized. The stonemason, rising slowly, was a cresting wave, tense and constrained, yet full of colour and grace. While the child...the child was dust and ash and every regret he'd ever felt.

It spoke, using the man's lips. "You are blind, Wizard, and powerless."

"You are found, soul-eater," Cenoté said, and in her voice was a hurricane's wrath. "And I'm not alone." Her hand lifted from Hunhau's, joined the other in a sweeping summons.

Water burst from the walls, rose from the floor, water that formed itself into nightmare shapes. Hands with shattered fingers reached. Legs that were stumps walked. Faces, ruined and rotted, opened what remained of their mouths to shout curses without sound. All aimed for the child.

The stonemason leapt forward, tools raised. "Stop me!" he pleaded as he splashed through the watershapes. They reformed at once, oblivious to all but their tormentor. "Stop me, please!"

Time didn't pass as it should. The maskmaker saw every step the man took, felt, as if it were his own, the sick horror filling the poor man's eyes.

Stepping forward, Hunhau pulled his beloved mask from his belt and smashed it over the stonemason's head.

The thick wood cracked and split. Staggered, the man fell to his knees, pieces of mask dropping beside him.

Hunhau quickly grabbed the tools from the man's hands and

tossed them as far as he could. They disappeared within the rising flood.

"You haven't won," the stonemason's mouth said. "What I've birthed will burrow under this city and find the Afterglow. We shall have its power!"

Water surged to lift the child and pin her against the wall, thin legs and arms at awkward angles. "'We,' small one?" Cenoté mocked gently. "Your masters share nothing with the likes of you. If I thought you knew anything of their true intent I'd grant you safe passage from this city in return, but you are a thing shaped from lies and ill intent."

Black drooled from the child's mouth. Her puppet's lips twisted and spat. "And the name of he who betrayed you, Wizard? What will you grant for that? I know it, I do. I know all the dark secrets. Even yours!"

The watershapes faltered, then straightened. "By the Shining Sea, take them to hell with you!" Cenoté stepped forward, or did she flow with the water, become one of the shapes?

The child's mouth gaped impossibly wide and she vomited a vile black dust. Hunhau shielded his face as it struck, coughing and gasping for breath.

"See her!" Cenoté commanded.

He dropped his hands to stare at the soul-eater as it dropped all pretence.

No longer a child. No longer small. It spread itself over the stones like a foul stain, black hooked edges digging into cracks and crevices, pulling.

It wasn't trying to escape. It scrabbled at the stone, making a dreadful sucking sound. It was feeding! Growing larger!

"This ends," Cenoté said, ice calm, and raised both hands. The watershapes flew through the air to crash against the wall!

A wave would have receded at once, but this wasn't a wave. Tortured hands gripped. Broken mouths chewed. Given form, the dead fought for themselves and for Taux. The now-desperate soul-eater tried to consume them, but these had already lost their souls and could not be touched.

The stonemason wailed, then fell silent.

When at last the wave did recede, draining down through the tile floor, the black stain was gone and the wall, new and white, glittered in the torchlight.

Hunhau noticed the figurines between the stones for the first time. Little faces gazed back. Those at head-height laughed. Those above seemed to sleep. The lower rows held lovers, their limbs intertwined.

He took a cautious sniff, then a deeper one. The air was as fresh as any he'd smelled.

"Zotz–" The stonemason sat on the floor, his eyes dazed. Not, Hunhau thought, from the blow. "Is she gone?"

"This one," Cenoté said disconcertingly. "The prize is too great. They will make more. They will try again. Whoever they are."

Hearing the weariness in her voice, Hunhau turned. With one hand, she held a mask of crude wood over her face, its colours run into lines and splotches of black, blue, and grey. As he watched, the floor beneath her dried; slender toes peeked from under her hem. "You're free," she told the man. "Hunhau?"

The maskmaker helped the stonemason to his feet. "Sorry–"

"For this?" The man touched his head. "I thank you for it." He had a strong and pleasant face, now that the horror had left it. "My name's Ghanan. I'm forever in your debt, good lady." He gave the wall a look of wonder. "I believe I'm not the only one."

"Speak not of debt, Ghanan. You fought her will all this time. That kept her small. That gave us this chance."

Hunhau could hear the dimple. Collecting Cenoté's hand, he led it to his shoulder. "It's time we left. I don't think the riot will last much longer."

Ghanan chuckled, a warm rich sound unlikely to have been heard in this place before. "I don't think I'll ask." He nodded at the stairs. "Shall we? I need to see my wife." He made no move to collect his tools.

For some reason, perhaps the same one, Hunhau didn't want the pieces of his mask. He tapped the side of his great nose instead. "I'll lead the way."

And he did.

È

There are those who come to Taux to steal and prey on the weak. There are those who seek a hiding place or new victims for their play. And there are those who sense a hidden power and would claim it for their own.

But there are those who live within Taux's walls and stand in her tower who will deny evil with their last breath.

Given a chance.

Addendum: Taux and the world it inhabits, including the cursed bleeding stones, were created by R. Scott Taylor for this project. The character of Tohil was created by Rob Mancebo and that of Tlacolotl Vash by Mike Tousignant. Others who wrote stories in this project include: Lynn Flewelling, Martha Wells, Harry Connolly, Juliet McKenna, Todd Lockwood, and R. Scott Taylor. A pleasure creating with you, my friends.

A Taste for Murder

~ 2014 ~

by Julie E. Czerneda

Author's Note: My parents' library was filled with mysteries and detective stories, slim little war-era books I devoured from cover to cover. I wanted to write one of my own, and my chance came when Ian Whate asked me for a story. I'd been researching genetic modifications and watching home DIY shows. The two seemed to me heading for a collision and how better to show that than a murder mystery! I'm also fortunate to have two close friends who were police officers at the time. Anything I get right is due to Kevin and Simon. Thank you!

Thursday was dialled warm and sunny, with a soft breeze aimed straight over the rose arbours. Perfect for a funeral.

I should know, I'd been to more than my share this week. Before you ask, that's because I'm sitting a homicide desk while Ortmer adapts to his clin-mod—poor blighter's regrowing fingers bitten off by an argumentative drunk—and the newest face always gets stuck in a suit to attend funerals. Not any or all, mind you. Just those of particular interest to the department.

Judging by the glitter of media eyes amid the branches of the nicely groomed trees edging the high-class section of *Glendale's Forever Gardens*, we weren't alone in wondering about the untimely death of Marie-Jeanne Baptiste, tastemaker.

Me? The name's Martin. Denny Rashid Martin. Probably the only one unawed by present company. Back when I was a street cop, as in last week, the Fashion District was my beat, making Baptiste's funeral like being home. Most of the celebs here I'd watched slink from the synth clinics through back doors or after hours, desperate to avoid the paparazzi until their friv-mods had taken hold and they could show off the result. They'd spot me and demand to know where their limo or taxi was waiting, as if I was someone who gave a shit. I'd tell them to take the first available right turn, while trying not to look too close. Trust me, you don't want to see skin ripple as it changes colour or texture—or facial bones melt and reform—and as for horns bursting from boils? Then there's the screaming when the drugs wear off...

No thanks.

Perishing chance any of them would recognize me out of my blues. A uniform's better than an invisibility cloak.

I recognized them, as I'm sure they'd expect, and could make a good guess as to the clinic responsible for their mods, which they wouldn't.

Scuttlebutt claimed a senior investigator wanted this assignment and was refused. A fan, I suppose. I wasn't. The District is pure theatre. The ground floor clinics are fronted by gorgeous facades and glamorous waiting lounges, with staff who are oh so professional and smooth and reassuring. All have booths where you can preview your perfectly modified self. Oh, and every one discreetly offers credit, if you can't afford the fee, at interest rates to make a loan-shark blush. Get you coming and going, they do.

Gag a maggot.

Their back doors opened on the truth. Cramped incursion rooms, illegal biowaste digesters, poorly-trained techs. Dreams forced into unwilling flesh; nightmares, often as not, the result. The alleys crawl with addicts hooked on whatever they'd been given to shut them up when their mods went wrong; late night deliveries of questionable supplies have them scurry into the dark. So do the gangs sneaking in new members for tag-mods because, hey, nothing says you belong–and keeps you belonging–like the same bargain-basement fangs or claws.

No hint of cheap here. Or failure. To ogle high-end friv-mods like those on display at Baptiste's funeral, you'd have to pay a fortune for a seat by the runways at Fashion Week, when mod developers reveal their latest wares.

My maternal grandfather once told me "you can't teach an old dog new tricks." Maybe then. These days, dogs don't age mentally any more than people. It's coming up with new tricks for them that's troublesome. They get bored.

So do we. Which explains quite a bit, in my opinion.

Right around the time clin-mods became the cure-all everyone had hoped, with genetic tweaking leading the way and biotech taking up any slack, synth clinics like *Star Power Inc.* sprang up to offer custom career-enhancing modifications. Not so essential to health, but popular. Society barely gasped for breath before true friv-mods appeared–guaranteed safe, mind you, as if...–the results sweeping like a contagion across the world. Want a new skin colour? Different eyes? Sex? Nostril hair? DYIbio kits offered anyone the chance to create the next must-have mod. Anything seemed possible.

Maybe it was, but possible didn't translate to prudent in any way, shape, or form.

As usual, regulations couldn't keep up with the inventiveness of people who could now change themselves. Wasn't long before clin-mods were necessary to reduce the harm done by poorly planned friv-mods. Changes piled up like garbage during a strike.

Case in point? Well before my time, synth clinics advertised a friv-mod to remake feverish young fans into the "type" reportedly preferred by their teen idol. Enough took the plunge there was a bump in honey-toned skin and round dark eyes in the populations of every city.

No one knew—or rather no one paid attention to those who did—that some of those "tweaks" would prove epigenetic and express themselves happily, or not so much, in their children.

And grandchildren. Within two generations of such modifications, human diversity had blown the old racial distinctions away. Newborns still had their genomes tagged and registered at birth and clinics were supposed to update records with any mods. Right. These days, who could prove they had 100% virgin DNA, or be sure it would express as it had in their ancestors?

I'm fond of my grandfather. We look alike simply because we're related and that's not only old-fashioned, it's rare. My other half, Daisie, insists on carrying a dige of him in his forties in her grab to flash any doubters. A sweetheart, Daisie, and the light of my life. She's also 60 kilos of pure genius, spiked with enough drive to power one of those starships she's busy designing, which goes to prove love don't always make sense.

'Cause me? I'm the definition of bland in a world gone to extremes. Unlike my to-the-future-and-beyond darling, the only drive I've got is to do the job and make it home at the end of my shift—oh, and to retire with my original parts. That'll be in eleven years, five months, and twenty-two days. I plan to sit on a dock with a keg of beer, watching folks with more money than sense struggle with boat ties and sails.

Till then? Well, being a cop is one of the professions that

keeps going no matter how the world changes around us. Easy to see why. Mods or not, people don't change. Not in the ways that make them bump into each other or into walls. Maybe I see that more than most, being a beat cop. Never wanted a desk. I like my streets. My people–decent, dregs, something between–and I have an understanding. This, I might put up with; that, the hell I won't. Good days, some need an ear; others to be politely told to shut up, sit still, and listen.

The bad days? All I'll say is mine end better than theirs.

I go home.

So I've no problem when I can be more counsellor than authority figure, even if it screws my record. Daisie claims I'm a throwback to a time before we–the civilization "we"–began moving faster than we could parse our course. That's how she talks; I don't always get it. Me, I go by what I see. Her smile. The look in her eyes when I come through the door.

Yup, I've a good life.

Life had been good to Marie-Jeanne Baptiste too, until its end. That had been nasty.

I stood in rose-scented shade, close enough to the cluster of funeral staff to be mistaken for one of them, and watched the Who's Who of synthetic graft and genetic transfection mill around the open grave. Those who gawked at their neighbour's mod were likely the ones strutting their first extremes in public. Those who'd missed the trend boat did their pathetic best not to appear envious or dismayed, though I was amused to see the hornies edge almost by instinct away from one another. Too late, I'd have told them. Antlers were over. It was all about skin this season. The pleasant weather arranged for Baptiste's graveside service meant most of that skin was exposed.

I got looks because mine wasn't. What was different about him, they wondered, certain something was. Who didn't have a mod of some kind, if only to avoid wearing sunglasses or having to–shudder–carry a cell?

Oh, I'd my share. They just weren't flesh. Department-issue

ceramic soles on my feet, department-issue liner in my gut, swallowed this morning. I could walk forever and my body exist on any combo of fast food and caffeine without harm. More importantly, calls of nature waited till I was off the clock. Basic beat-cop tech. The union paid for it. If I wanted the homicide desk for good, they'd haul me in for scene analyzer implants, truth serum spit, and who knew what other nonsense.

Not that I needed any of it today. There were department eyes among the media for the routine record. Me? Try as they might, despite union protest, nothing performed an on-the-fly analysis of human behaviour better or cheaper than another human. My report would be more impression than detail, but it mattered. A quick scan of the crowd gave me the faces I'd flag later. My gut—the real one—told me which of those to keep watching now.

Like Kamea Hale, Baptiste's former boss. The Hales had started in cattle—not that she owned any now. Free range animals were scarce and pricey, not to mention the idea of consuming parts of one nauseated the majority. Instead, Hale owned *All Your Favourite Strains*, the world's largest producer of vat-meat, patent-protected and available in any flavour of fish, fowl, or mammal desired. A success due in large part, according to the background, to the infallible taste buds of Marie-Jeanne Baptiste.

Baptiste was—had been—an epicure. Made her rep as a food critic, then moved on to become premiere taster for *'Strains*. Their slogan was "We feed you too." and it wasn't a boast. After fifty plus years in uniform, not much surprised me, but I'd whistled once at the company's size and scope, then again at Baptiste's reported salary. Before perks.

Hale's mods were tame for this group. Enlarged eyes, purple feathers on her head. Her skin—more likely its hairs—had grown overlapping scales that sparkled like the side of a dying fish on a sunny dock.

Was she here to mourn Baptiste or her valuable mouth?

Another A-lister, Sir Bolivar Walczak of *Star Power Inc*, stood nearby, his none-too-subtle security a step behind and glowering. His presence accounted for most of the crowd and all of media. Walczak was the prime mover behind *Star Power Inc's* latest "We Can Make You A Star," campaign: part reality show contest and part re-makeover; he was rumoured to have single-handedly created the current skin-mod craze. Me, I like my DNA as it is, thanks. Okay, as a teen I'd kept *Star Power* brochures under my pillow and dreamed about becoming a superhero. Or taller. Who hadn't? But my family was too poor–or too sane–to mod me. Once I gained some years and smarts of my own, most notably Daisie's, I was fine with the existing me.

Walczak was a virgin himself–or had everyone believing it. In this crowd, his bald head and ample girth looked more exotic than Hale's feathers and scales. A busy man and a notoriously media-shy one.

Until today. What was he doing here?

Despite the circus atmosphere–helped along by the vintage calliope being played quietly but with a snappy beat–there were a few sincere mourners graveside. I'd done my checks during the sermon. Baptiste left two daughters, both in their teens, and two husbands, only one in his teens, the other possibly my age or more. The older man had gone for blond and stalwart, or was it elf?, with pointed ears and sweeping eyebrows. The younger looked to be a trope–one of the unfortunates who continued to express their grandmother's idol choice. Or round dark eyes and honey skin were making a comeback. Odder things happened.

Dual spouses weren't unusual. Marriage had come to accommodate any combination who wanted a lifelong commitment. Many did. According to my Daisie, when what was human began to change almost daily, relationships had to expand as well. As a cop, let me tell you domestic violence went along for the ride. Don't get me started on families torn apart by one partner's mod-addiction.

Among other minor mods, the daughters' arms and legs were in different primary colours, which made them look like poorly assembled dolls. All four seemed appropriately unhappy and uncomfortable.

Other than the human scenery, Baptiste's funeral seemed no more interesting than any of the others I'd attended until the unicorn showed up.

ଓଃ

He was late, in a rush, and I knew him. Who didn't? All-star goalie Kris Rebane had been fans' MVP pick when a stick took out his mask and most of his face in game seven of the playoffs. Instead of regrowing what he'd had, he'd taken a buy-out and opted for full unicorn, complete with horse nostrils, goat beard, and the trademarked spiral horn erupting between now-violet eyes. His skin was covered in fine white hair, what showed beyond the kilt, and he'd added a mane since I'd seen him last. A gold, sparkly one. Heroic as hell.

Ridiculous on a lesser man; Kris had the shoulders and bearing to make it work. Not to mention attitude.

He was one of mine. Grew up in a tiny apartment below the clinic where his mom worked as night sterilizer. Hot-headed, impulsive, with a heart bigger than his brain, he'd find trouble faster than any kid I knew. Won't say I got him into hockey, but I helped make sure he stayed there.

Unicorn. I'd told his mother it was better than bull.

He spotted me and changed direction, charging through a trio of bunny boys who scattered, then regrouped, noses atwitch with interest.

"Constable Martin, sir." When a unicorn comes to attention, it causes a stir.

A stir I didn't need. "Hi, Kris." I didn't bother mentioning I was "Inspector Martin" for the funeral and was about to politely brush him off when I realized the mauve streaks down his cheeks had to be from tears. I'd no idea how his path crossed Baptiste's; celebs had their own circles. "Sorryforyourloss."

"I didn't think anyone took me seriously," he said with relief.

"Thanks for coming."

That couldn't be good. One of the daughters looked our way, a green hand drifting to her purple throat in almost theatrical dismay. I gave her my "move along" glare and she glanced away quickly. "Don't be sure anyone's taking you seriously yet," I warned Kris. "What's this about?"

"M.J. was murdered." The whites of his eyes fluoresced. It didn't look like grief, but that was the problem with many mods: the unexpected extras. "Isn't that why you're here?"

No, I was here because Ortmer hadn't kept his fingers out of a drunk's mouth. "You didn't file a statement." It wasn't a question. If he had, and it'd reached homicide, I wouldn't have been sent.

"They wouldn't listen!" He snorted like a horse.

Which wouldn't have helped the be-taken-seriously part. I sighed. Even before growing a horn with a sharp point, Kris in full righteous rage had never been good for those around him. And he was, as I said, one of mine.

Maybe all he needed was to vent. I resigned myself to the inevitable. "I'm listening."

He lowered his voice to match mine. "However they said M.J. died, it's a lie."

I'd seen the autopsy report. The term was CMF. Catastrophic Modification Failure. In other words, the unexpected. Techs from the synth clinic responsible had been questioned and her DNA examined; nothing culpable, concluded the department biotechs before moving to the next case. Between the ever-present risk of a new change interacting with something previously unexpressed, and the simple reality that we still didn't know everything about our own coding, it was no wonder the waivers required before any mod were the tightest legalese known to humanity.

"CMF's happen, Kris. You know that."

"Not like this. It was murder."

It was gruesome, I'd admit, which didn't make it murder but did make me question the competence of the clinic. Baptiste had wanted to enhance her ability to taste – maybe someone was on her heels for the same job – and had ordered a forked tongue with a greater surface area for tastebuds.

What they'd done was ciliate her tongue, using the portion of her DNA that coded cilia for the inner ear and many other parts. Vid from the clinic, a cheery voiceover describing the design features, showed a tongue made of separate thickened threads able to spread apart during tasting, then to collapse into a normal-looking tongue once done. Handy.

Unfortunately for Baptiste, her cilia abruptly grew past their intended design limit. They'd filled her mouth, sinuses, and throat then punched through to her brain. The younger husband had found her when he'd gone to her bed that morning. His screams had set off the building alarm.

"CMF's don't happen weeks after the mod's settled. Not without some warning. Someone did this to her," Kris insisted.

The details of Baptiste's death had been kept–supposedly–to immediate family, the department, and... "The clinic," I nodded to myself, putting it together. "It was one of yours." His mother had insisted he invest; I doubt she'd foreseen the unicorn.

Kris shuddered, mane sparkling in the sun. "Yes. I asked to see the–they showed me–" Beneath the white hair, he turned green. His throat worked convulsively, jiggling the goat beard.

The funeral staff came to the alert, presumably ready with a bucket. I waved them off and, taking his arm, escorted my unsettled unicorn to the chapel building. We weren't alone. Media drones now hovered over the arched door, hunting tears as the mass of funeral goers were cued to retire to the waiting reception. Serve them right if Kris vomited on the marble steps; wouldn't serve Kris at all.

Or Baptiste.

Murder?

They'd have sent someone else–anyone else–if that'd been remotely on the radar. My assignment was to observe the people drawn to this death. Who talked to whom. Who wouldn't and why.

Gossip was grist for the department info mill and funerals made for easy pickings. The most private of people would talk to a stranger, given a sympathetic look. I could look sympathetic.

No reason I couldn't ask a few questions, clear this up for Kris, and be done with it. I owed him that much.

I should have known better.

CB

Glendale's Forever Gardens' chapel lay within a sprawling edifice of reused stone, glass, metal, and wood, each and every component labelled with its source. Maybe they meant to be respectful. Historic, even. Ask me, it was annoying. When I finally located the restroom for Kris, it was unhelpfully labelled the "Old Montrose Railway Depot." Though I did like the coat check. Its long polished counter had once graced "Darby's Fine Meats." Nice.

The reception was in the main hall, named the "Bradley Greenhouse No.6," presumably for the glass ceiling. The hall itself was a maze of tables covered in soon-to-be-compost flowers and unrecognizable food. Beverage fountains tinkled gloomily. Windows, curtained in dark velvet, were set deep within semi-private alcoves for those overcome. I'd have said by grief but it was doubtful most of those here had even met Baptiste or her family. Eaten food she'd tasted for them, yes.

Eat the food here, definitely. Hungry work, a funeral. And thirsty, by the swarm around each fountain. Other means of dealing with sadness were changing hands or whatever in the Railway Depot. I wished them luck. Sex-mods were no more reliable than the basic model and some required a manual to even rev up.

I'd parked my unicorn with two of the bunny boys. Turned out they were hockey fans and Kris, rightly figuring I didn't want him underfoot, resigned himself to adulation.

I moved through the hall, listening more than watching. Most conversations, predictably, were about anything but the woman now dead. The few of interest to the department I noted as I passed by, feeling more ridiculous by the moment. Kris had no motive or suspects, just his guilt and an overblown desire for justice. The same desire that had got his face rearranged, truth be told. Unicorn.

After half an hour. I'd made one circuit of the tables and alcoves and was starting my next when,

"–you know it's your fault she's dead."

I feigned a craving for some green goo and crackers on the nearest table. Whatever was in it, my gut liner could manage. I hoped.

Who'd spoken?

"Don't be ridiculous. I never blamed M.J."

That voice I recognized. Kamea Hale had given a short eulogy at the service. She was holding court in the alcove behind and to my left.

"What'd you lose–billions? You couldn't afford another mistake."

Male, older. I reached for a napkin, managing to avoid the red-dappled ribcage of the nearly naked lady doing the same. Skin-mods. The air was cooler in the hall–for the food and flowers, I assumed–and gooseflesh marred most of her pattern. Still, it was prettier than some. Almost like rose petals.

As we exchanged the tight-lipped smiles and compassionate nods of funeral-goers, I got the glimpse I was after.

Hale was sitting with Walczak. His security, stationed on either side of the alcove opening, noticed my interest and gave me the eye. Three each.

As if. I lifted a green-smeared cracker at them and popped it in my mouth before turning away again.

The taste curdled my toes in their ceramic soles. Wishing I could spit, I swallowed hastily, then helped myself to something sweet and bubbly from the closest fountain.

From the mouthful, it had a good kick to it, if I hadn't already guessed from the rising volume of voices to every side. Oh, I wasn't drinking on duty. You kidding? Another perk of my cop's gut. Alcohol's just another source of hydration.

I smelled unicorn—cloves and day-old armpit, I kid you not—before I turned my head to confirm that yes, Kris had run out of patience and found me.

His eyes glowed white around the violet again. Not a sign of calm. "He could have done it." Which "he" wasn't in question, given the swing of that wickedly pointed horn towards Walczak.

Security tensed as security is paid to do. I took Kris by one thick arm, again, and steered him out of their sight. "Walczak's not the only mod designer here," I reminded him.

"He was M.J.'s."

A tidbit not in any report I'd seen. Had I gone for ears able to prick up, mine would have stood on end. Means and opportunity. If, I reminded myself, it'd been murder and not tragic error. Still, an error this big wouldn't help the next season of "We Can Make You a Star."

Who was I kidding? Of course it would. The risk was the draw. New question. Why the secrecy? "Keep your voice down," I grumbled. I shouldn't encourage this; my mouth kept going anyway. "Walczak could buy a middling country. Why would he bother with a career mod?" Something else niggled at me. "And why did Baptiste? Was someone after her job?"

"Don't you remember? The Veggie Turkey."

Right. Last year's Xmas dinner had cooked up more like broccoli than fowl. Consumers had howled. *'Strains* had released a statement about a mix-up with their vegan option ordering and given credit for a month's supply to any affected family.

Whose wasn't? Billions lost it was.

Hale had claimed not to blame her. "Think the company insisted on the mod?" I asked. Insisting was illegal; hiring based on a desired mod wasn't.

Kris looked offended. Unicorns did that exceptionally well, which gained us a modicum of privacy as people edged away. "M.J.'s–she was their best. Beside, it wasn't her fault. Production had rushed ahead for the holiday." A huff, then he unwound a little. "Sure, she worried about missing the next mistake. She was like that, wanting to be better. Someone could have talked her into the mod and then used it to–" he closed his wide lips over the rest.

"Or maybe–" I used my let's-be-reasonable voice, the one before don't-give-me-that-crap. "–the mod failed, as many of them do. Murder takes motive, Kris."

"You're right." His nostrils flared thoughtfully. Then, "What if we have it wrong? What she was murdered because of her mod?"

Judging by conversations I'd overheard, there were plenty of people in this room willing to murder to keep whatever they'd painstakingly built into their flesh exclusive. Didn't mean they would. Still...

My pause let Kris keep on thinking. Not good. Sure enough, he ducked to bring his face next to mine, horn passing alarmingly close to my nose, and whispered hoarsely, "What if *'Strains* is putting something it shouldn't into the food stream? Something M.J. would have tasted with her new tongue. They'd have to be rid of her!" He straightened and tossed his mane in triumph. "It was a plot!"

First murder; now conspiracy. I was done here. I pulled out my compassionate voice. "Look, Kris. I get it. A person you knew–you respected–died at the hands of people you employ. It shouldn't have happened–to her or to anyone. You need to make your–" At his now-stricken expression, I changed "peace" to "–need to think of those still alive. You don't want to upset the family." With a nod to our people-filled surroundings. "Or anyone else."

I was reaching him. Maybe. Then he grumbled, "Why would they be upset? None of them care. I don't even know why they're here."

"For the media—"

I'd forgotten who I was talking to; Kris Rebane made the news when he ordered a multi-grain bagel at *Tims*. He shook his head. "Not one posed for a feature grab or waited on a personal. They came in here, where there's no coverage at all."

Not even the department's eyes, this being the private part of the function. The more we watched ourselves, Daisie'd said once, the more important surveillance-free space became. I'd laughed and called it nuisance-space.

What I'd meant was scary-space, but I wouldn't say that to her. No watcher meant no backup, no record, just me.

Like now.

The unicorn looked as uneasy as I felt, so I put on my best everything's-fine face. "Free food and drink, then."

"That's the other thing." Kris lifted his head to gaze around the room, something easy from his height, then his eyes came back to me. They glowed. "Skin-mods show every calorie."

And the crowd was gorging itself, not to mention draining the beverage fountains.

My street-sense twitched. Not that I was an expert on celebs when they let their figurative hair or feathers down, but something wasn't right in this room.

Fine. There was someone left to question; someone who'd know all about this crowd, as well as Baptiste's death.

After all, he'd had his hand in creating both.

Sir Bolivar Walczak.

                                        C03

Funeral homes have their egalitarian side. Coffins might range from minimal to ridiculous but, no matter who you were, eventually the food and drink would sent you to the Train Depot.

Unless you were a cop with a liner, but I could fake it when necessary.

It became necessary when Walczak finally made his excuses to Hale and stood. I made sure to leave promptly enough to be inside the restroom before his security. No chance they could clear the public facility for their boss, not with Baptiste's former husbands cuddled in mutual misery on the anteroom couch.

I judged the private Sir Bolivar Walczak would have had his fill of the crowd outside. Right I was. I heard him order his protectors to stay with the husbands.

I delayed in the stall till he put his hands in the sterilizer field, then came out. He turned his head and fixed me with a blue-eyed stare as cool and collected as any I'd seen. "Cop."

Two kinds of people greet us like that. Those with experience avoiding us and those who've hired those with experience avoiding us.

Interesting.

"Homicide," I returned agreeably. "Inspector Martin. Sorryforyourloss. Were you a friend of the deceased?"

"Her designer."

I didn't pretend to clean my hands. "So you're responsible for the mod that killed her."

"Far from it." Walczak paused to suck some rinse and spit. Why the stuff always smelled of mint, I don't know. "I recommended against any mod. M.J.'s job was to taste new products the way any of us–any unmod–would. What was the point of her becoming a living chemoanalyzer when it was her discrimination and sense of taste that mattered?" He ran a towelette over his sweaty head and nodded to his reflection. "She listened. Seemed to like what I said and agree." Tossing the crumbled towelette at the disposal, he turned back to me. "Then…this tragedy."

If an act, it was a good one. "What changed her mind?"

"Who," he answered promptly. "That's why you're here, isn't it? To uncover the truth about her death."

I was here because Ortmer–I gave up making the excuse to

myself. I'd blown my original assignment the moment I'd listened to the unicorn. "There've been–questions–raised."

"You think she was murdered." Walczak smiled. "A CMF would be the perfect weapon, wouldn't it? Talk someone into a cutting edge mod–untried, exciting, risky–and design it to be fatal. Not right away, of course."

"Why not?" Was I hearing a confession? Maybe homicide wasn't as hard as I'd thought.

Maybe dogs could learn to juggle geese.

"The clinic would be accused of a poor incursion. There'd be an inquest. No, the mod would have to settle in and work as promised first. Anything goes wrong after that, well, it's a skeleton in the code." At my frown–who doesn't hate jargon?–he went on, "an undetected conflict within the client's genome."

"What are the odds of that?" Though I was becoming convinced how Baptiste died wasn't going to clear anything up. To be murder, someone had to want her dead.

"Higher than we like to tell clients, but slim." Walczak took one of the two easy chairs at one end of the restroom. There were such paired conversation spots everywhere in the *'Forever Gardens,* each with its small table bearing a box of tissue and bowl of candy. He waved me to the other chair, clearly in no hurry to return to the funeral.

I obliged, well aware he wasn't trying to be helpful. This was no unicorn. This was a highly intelligent, self-assured villain. If he'd frequented my streets I've have ordered up all the surveillance the department could muster. Surveillance that wasn't in this both public and very private space.

For some reason–maybe for that reason–Walczak smiled again. Then, as if he'd pulled the thought from my head, he commented, "The real question is why."

I didn't smile back. "Any ideas on that, sir?"

"If I were to speculate..." He leaned back–his belly testing the buttons of a suit that likely cost more than I made in two years–

closed his eyes and worked his lips in and out.

Bullshit. I stood to go.

His eyes shot open, anticipation gleaming in their depths. "You really should speak to Kamea, Inspector. Mention the Ministry of Health and–oh yes–do ask her about using the consumer food stream as a delivery mechanism, will you? And what M.J. thought of it. If you're any good at your job, you might find your reason. If it was murder. These things do happen, you know."

My words to Kris, back in my face.

I didn't bother to respond.

As I pushed my way past Walczak's waiting security, I found myself hoping that if it had been murder, I'd be able to nail their boss with it.

So I turned at the door, looked the nearest goon in all three eyes, and said pleasantly, "Make sure Walczak stays available."

"Sir Walczak."

As if.

⅓

People killed each other every day for the simplest of reasons. You smell funny. You're in my way. You have what I want. You took what I had. You don't love me. You love me too much.

Baptiste?

Maybe one of the husbands decided to do in a rival. Who was the rival remained moot, considering I'd last seen the two in a tight embrace, but they could have worked together. Then there were the daughters. Not an uncommon motive, impatience to gain an inheritance. Didn't wash here. Both had substantial trusts waiting tied to their ages, not their mother's life.

Which took me back to what was way past my pay grade, Kris' notion of a conspiracy by *All Your Favourite Strains* to be rid of their top taster because of something they intended to put in our food.

I really hated that idea.

For one thing, it'd mean recalls and shortages and nothing got the streets uglier than shortages–real or imagined. For another, Daisie didn't have a cop liner in her gut to protect her. If there was something wrong with the food on our table, if something might have harmed my family...?

I stopped myself there. We'd have to know. That was what mattered. Again above my pay grade.

Give me an angry guy with a bat standing over a still-twitching body any day. For an instant I considered calling Ortmer, though I knew he'd be in a foul mood being interrupted. Fingers? He was probably working on his golf swing.

I could take Kris to the station, unicorn head and all, sit him at my pretend desk in homicide, and start a file. They could stick me with it. More likely they'd hand it to someone who didn't know him or the District.

For a moment I thought of begging off, of reminding Kris I wasn't his cop any more.

But I was. I'd wiped his bloody nose after a fight behind the arena. Gone to a game or two or ten when his mother couldn't be there. Taken him to a synth clinic where they wouldn't ask questions when he'd gotten himself twisted about trying to get back his game during the strike.

Hell, I'd even helped his mother find polish for his stupid horn.

Kris, who'd met me outside the Train Depot, gave me a bright-eyed hopeful look that meant all my thinking had shown on my face and I was toast. "I want to talk to Kamea Hale," I said, giving in.

"Great. I'll come with you. She knows me," this rather urgently.

I recognized the light of battle in his eyes, despite their lilac. If I didn't let him tag along, he'd start asking his own questions.

Great. "You," I told him, grabbing the horn and using it as a handle to shake his head in emphasis, "will leave the talking to me. Got it?"

You'd have thought he'd won the Cup. "Yes, sir!"

℃

All I had was a dead taster, a unicorn, and a villain. Not even a murder, not for sure. Yet I trusted my instincts. Something was off in the reception hall. The crowd of brave new humans–or crazy fashion extremists, take your pick–had gathered for another reason than a funeral.

Kamea Hale? Her scaled hands trembled as she lifted her glass to her lips. Her eyes, unexpectedly normal, human eyes, were haunted. As Kris and I sat across from her in the alcove, the couch creaking under his weight, she sipped and swallowed and looked as guilty as anyone I'd ever seen.

I showed her the palm of my hand, activating my badge with a tap of my ring finger, then shut it off again. "I'm sorry for your loss–"

"Kamea, did you kill M.J.?"

What part of–? Using the tissue table for cover, I tromped on Kris' bare foot, ceramic soles being good for that too. He shut up, giving me a hurt look. Unicorns.

"There've been some questions raised," I said smoothly, ignoring their source. "Sir Walczak suggested you could be of assistance. If you have a moment."

"Bolivar?" Up close, the scales of her skin-mod didn't touch one another, letting me watch her cheeks go ash white. She set her cup down without taking her eyes from mine. Kris quickly saved it from missing the table; I doubt she noticed. "This doesn't–I don't see–" Her voice firmed. "This is hardly the time or place, Inspector."

Couldn't argue with that. "You'll come to the station, then," I said cheerfully. "Thank you."

Hale collected herself, a glint of what helped her successfully run an international megacorporation in the lift of her head. She looked at me, not Kris, but her first words were to him. "I most certainly did not kill Marie-Jeanne. She was one of my dearest friends as well as a valued employee." To me. "As for questions about her death? It was horrible way to die and a tragic waste of a life. What else could you want to know?"

Walczak thought he was using me. The difference between us was that I didn't care. "What did the deceased think of the government using *Strains'* consumer food stream?"

"M.J. hated it," Hale replied without so much as a blink. Good or honest or both. I reserved my opinion. "Not the reason–who could argue with testing our ability to deliver emergency rations in a crisis?–but how it interfered with her work. She didn't like any strain being released to the public without being tasted. She was a proud person. Responsible." She dabbed her eyes with a tissue. "Irreplaceable."

Kris' horn dipped and rose as he nodded.

"Her sense of taste was that good?"

"Better than any analyzer money could buy, Inspector. Raw components don't matter. M.J. infallibly predicted consumer mouth response to any food we dreamed up. She guided the research responsible for putting *'Strains* into almost every home. Including yours." Hale frowned and leaned forward. "Bolivar told you about the ministry. That bastard." She pointed a scaled forefinger at me. "There's your suspect, Inspector."

"What's *Star Power* got to do with food production?" Kris asked, looking as puzzled as I felt.

"I've no idea," Hale admitted, sitting back in her seat. The frown, I noticed, remained. "Bolivar tried to hire M.J. away from us. When she refused, he bribed someone in production to discredit her. He denied it, but I have–" another glint "–a very efficient security staff."

"What else did they learn?" Her hesitation as good as an admission, I pressed. "Ms. Hale, it may be relevant to the death of your friend."

"Nothing concrete," she said after a long pause. "A rumour at best. They could be using grey source DNA to shortcut their mod development."

Great. Now vice would be interested. "How grey?" It used to be grey meant corpses. Now it could be anything from trafficked children to some test tube concoction.

Her lips twisted. "Animal."

On the face of it, using DNA from other species wasn't a big deal. We shared most of ours with everything from bananas to whales. But the devil, as my grandfather would say, was in the details. In some instances, our cells didn't use interspecies DNA in the same way, or to the same results. The earliest animal mod attempts–because oh, yes, they tried–had been so horrific the entire world had agreed to ban them.

It hadn't slowed the synth clinics; our own DNA has virtually no end of possibilities. Turn on the right gene and you've a penis to your knees.

The unicorn made an unhappy noise. "What does that have to do with–"

Hale cut him off, rising to her feet. "What's Belle doing with him?!"

I stood and turned to look, Kris looming like a golden-maned monolith beside me.

Sir Bolivar Walczak stood in the doorway to the reception hall, one of M.J.'s daughters–the elder–snug at his side. As my thoughts immediately turned to a less complex and time-honoured motive for murder, namely a mother with better taste, the air above the couple filled with incoming media eyes.

Then the lights went out.

♋

The unicorn's eyes glowed in the dark. That, I'd expected. The glowing horn, not so much.

The skin of everyone in the room emitting light?

Okay, not mine. Yes, I checked.

We seemed the only ones shocked. Chants of "*Star Power*! *Star Power*!" mingled with cheers and the joyful smashing of glassware.

I looked over my shoulder at Hale. I'd been wrong to think it a glow. Her skin pulsed with fluorescence, greenish light marking her every vein. No, moving through her every vein. She stared at her bare arms, her face a ghastly mask, then her mouth opened and she screamed.

Kris moved faster than I did–or could–easing her down, taking her hands in his. He looked up at me. His skin, I realized numbly, hadn't changed like the others'. He said something I couldn't hear over the bedlam.

Not that I needed to.

Walczak.

Maybe he'd murdered Baptiste. Maybe he hadn't. But this stunt at her funeral?

That he'd planned.

CB

Finding Walczak was easy. He'd stayed by the doors, surrounded by adoring masses and the media. I found myself more invisible than usual, being the only one not generating their own circle of light, and moved to stand close enough to Belle Baptiste to smell her perfume.

I resisted the temptation to whisper in her ear, "what would your mother think?" Besides, Walczak was holding forth.

"—permanent? Yes, of course. Bright Skin is *Star Power*'s latest friv-mod, guaranteed to last until the owner wishes a new look. And that, my friends, will be as easy as drinking your morning coffee, won't it?"

Cheers and whistles drowned out the broadcaster's next question.

"—all volunteers. And why not? This will go down in history–" Walczak paused, as if savouring the words "—as the first flash-mod in history. Won't be the last, will it?"

"Nooo!!!!!"

They were all certifiable. Certifiable and drunk.

"I didn't agree to this!" Media eyes zoomed close as Hale staggered forward, hands grabbing for arms and shoulders, sliding over glowing skin. "You'd no right to mod me!"

The unicorn was right behind, horn lowered. I was amazed at his restraint. Wouldn't last.

"I warned you not to drink, my dear Kamea."

Walczak had put his "Bright Skin" mod in the fountains?

Daisie'd said there'd be a breakthrough one day, something to take the sting–literally–out of mods. She'd called it a world-changer.

Then, I'd chuckled. Now, the urge to vomit almost overwhelmed me. What if I hadn't used the liner today?

I'd be glowing. And look ridiculous.

And be unable to do my job. A glowing cop?

More importantly–far more importantly–if so, he'd done what everyone said was impossible: to deliver a mod into a body through ingestion.

There must have been another question. "—being available through regular retailers is the long-term goal, but for now we're giving "Bright Skin" away. This is the future. Mods without pain. It's the end of expensive synth clinics. Drink up to be what you want. Whatever you want! The essential precursors went out in the latest shipments from *'Strains.'*"

Shipments Baptiste hadn't tasted, being dead. The bribes to production hadn't stopped with vat-turkey.

I had him.

No, I realized a sickening heartbeat later.

He had us.

Silence spread through the hall as even the drunks realized something more was happening here. Something dreadful. Hale whimpered. She wasn't alone.

"The precursor transinfects the DNA of every cell in your body, ready to accept whatever mod-code you ingest. No need for nanovectors. Total efficiency. Mods activate the moment they enter cells." Walczak chuckled. "Unless stopped. The real market will be for what I call "code-glue." If you want to stay as you are, you'll need to take code-glue to suppress the precursor. Elegant, isn't it?"

Hale was speaking frantically to her elbow–shutting down distribution centres, purging tanks, trying to stop this.

Too little, too late. "First you had to murder Baptiste," I said, the words echoing. Media eyes whirled to focus on me, but it was the department I hoped heard. The department, and one other. "M.J. was on to you, wasn't she? Your little plan to blackmail the world." The murder weapon hadn't been Baptiste's mod; it had been whatever Walczak–or her daughter–had put into her food or drink. How didn't matter. This was why. "Aren't you rich enough?"

Walczak's laugh drew back the eyes and sent cold fingers down my spine. "I've rewritten humanity, Inspector Martin, and signed my name in every one of its cells. You're all mine now! It's the greatest–" Blood, not another word, spurted from his mouth as the unicorn's horn went through him.

Cঃ

I'm not proud of what I did, but I'm satisfied I had no other choice. Kris? He's a hero.

The rest of us? Life's about change, Daisie says. Humanity's been changed again, this time at one man's whim, this time in a way that accelerates the pace of our evolution.

No one's willing to say what we'll become.
My guess?
I'll still have a job.

Duck, Duck, Goose

~ 2019 ~

by Julie E. Czerneda

Author's Note: I was approached by NIXs magazine to contribute to their issue exploring, through art, algorithms and communication. What they were after was something different and I was delighted to be asked. That said, each work was to flow or be inspired by the one preceding it. Mine? A pastiche of line drawings depicting restaurants. I studied it, then spotted some words I recognized. Duck, Duck, Goose. I was off! It was also a pleasure to revisit the notion of first contact and technology. What goes around, keeps coming around.

"Emotional content will be a factor in communicating with these people."

Duck, duck, goose. Like the game children played. You picked an entry point for communication from the choices available, hoping you'd tagged the right "it" to allow success.

Waiting in the airlock to enter ORBIT40, Lambert Sing tucked his case under his arm, mentally reviewing the experts' final briefing, looking for "it." He did his utmost to convey professional dignity, despite a body suit adhering to skin stripped of hair and earthly microbes because you didn't know, ahead of time, when biota crossed the line of courtesy. They'd stopped short of an enema.

He ignored the burning itch. Ignored how the suit drew attention to knobby elbows and knees, and crawled up his crotch. With any justice to the universe, his counterpart had the manners to undergo similar discomforts. If not, the experts would gleefully suck every biological particle his clothing acquired during their meeting.

Lambert couldn't see outside and was glad. The visitors' massive ships dwarfed the great ORBIT40 and her sister stations, a potent threat over the fragile ball of blue he'd left this morning.

He removed the word "threat" from his train of thought. His role was to open the dialogue, determine, if possible at this early stage, what the visitors had in mind, and create a negotiation framework.

Harder to be rid of "emotional." Lambert pressed his elbow against the case. Inside was his comp system, newly loaded with the latest facial algorithms. Facial as in able to interpret a human face; apparently his counterpart would present one. Giving him a nightmare of aliens ripping faces from people he knew, to hang their lifeless features over gaping mouths—

—a nightmare he'd not shared, or another would be here.

What role would "emotional context" play in this negotiation? Were the visitors prone to threatening frowns or intimidating teeth gnashing? Or was their idea of negotiation more intimate—more revealing?

In human-human dialogue, as a negotiation intensified, emotion became calculated. You avoided random elements. A tightness near the eyes at the wrong time might skew value. A smile, if forced, imply an entrenched position. As a top negotiator, Lambert had perfect control over his own expressions.

Now help or hindrance?

Duck, duck, goose.

☓

The station's communications chief briefed him as another of ORBIT40's crew towed him through corridors. "No prob conveying the basics of approach and docking, Envoy Sing, but they weren't happy till we warmed the pod environment."

Technological congruence was reasonable; psychological was not. "You weren't to elicit communication."

"Didn't. They sent images of a sad face, then a happy one." With smooth synchrony, the two stationers took hold of wall bars to ease Lambert around a bend. "Not far now."

Emotional context. Happy/not happy. "What else can you tell me?"

The chief tugged him until they could see one another's eyes. "They're using the freight door. Guessing they're big."

"Security risk?"

The chief gave the lift of a brow that was a shrug in null-g. "Nothing here to stop them."

Duck, duck, goose.

☓

They floated Lambert through the airlock and hatch into the pod, granting him sufficient momentum to reach the waiting chair and grasp the takehold to pull himself into place. On contact, the chair gripped the fabric covering his buttocks and thighs; the table contained a similar spot to receive his case. The pod was otherwise featureless, a reusable cylinder to ferry goods between stations, configured as needed, shortly to be the most famous—or infamous—meeting place in human history.

Warm as a summer's day in Florence. Lambert opened his case. Paired monitors rose to attach to the ceiling, leaving behind keyboard and screen.

"United Earth Envoy Lambert Tyler Sing, ready to greet our guest." Words transmitted around a world not as united as a planetary government suggested, but in this moment of first contact?

Linked indeed.

The freight door at the cylinder's end spun to align floors. Lambert flashed on another nightmare, where what he faced would be a giant spider, clung to the ceiling.

Atavistic reactions. He'd medication should those become overwhelming. Beyond a last resort.

A muted clang of released clamps. The inner hatch receded into its housing, the outer opening on an airlock full of spare parts.

Spare parts imbedded in a two metre per side cube of transparent pink goo, the result like fruit bits in jelly, atop a flat trolley that rolled inside, somehow gripping the floor.

An office chair. He could deal with that.

What jiggled atop the chair—their visitor–was held by a net up two sides. It came to rest opposite the table from him.

Parts shifted within the goo. Too many and strange for him to detect correlations to human tech and he'd no idea if he faced a person in a suit, or a blend of machine and flesh. No need. The monitors collected all imaginable data; analysts were ready to assist.

A bead of sweat left his forehead, to float near the corner of his eye. Lambert opened his mouth to speak.

A face pressed out from the goo, a human face—male, middle-aged, hairless.

A prisoner? Lambert's muscles tried to thrust him from the chair, tightening the suit.

Eyelids stayed closed. The mouth moved, stretching in a bizarre smile.

Representational. Emotive. Creepy as hell.

Lambert risked smiling back. "Hello, my name is Lambert–"

The face rotated into the goo, another taking its place. This female, older, the expression almost a caricature of anger.

What had he done? Not done? Should do?

Duck, duck, goose.

Face set to neutral, Lambert pressed a button. His screen came alive with the facial algorithm's assessment: *displeasure/ repudiation/repugnance/anger.*

In a human, yes. He ignored the list, concentrating as covertly as possible on the face displayed beside it. The Goo Being's chosen face looked familiar.

Lambert sent a request. The display filled with myriad boxes, each with a human face, shifting through expressions. The algorithm's real-life models. Words appeared at the top of the screen.

<u>Analysis: Same algorithm.</u>

A box enlarged to show the face that looked out from the goo, clouded with anger.

Lambert held up his hand, palm out, and deliberately smiled. The goo face revolved, and out pushed another, a smiling younger man, *pleasure/acceptance/friendly.*

They'd tapped into human emotive constructs. Were using those to aid communication.

Sitting back, face arranged in *polite interest/attention/ goodwill,* Lambert summoned the first preset hologram. An image of the visitor's ships, arriving in orbit, appeared above the table.

He raised his eyebrows. *Curiosity.* Hoped for meaning: why are you here?

Another revolution. A child's face, filled with *remorse/regret/guilt/anxiety.*

Years spent at tables almost as fraught as this locked Lambert's face at *calm,* though it was a strain when pieces shifted within the goo and something pressed outward until it popped free to soar towards his nose.

The disc stopped short, sank to the table, and aimed a blue beam at his case. The screen's display changed to show an incalculable number of alien ships in a space strewn with rocks. Asteroids?

<u>Analysis: Neptune's rings.</u>

A hidden invasion fleet—? Lambert flinched. *Fear!*

The goo offered a new face, an older woman's. *Soothing/reassuring/maternal.*

Lambert fought to compose himself. Managed *curiosity/question,* certain of *anxiety/fear* in the mix.

The display switched to a Goo Being ship, at a distance from what were now clearly the rings around Neptune. An image of just the rings. All at once, sound. Pings. Hums and clatters. A profound hiss.

<u>Analysis: ring sound, recorded.</u>

Lambert looked up to find a smiling young man's face. *Beatific/joy-filled/happy.* Looked down as the display changed. More ships, many within the rings.

"You're tourists?!"

No sooner had the exclamation left his lips than the face flipped back to scowling old woman's, with its *displeasure/defense/repudiation.*

No trained thespian could have portrayed *apology/contrition* any faster. Lambert gestured to the image and gave a big smile, nodding for good measure.

The goo went back to *happy* face.

He relaxed.

The child's *remorse/regret/guilt/anxiety* face reappeared.

Lambert replied with exaggerated *curiosity* and this time allowed *fear*, not reassured when the next face pressed out with a look of *compassion/understanding/regret*.

He dragged his eyes to the display. Saw a collision, an explosion. Ships evacuating, some towing others. Three speeding ahead of a glittering mass of ring material.

Last, the image of an exquisite gem of a world, blue and white, with greens and browns, and every other colour.

Analysis: ring material on Earth trajectory.

His screen went blank, eloquent of futile, global panic.

Lambert looked at the Goo Being. Faces pressed out from every portion of goo, a spectrum of humanity, each with the same expression.

Contrition/apology/regret

Duck, duck, goose.

They were it.

A Pearl from the Dark

A Story of Night's Edge

~ 2022 ~

by Julie E. Czerneda

Author's Note: What's ahead for me? For the next while, I'll be back in the valley of Marrowdell to add to my fantasy series, Night's Edge. House toads and dragons. Nyims and ylings. All the characters I've dearly missed and hope you have, too. To complete my anniversary collection, to thank you and bring you, dear readers, with me into the future...a brand new story.

Prologue

*L**ast Autumn, Within the World of Forgotten Soldiers...*
On the day the peace treaty between Rhoth and Ansnor was signed, sealed with wax and ribbon, and proclaimed loudly throughout those lands, prison gates quietly swung open, releasing soldiers captured by either side during their lengthy and bloody border dispute.

In the treaty, Rhoth ceded half of Vorkoun to Ansnor in return for an agreement to permit the Eldad's new train, rail already being built from the south in Rhoth, through that city to reach Ansnor's mines. Economies and cultures were set to blend as never before, with fortunes ahead for all.

According to Prince Ordo Arselical, leader of Rhoth, whose many and secret plots were at last coming to fruition and who cared not a whit for fortunes made by anyone but himself.

According to neighbouring Mellynne, outside the blend if not the plots, the prince was a dangerous fool. Mellynne knew of other forces at play in the world that cared nothing for the schemes of those in it. Knew to fear what might sleep beneath Ansnor's mountains. To grant access to the Eldad, who denied what they couldn't see or touch, put all in peril.

While rulers argued and traders filled warehouses in anticipation, forgotten soldiers shuffled uncertainly into the light, to start their lives again. Each received a bundle of civilian clothing and a pair of new boots, plus a small purse of coin. They signed discharge papers full of words about peace and forgiveness, with a clause stating it was up to them to leave at once. There was no welcome from former enemies and none from friends with newly peaceful streets.

For the Ansnans, it was east to the mines or north to the Barrens, there being no road south, ironically, until the Eldad built their train.

And only the stars knew when that would be.

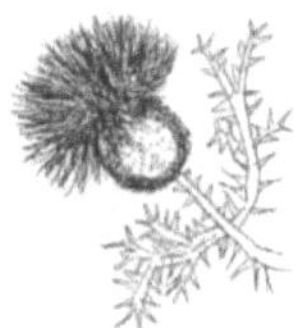

Four Hundred and Seventy-one Years ago, Within the World of Toads and Dragons…

There was magic, enough. Beings who used it, or were it, or both. There was sky and earth and seasons, of a sort, though it didn't snow. How could it? Water stayed where it was summoned, in fountains and wells, and what rained from sky to earth in its seasons was mimrol. Silver and warm, mimrol carved rivers and filled lakes, spreading magic as it flowed.

Dragons hunted the air, kruar the ground, and toads, though cousins, stayed out of sight. Terst farmed and built, bringing peace where it could flourish, and avoided dragons and kruar too. All had their place, whatever they thought of it, or if they even did.

But there were those, the sei, who thought a great deal. Sei pondered what was beyond the ken of others, being as curious as they were powerful, and one fateful day the sei wondered…was there more?

And one day wondered…could they touch it?

And all would have remained as it was, with magic enough and peace, but on a day when the light of an unseen sun dimmed, on a day when anything seemed possible, one sei reached from the world of dragons and toads, into that of trains and soldiers…

Tearing both worlds open.

Making both worlds bleed.

Spilling magic.

The sei mended that tear, as best it could. Used itself like thread. Held on, accepting that penance.

While dragons and toads, as well as kruar and terst, explored what the sei had wrought.

This spring…

There's a world of forgotten soldiers.

There's a world of dragons and toads.

Writhing through both is the edge where they meet, for the sei holds, still.

Magic, wild and potent, lives there. In the valley of Marrowdell. In the canals of Channan's Shadow District. On a hill behind a summer house. In so very many places…

…magic waits to be found.

One: The Dreamer

The first dreadful dream of Roche Morrill entered his sleep when he was a child of seven and he never forgot it.

He hurried through the playroom he shared with his younger brother Devins, chased by shadow hands that crumpled the familiar walls and furnishings around him into swirls of dust. He tried—oh how he tried—to pick up every beloved toy and treasure before the shadows took them too, but he'd very small hands and kept dropping what he held and the shadows wrapped around him and what he did hold became dust, pouring from his fingers, pouring into a carpet of dust and a floor of dust and through it he fell and fell and couldn't breathe-

He'd waked, screaming and inconsolable until his father, the great Baron Reidd Morrill, came himself, still in his velvet and fur robe from the House of Keys, to sit on his son's bed and hear a spate of tearful babble. When Roche sputtered to a stop, his father gave a grave and sombre nod, the heavy chain and key around his neck catching the light. It hadn't been a nightmare, his father told him, but a magic within his blood manifesting a warning dream. Roche's grandfather had been afflicted with such dreams his entire life and it meant their lives were about to change. They would be extra careful, his father assured Roche. All would be fine.

Nothing was. When the sun rose, the Morrills, like others in Avyo with tainted Mellynne heritage, found themselves exiled to the far north, stripped of property and rank. Though the doing of a prince, it had been his dream. How could a child not blame himself?

The second dreadful dream of Roche Morrill came to him three years later, in Marrowdell, while asleep in the cramped bed he shared with his brother, in the hovel now their home, and he never forgot it.

He stood on a hill of bone, a wind like hands pushing him to the edge above the cataracts, and he couldn't save himself, couldn't stop, and he fell and fell into the water and couldn't breathe–

Roche told his father, who drew him close and ruffled his hair. Not every bad dream was a warning, the baron told him.

He was wrong. The next day his father was killed by his horse. Once more, the child blamed himself. Grief and self-loathing turned outward as a sullen rage; Roche began to lie and cheat, making a game of tormenting those closest to him.

The latest dreadful dream of Roche Morrill arrived fifteen years after his first, while dozing under a tree.

He stood outside the home of sweet Jenn Nalynn, watched by her mother's roses. Suddenly every stem and stalk pulled free of the wall, grabbing for him like hands, lifting him into the air. Even as thorns drew blood, the lovely scent filled him and he felt a stir of hope–until the roses threw him high in the air and he fell and fell...landing hard on the Northward Road, unable to breathe—

The next day, Jenn Nalynn, whom Roche boldly declared

would marry him—not that he loved her–told him she wished he'd tell the truth.

As had his mother and brother and Horst and most of the villagers over the years, but a wish by Jenn held singular potency. She'd been born at the turn of light, within the edge, and what she wished, Marrowdell made happen.

Every ill thought vomited from his mouth. Roche heard himself confess despicable intentions he hadn't known he had, as glibly as someone else discuss the weather. Ancestors Witness, if he'd stayed and kept spewing the truth, they'd have come to hate him as he hated himself.

When the Ansnan, Dema Qimirpik, offered to take Roche from Marrowdell and find him work, he left with his bow, a scant bag of belongings, and Jenn Nalynn's wish.

She'd meant well. He'd deserved it, he saw that, admitted it, but if she'd understood the consequence to his life, would she have stopped? Could she?

For Roche not only had to tell others the truth, risking their anger and scorn—he could no longer lie to himself.

Unlike his mother Covie, with her healing touch, unlike Devins, with his calm sure skill with beasts, and unlike Jenn Nalynn, Roche knew his only magic was to dream a warning of every disaster about to befall him.

And be helpless to prevent it.

Two: The Forgotten Soldiers

The farm clung to a slope better suited to sheep, thin fields stretched like fingers between the rock spires, the muddy ground steaming in the first heat of spring. Sweat glistened on tanned skin as the three toiled in silence.

The tall, lean woman pried another stone free and paused, holding it. She'd brown hair braided tight to her scalp, and worked stripped to jerkin and boots as did her companions. No farmer, this; it wasn't her strength or bearing that told what she'd been before, but rather the pale pucker of scars across cheek, neck, and forearms, the kind left by war.

A soldier, Edis Donovar had been; stars knew she was one no longer. She eased her weight to one leg, resting the old ache of a knee, and studied the vista below. The road twisted like a ribbon along the valley floor, matched by the tumble of river. Farms there were rich, fertile—and didn't hire ex-soldiers.

Edis found herself tempted to fling the stone down the slope to see how far it would tumble, though it wasn't the road's fault it couldn't take them anywhere better.

As for the stone…

Half covered in mud and pale grey, it looked like the skulls they'd pull from Rhothan cairns to smash for spite, their enemy worshipping the gory remains of their dead instead of showing proper reverence for the peerless beauty watching from above.

A petty vengeance. She wasn't proud to remember it.

The stone in her hands…remembered. Ice. The slow relentless rise of frost, nudging it up and up through the soil to face the sun and stars and sun and stars and…

She blinked free. Useless, to feel a stupid stone's version of history. Her father's aunt's nose for copper or iron—there was a gift worth having. If she'd that–Edis turned upslope to heave the annoying thing away.

"Comet's curse, Edis. You almost hit my shin!" Jon Palyenor pretended to stagger as he added the stone he'd caught to the pile. "I go lame, you'll be carrying me."

She grinned. "'Long as you're breathing, that's the vow." Hearing what she'd said, Edis made a face. "Habit."

A keen look from under grizzled eyebrows. "Not the worst to keep." Jon was older, thicker, and his scars covered the holes where he'd been shot, twice, by a pistol, then again by an arrow. Surviving each time had been, according to Jon, due to his soldier's luck; what help a little bag containing a twist of his mother's hair, a mummified rat tail, and an old cork could be was beyond Edis, but most soldiers carried them.

Stars knew the man was tough as granite; no one in the prison had dared try to steal from him. Jon might have led their seven in the marches instead of Edis—

Had he the least interest in command. Or strategy. Or, she smiled to herself, a thought beyond tomorrow.

They'd saved each other's lives time and again. A good man. A trusted companion.

"I win," crowed their third, admittedly neither, but hers nonetheless. Deter Elenyas opened his fist to show the short straw, blue eyes dancing. "My turn to go to town for supplies."

"We didn't draw—" Jon protested.

"Because Deter always cheats," Edis replied mildly. A habit the younger man brought to the marches, made worse by two years behind bars; not that his skills hadn't proved an asset at times. She frowned at him. "Why do you want to go?" It was no less work. Lumps was a cranky old ox; once he felt a load in the panniers on his back, it took constant prodding or a snail would outpace him.

Taking up his pickaxe, Jon chuckled. "Deter's hoping we'll finish the field before he's back."

The stone remembered. No matter how hard they worked to clear it this year, the field would be strewn with rock again the next. And the next. Edis sighed to herself. "No fear of that."

That oh-so-charming grin lit Deter's still-beardless face. "I'll buy some candy."

She aimed her finger at him. "We can't afford it. Stick to the list." They wouldn't be paid till the ground was ready to plant. Weren't welcome in the kitchen either and slept outside, camped upstream from where the oxen and hogs watered. "And stay out of the inn."

"It's hot. I'll get thirsty—"

Eying the stones still to be pried free and moved, Edis felt a rare stir of rebellion. "Maybe we should all go—"

Jon straightened and took hold of his pickaxe, head cocked in warning. Edis turned her head. The owner of the field—and their contracts–had stuck hers out the window of the farmhouse to watch.

Ready to fire them on the spot. Plenty of others on the road, hunting work, hunting anywhere to stop and earn a wage. Forcing a smile, teeth gritted, Edis waved an acknowledgment. "You go, Deter, get what we'll need for the next three days—no more–and be back by dusk. Hear me?" With a snap.

Deter went to salute, spun the move into a cheeky little bow. "Aie, aie."

"Away with you," she ordered, giving him a shove. "And be

careful," she finished fondly.

Deter

He owed Edis, he and Jon both. She'd kept them alive when the cursed Rhothan patrol surprised theirs, that cloudless night. Stars knew. Stars saw.

Wore the guilt of those she hadn't saved, a pierced copper lug for each on a string around her neck. A pointless waste. The four died of stupidity, charging when she'd signalled to hold position, not that she'd listen. Sentimental under that tough hide, Edis refused to spend one, even when it meant they went hungry.

And kept saving him and Jon, Edis did, first in prison, then finding them work, shoving them along to the next hole of a town or village, as if anything would change. As if they were living, like this.

Stars knew he needed a break from it.

As Deter had anticipated, pilgrims jammed the *Inn of the Blessed*, the roads newly opened to the Celestial Refuges after a hard winter. "Not," the innkeeper assured him, "that they'll have an easy trip of it. Poor sods." Refuges being where the holy stars were closest to the world, atop mountains, the better to stare down and judge.

Wouldn't catch him in one.

"The business is welcome," she finished, with a pointed look at his empty plate and mug.

Deter gave his charming grin, a dimple in his cheek, and flipped the woman a coin. "Another ale, if you please."

She caught it with a practiced hand, then hesitated. Her voice lowered. "Seen others like you lately, with cheap new boots and the same small purse. Pretty sure this is your last." The innkeeper opened her palm and held out his coin. "Don't waste it on drink."

He'd already gambled what he'd brought to buy supplies along with the ox—making a tidy profit. Nonetheless, Deter let his expression fill with woe. "This is the best place I've been in two years. I don't want to leave, good 'keeper. Please. Take it."

She turned her hand, planting the coin on the table. "I'll bring the jug." With a gruff shrug, "Not all of us forgot you."

Most want to. A thought he kept to himself as he nodded gratefully. "May the blessed stars see and bless your kindness," he murmured huskily, and if there was a tear glistening in his eye?

Day he couldn't make one of those on the spot, he'd turn honest.

Deter pocketed the coin once the woman disappeared into the crowd. A slouch drew his face within the shadow of his coat's collar. He wasn't done here. Not if those he watched were as predictable as the innkeeper.

The one disguised as a lowerclass merchant had arrived first, claiming a prime table by the fire only to sit there alone, oblivious to glares from the pilgrims forced to stand and juggle their bowls of stew.

Unearned wealth brought about that blind arrogance. Akin to a flower's scent to a bee, the draw of such a target to Deter. He'd always had a knack for sniffing out what could be parted from its owner, to his profit.

At a guess, the fool had eluded his protection, the guards who would have known better, and thought himself clever.

Deter fingered his dagger. The sun was about to set. He'd wait and follow. A casual bump in the shadows. A quick stab up and under the ribs. He'd find whatever riches the fool carried then slip back inside. Be righteously indignant with the rest when the news broke of a murder close at hand and have another drink.

He licked his lips. Like the old days–

–except he wasn't alone anymore. He'd companions waiting for him, the ox, and the supplies he hadn't bought. Edis would be pissed.

Maybe he owed them the chance to be smart. Jon would see it, how they had to have a score like this to survive. Be grateful.

Impressed.

Edis, though—

Someone joined the would-be merchant, a challenge to Deter's plan. Still, he waited, watching over the rim of his newly-arrived ale, biding his time. The new arrival tried to get the other to leave. Failing, he sat, shaking his head. They conversed, low and hurried. The wealthy fool opened his coat to show a fat moneybelt.

Better and better.

The new arrival brought out a fist-sized box. Deter could see the naked greed on the fool's face from here.

A thrill coursed through his veins. He fought to keep slouched but this—this could be it.

And if Edis kicked a fuss.

The starless pits with her.

Three: The Apprentice

Watched over by the serene and sacred Seventh Refuge of the Blessed Celestials, the town of Loudit nestled in a narrow valley within a collision of mountain ridges, the last Ansnan holding before the road climbed the border to Rhoth. Its streets were aligned with the most beneficent constellations, as much as possible, with intersections prudently framed by astronomical obelisks inset with precious gems, accounting for any flaws.

Loudit was justly famed for the quality of its lenses and mirrors–and for keeping a useful neutrality during the conflict to the south, having customers without as well as within Ansnor. It was said those of Loudit spoke Rhothan as readily as their own tongue and that was true for most. The treaty thus had little import, other than as a topic of conversation less interesting than bets on the building of Eld's preposterous train. Those who'd settled here understood the construction of tunnels and track, having mined for generations until the veins of ore ran dry; their descendants were highly critical of foreigners who professed to know more.

And foreigners in general, were any asked, being anyone from outside their town.

Other than young Roche Morrill, the lensmaker's new apprentice, sponsored by the Refuge's esteemed Dema Qimirpik himself as an honest, hardworking fellow of good character–despite being born in Avyo and a descendant of ill-reputed Mellynne, his own family disgraced and exiled from Rhoth, truths another might hide that Roche spoke plainly to any who asked, earning respect.

Then pity, when he told them he'd no choice but be truthful.

When the elders might have objected to the presence in their fine and prosperous town of someone clearly under the influence of a magic spell, Lensmaker Lapec had argued surely the stars regarded the Rhothan with favour, since he'd come with the demas, whose sponsorship came with a large chest of coin and a vow to add the lensmaker to his weekly exhortations to the celestials.

Though if the elders of Loudit fully appreciated the risk posed to their town and livelihoods by someone compelled to be truthful, they might have changed their minds.

For they kept a secret.

Roche

Every foursday night, Lensmaker Calym Lapec closed the workshop to her juniormost apprentices to concentrate on more exacting work with their seniors; the juniors to take other gainful work in town until sevensday, what they earned going toward their debt.

His first sevensday morning, Roche had hurried in as soon as the shop reopened, curious to see what marvels had been created in his absence. But there was nothing new. In fact, the furnace was cold and work already underway had been moved aside, as if to make room. The other juniors didn't appear surprised. Roche spent that day helping put all back to rights, careful not to ask questions and avoiding any thoughts of a secret belonging to the lensmaker and her seniors.

Ancestors Witness, if he learned it, he'd tell it, surely as the sun rose, and be sent packing or worse, to prison, whatever it was.

To his dismay, when Roche went to leave that evening, a senior beckoned him to stay behind. Wibler the Great they called him, oldest here and more skilled than Lapec herself, his task the final delicate polish of mirrors for the great telescopes used in Ansnan refuges, and there was no reason for him to speak to the most junior here.

Except there was no mistaking the crook of that gnarled finger. Roche walked over and stood waiting, glimpsing himself in the mirror on its turntable—brown-haired and green-eyed, as no Ansnan was–and desperately hoped the man wanted his floor swept, though it shone, being the cleanest part of the shop.

With the thought, his mouth betrayed him. "Your floor doesn't need sweeping, Master Wibler." Roche pressed his lips together.

Wibler had a perpetual squint that made it hard to read his face. He regarded the floor. "It does not," he agreed. His voice was a hoarse whisper, as if hardly used. He aimed the squint at Roche. "Stars know. There's danger here for such as you."

A knot tightened in his stomach, but the words came out. "Because there's a secret. I don't know it," Roche added quickly. "I won't learn it. I swear by my Ancestors."

A gnarled finger tapped his chest. "Best you leave and be safe."

For once, the truth suited him. "I won't be safe, Master Wibler. If I leave, the demas would be disgraced and I'll be hunted as an oathbreaker. And I like this work." The last surprised him, but it was, of course, the truth. Having seen what could be created with molten glass and skill, Roche longed to do the same.

A tiny smile appeared within grey whiskers. Was gone. Another gentle tap. "Then my advice, truthteller, is that while the shop is closed, you be far far away. You needn't fear those in town, they won't speak of it. You must avoid any strangers who come."

So on his second foursday, when the shop closed Roche grabbed his bow and quiver of arrows and headed up the mountain to hunt, not returning until sevensday morning. Having killed and butchered a deer, the meat and hide of value, Lensmaster Lapec seemed well pleased and encouraged him to continue.

Which might have been the venison, for there were few hunters and the innkeeper was delighted to add it to his menu, or might have been guilt, the lensmaker also aware Roche told the truth.

Roche

Every foursday morning, Roche continued to take the good master's advice and leave town. Fortunately those who'd questioned him in the beginning were satisfied by a single truth, that he slept in the entrance to an abandoned mine, there being many such, and didn't press for more.

Spring chased away winter, as it was wont even in the heights. By now, no one gave a thought to his habit. No one but his friends, who'd pulled him from bed this night for an adventure before he left them again.

Staring up at the rock wall, Roche shook his head. "Disel should go first," he shouted over the din of a waterfall closer than he'd thought. "She's strongest."

The smithy's junior apprentice took the loop of rope over her broad shoulder, saluting him with two fingers. She shouted back, "Never argue with the truthteller!"

He rolled his eyes, muttering. "How many times–"

Lenert, the miller's apprentice, leaned close. "Might as well give up. Ready, Flam?"

The musician—when not clearing tables at the inn–raised the plump flasks he held by their strings and gave them a shake, then pointed wistfully at the ground.

"Up it is!" Disel jerked her thumb at Roche, who'd be leaving in the morning.

"And tonight the stars can't see us," Lenert shouted with a pious gesture to the overcast sky.

Flam snorted. "Roche would tell on us anyway."

"Only if someone asks me," Roche returned equably and they laughed.

What a gift that was, to be accepted as he was, to have gained friends despite it—or because of it. There was a lesson there, Roche suspected, not that he tried hard to find it. Not on a night of fun.

The three had made their way past workshops and mills, entering the pine forest beyond, until what had been a distant roar, constant and familiar in town, grew louder and louder and talking became shouting. The noise and growing vibration underfoot brought back memories. Not that he'd been here before, but Roche had hunted the base of the cliffs where Marrowdell's river split, half tumbling in a wild cataract from the valley. He'd explored, curious where the water went, but been thwarted by the mists and slippery rocks.

His friends took him to see the Loudit Portal, the opening in the mountainside through which poured another river, the one that nourished the town and powered its mills. A river they claimed came from deep underground, through a tunnel made by their ancestors. Roche having scoffed, they insisted he see for himself.

Still chuckling, Disel started up the wall. The three waiting below craned back their heads as she climbed, so intent Lenert jumped when the rope dropped, the end at his feet. Roche felt a smile pull his lips. "Flam, you next."

"Aw. You can trust me—"

"With wine?"

Flam chuckled and hung the flasks over a shoulder, jumping to take hold of the rope. Lenert followed, both on the rope at once, using their feet to walk up the wall.

Which wasn't natural rock, Roche suddenly realized, going closer, but fitted massive stone. Ancestors Blessed. Someone had made this—

"Come on!"

Roche jumped for the rope, swung wildly as if about to let go and splash in a swimming hole, not that there was one here, then steadied. Before he could lift his feet, the rope rose, his friends pulling him up.

"You didn't let me try," he complained when he could see over the wall.

Tugging him to his feet with one hand, Disel gave her deep-throated chuckle. "Next time," she shouted. Her other hand fell on his shoulder, spinning him around. "Watch your step!"

Roche caught his balance as she let go. They stood on a huge pavement of fitted stones sloping to either side, behind them a sheer cliff rising out of sight. Ahead?

Ancestors Dazzled and Delighted. The view! He could see across the valley to the other side, see the mountains he'd passed through with the demas last fall, some Rhothan. See the gleam of white nestled on the highest peak of all, the dema's refuge, and trace the sliver of road zigzagging down that was its sole access.

Lenert walked casually to the pavement's lip, overlooking the world below, and sat, taking a flask of wine from Flam, who joined him.

Disel gave Roche a nudge. He shook his head wildly and she shrugged, going to join the others.

He had to go or they wouldn't like him anymore.

Which wasn't true. He was afraid and shouldn't be; his friends proved it was safe for him. Straightening his shoulders, Roche walked straight to the edge.

Flam grabbed him, as did Lenert, pulling him safely down between them. Roche found a flask of wine in his hands and a waterfall at his feet.

It was true. The river erupted from the mountainside, arching out in a smooth powerful curve, the ceaseless pound of it striking below deafening. It emerged through the opening of a tunnel the size of which he could barely comprehend, constructed like a straw punched into a sweet melon, powering the mills, watering the fields and all that lived below.

Built by people.

Roche's heart pounded. This was what he yearned to do. Not blow glass, however beautiful and useful the result. This. Build what changed the world. Build what would last beyond his bones and hold his father's name.

"I want to do this," he shouted, the words a promise.

He doubted his friends heard him over the noise, but they lifted their flasks with his, and that was enough.

Edis

While the stars came out, Edis brooded over the embers of their fire, Jon silent company, thinking it was damned inconvenient how the Blessed Celestials waited until after you died to render judgement on whatever they witnessed.

Not that she needed the stars to tell her why they sat without supper, or the fate of their meager funds and cranky ox. Nor need for Jon to tell her working this farm had been a mistake—hers— driving Deter away from them at last.

Deter, more boy than man, thinking he knew how the world worked. He'd have been dead years ago on his own–with that feckless grin on his face, because nothing was ever his fault, and she'd give anything—

Edis raised her head, fingers on her knife. Jon stirred, notching an arrow to his bow.

"Miss me?" Deter called from the dark, having at least learned not to approach unannounced.

"Depends what you brought," Jon growled, putting aside his

bow.

"Stir up the fire. I'll show you."

Edis kept quiet, watching Deter ease into the light. His sleeves were stained dark with blood; by the way he moved and the half-mad glitter of his eyes, none was his. He handed Jon a jug then sank to a comfortable squat by the fire, meeting her hard stare with that grin. He produced a small bloodstained box and opened it, tipping the contents onto his hand.

Jon lowered the jug, having taken a quick drink. "What the–?"

The gleaming pearl almost covered Deter's palm. "We're rich," he declared, bold as could be.

She didn't move. Barely breathed. Stars knew. Whatever its worth?

Wasn't close to its cost. "We're not rich. We're dead," Edis countered, her voice that of a stranger. "A thing like that has a name. A history. It'll be tracked—"

"No one saw me—"

She snatched it from Deter's hand, waited for him to ease back, for Jon to take another hasty drink. "You killed for this," she accused. "We get caught with it, we don't go back to prison, we hang. I didn't save your sorry ass for that."

"Didn't ask you—" Deter snarled then stopped, eyes down, hands clenching.

Thought about trying her, she saw with a pang. Gave it up, having some sense still, and she relaxed. "Doesn't matter what's done. We stick together, like always. I'll fix this. Hear me?" She waited until both were looking at her, until both nodded, Deter taking his sweet time about it, but the boy had his pride. "Tomorrow, this goes in the river. Hope you ate well—we'll be working twice as hard in the field."

Deter wasn't done, not yet. "We can sell it. The owner said there's a buyer waiting in Loudit, the border town next on the road. You ask for Lapec. No questions asked, top price." His voice became ever-so-earnest. "Edis—no one wants us. No one cares.

What you're holding—" His gaze locked on her closed fist, then rose pleadingly. "It'll buy a new life for all of us—Jon, tell her."

The older soldier pointed up. "Stars are watching, lad."

"They've seen our pathetic lives—let them see us succeed! Edis–"

"I'm for bed." She shoved the pearl inside her jerkin. Got up and walked away from the fire, leaving them the jug.

Leaving Jon to calm Deter down. Stars knew, he'd done it often enough, the boy chafing under restrictions for his own good. Like family, the way they'd bicker then pull together.

Like family, safer that way.

Edis

They came for the pearl before dawn. Edis woke, amused by their antics as they went through her coat, clumsy drunk. Was less amused when the pair suddenly landed on top of her bedroll and started pawing at her, a feeling she expressed with hard open-handed slaps at whatever part came in reach. Got a high-pitched yelp from Deter, a low breathy curse from Jon, and if they'd had the sense to stop, she'd have let be and they'd have laughed about it in the morning.

But then a fist struck and a boot stamped and Edis found herself fighting for her life. She'd have given them the damned pearl before it came to this, but they'd passed beyond reason. Taking the punishment, she concentrated on getting free of the blanket. Got an arm clear. Chose to punch back instead of reach for a knife because they were family and friends and, stars as her witness, she refused to kill the fools—

–and that was all she knew until waking in the river, tossed there instead of the pearl, sinking—

She'd the wits to stay under, letting the current drag and bounce her against rocks, stealing quick gasps of air. Felt the rocks remember…*windy peak, tumble tumble rub and rumble splash and sink and roll and tumble tumble tumble.*

When she'd tumble enough of her own, she pulled herself from the river. Rolled over, gasping, to stare up at the sky crusted with blessed stars, so many, so cold and distant. Witness.

"Stars saw. I taught you better." Edis spat blood. Rose to a wavering stand. "Stars as my witness I called you friends. Family, all I had. You were my boys…my stupid stupid boys…and for what. A pearl that'll kill you both." Her breath caught on what wasn't grief and her voice turned thick and hard.

"You should have made sure I was dead."

Four: The Hunter

Dew bent the grass and trailed dark fingers across his leather pants. The sky brightened behind the Crow, dawn's promise a glisten on the snow and ice still clinging to the mountain's peak, doing little to reveal the ground at his feet, but Roche didn't need to see it. By now, he could have climbed this wandering path through the foothills with his eyes closed.

He'd a pack on his back and his bow over a shoulder, fresh arrows in his quiver and pebbles in a pouch for his sling, making it plain to any watcher he left to hunt. And would. Deer and elk roamed the woodlands above the town, of no interest unless he brought an ox to pack out the meat, but the sloping meadows hosted an abundance of rabbits and squirrels, smaller than he was used to but tasty. Not to mention fat slow woodchucks, wary and ever near their dens. He'd marked the openings of several, needing only an arrow and opportunity.

Two days hence, he'd return with variety for the inn's pot, earning the cook's appreciation, and with hides to sell, a pittance against what he owed the dema, but a start.

What Lensmaker Lapec did while he was gone remained a

secret, one kept by the townsfolk and even his closest friends. Wibler had been right. Whatever it was held either profit for all or threat for any.

He was glad to have no part of it.

Today Roche's pack held a special treat, a bundle of letters from Marrowdell. Surprisingly early letters, the Northward Road closed for the winter by snow. He'd hadn't looked for more until later in fall, once the Lady Mahavar brought the valley's mail to Avyo.

These had been sent midwinter, according to Noabi, who handled the town's mail and tax collection between repairing wagon wheels and making toy carts. Midwinter and not through Avyo, but Vorkoun. Noabi showed him the seals and stamps, as impressed as Roche.

However they'd come, he'd wait to read them until in his sanctuary.

The path ended where the ground was levelled, hardened into a pavement cluttered with fallen, lichen-crusted stones. Beyond it rose a square of heavy timber three times his height, framed by shrubs and trees, built into side of the mountain. It was how Ansnans sealed the apit, or entrance, to a mine of no more value.

Or its true value had been forgotten. Roche had seen for himself how not everyone who left Marrowdell remembered what made it special.

Roche hadn't found the mine; it had found him, his first trip up the slope, though at the time he believed himself following a hunter's instincts.

It was only when he'd stood before the formidable seal, shivering in a downpour, that he realized where he'd been drawn.

To a place like Marrowdell. To magic.

Roche remembered turning aside, shoulders hunched in misery. There was no going back, not for him.

Remembered swinging around, the irresistible pull tugging his heart, tears mixing with rain on his face as he faced another truth lurking inside him. He missed his family. Missed his friends and everyone and everything of Marrowdell, even house toads, the sum a terrible loss he'd brought on himself, thinking all he wanted was to leave.

Yet…something of it was here.

Like the road into that valley, the way to it was hidden. Debris from winters past filled the bottom of the seal, piled to the right against a twisted tree larger and older than its forest neighbours.

A tree Roche recognized. It was like those in Marrowdell's forests, the kind you didn't cut.

As he had that first day, after a cautious look around, Roche stroked the lowermost branch. It slid aside in welcome and he ducked into the hollow, the branch creaking back into place.

Three steps took him to the small door set into the apit's seal.

He pressed the palm of his hand against the wood, as he'd been moved to do when he'd first discovered it. Lowered his head and murmured, as then, "Ancestors Blessed, I thank this place for its welcome."

Was faintly surprised, as he was every time, when the ancient door unlocked itself to let him in.

Edis

Edis Donovar staggered and stopped, her back against the trunk of a tree larger than most, hidden by damp and fitful shadows. Listened for pursuit.

None. They hadn't brought out dogs. Hadn't roused the town. Her lips curled in scorn. Of course not. She raised a blood-soaked fist. Uncurled the fingers.

The pearl filled her palm, streaked once more with blood. Some Deter's.

Most hers. Edis tucked her prize safely in a pocket, sucking a breath at the hot flash of pain as her coat pulled on the arrow stuck through her shoulder. She'd make no speed like this. Methodically, she pulled off her belt with her good hand and made a loop to put over her head.

Getting her right arm into the makeshift sling felt like being shot—again—but once done, Edis peeled herself from the tree. She'd get the arrow out later. First, to find shelter.

...up.

She eyed the steep, bushy slope. Among Deter's many faults was a lazy streak, but he'd climb for the pearl.

Had tried to kill her twice, now, for it.

The world swayed. Edis gritted her teeth, willing the dizzy spell to pass. There'd be more to come, if she didn't find help. A time they wouldn't stop.

...up up up.

Stone, remembering when it tumbled down the slope. But not. More like a voice, this pull in her head urging her up the mountain; she'd worry it was some foul magic, luring her from virtue, if she hadn't lost all claim to that long ago.

Common sense, that's what it was. Keep the high ground.

She began to climb.

Deter

Hag should be dead. Twice dead, Deter reminded himself as he climbed behind the others, panting and slipping on the mossy rocks, guarding his wounded face from the whip of branches. Stars only knew how many more deaths Edis Donovar had cheated in the marches and it wasn't fair.

Let alone the time she should have died fighting off the gang of half-starved thugs in the prison, thinking she saved him, never knowing her death was to be his entry fee.

A fool as long as he'd known her. A mark. That was all.

Deter stole a look at the men Lapec sent with him to retrieve the pearl. Strong and grim, both were, alike enough to be brothers except in size. They carried paired swords and axes, along with pistols, and the larger one had a crossbow on his back. At a guess, they'd orders to kill him and Jon as well as Edis, taking the prize for their master.

Stars knew, he would.

Strong, grim, and slow. He'd escape with the pearl while they tangled with Edis and Jon. Go to Lapec with the sad tale and complete the deal. Maybe do more business. He'd no problem with someone like that.

Edis—he'd a problem with people like her.

The smaller of the two pulled his companion to a stop. "The going gets worse. She'll have to come down. We can wait here."

Jon, in the lead, climbed a few more steps before coming to a halt. His broad back was a wall. "Not Donovar. She'll keep moving."

"He's right." Deter pushed forward to confront the pair. "We can't stop." Certainly not here where the lay of the land gave these two any advantage and was one reaching for a sword? "Jon and me—we'll go ahead when we find her. Get her talking. She won't be expecting you."

They liked that plan, he saw in their eyes. Of course they would. Let the strangers take any risk. Be bait. Easy to kill them all at once.

He would.

Not waiting for an answer, Deter briskly climbed to stand with Jon. "Still got her trail?" He could barely discern a path, let alone any prints.

"She's not hiding it," the older man said heavily. "She's losing too much blood."

Was that regret? Predictable. The real regret was Jon not firing that second arrow. They'd be done their business and drunk by now. Deter eased his voice. "Edis will see reason—"

A snort. "She'll kill us all. Stars knows we deserve it."

Edis Donovar, kill one of her own? Deter hid a smile. She'd hesitate that fatal second, especially if Jon went first. He'd seen it in her face.

Predictable to the last.

Five: The Olm

A sealed abandoned mine should have nothing in common with Marrowdell, with its homes and orchards and fields of grain but this one did. Its welcome. Its comfort. The apit wasn't at all cave-like, rather having a built feel, an airy space lit by a soft warm light produced by what looked to be moss growing from chinks in the rock walls. The floor was dry and flat.

And like Marrowdell, the mine had its unique citizens.

Roche set his pack and quiver on the bench he'd built of rope and branches, turning to warm his hands. "If you please, friend olm."

The enormous pale salamander curled within its shallow stone-rimmed well opened and closed its little mouth, then began to glow. Almost at once, water bubbled and steamed along its pearlescent sides.

Kneeling nearby, Roche took the cup he'd left waiting and scooped some of the heated liquid from a polite distance. He added a pinch of leaves, cradling the cup in both hands to inhale the rich fragrance; the bitter, cheap tea from the apprentice kitchen, transformed. As he sipped, he felt the knots in his body and mind let go. "Ancestors Gifted and Grateful," he murmured. "My thanks."

Another lazy gulp. Its eyes were clouded and sightless; nonetheless it reacted to his every move. A tuft of vivid red plumes adorned each side of the head, which tapered to a small mouth. He'd thought it a chubby snake before spotting the little limbs. He'd yet to see it uncurl or move.

In town, having a secret of his own, Roche took great care never to say where he went hunting, rebuffing curiosity with the truth, that a successful hunter didn't share his choice spots. He'd been caught only once, when Flam brought up caves and what lived in them, such as olms. Lenert claimed the olm were a myth, a story to scare children, while Disel sided with Flam. According to Ansnan teachings, pretty well anything that the "stars" couldn't watch was evil until brought into their light and cleansed— perhaps why the domain had so many mines.

Ansnans took the same course to divide the observance of magic. Above ground, healing or other gifts, though rare, were regarded by most as blessing from the Celestials. The use of tokens to conduct spells was tolerated–including a brisk trade in such items, usually not in the least magical, with Rhoth, where they were not.

Magic from underground was a chancier, perilous thing. The Ansnans believed those judged by the stars to be evil would spent their afterlife in the darkest of pits.

As for the olms, Roche's tongue betrayed him. He'd blurted out that olms were real, that he'd seen one up close in a mine. Knowing he spoke only the truth, his friends were forced to believe him.

Fortunately, they'd then had so much to say about olms— Disel that olms were incredibly rare and rightly persecuted as beasts of ill omens, Flam certain they were the spawn of dragons or maybe dragonspawn, and Lenert adamant Roche never approach one at risk of his soul, the rest nodding solemnly–none thought to ask him which mine, for there were several around

Loudit, or when.

They meant well, his friends.

They and all Ansnans were wrong about the olm.

To Roche, the olm was like a house toad, the keeper of this mine and deserving of the same wary respect. In Marrowdell, you left pebbles for your toad, receiving eggs and a home free of vermin in return. Toads best liked white pebbles, why no one seemed to know, but the villagers vied to collect them from the river.

Roche hadn't bothered, it being easier to steal his brother Devins'. Another truth laced with regret.

Though sealed many years ago, the air in the apit remained fresh, restored by airshafts deeper in the mine, its constant temperature that of a brisk fall day, a feature Roche anticipated he'd enjoy more come his first summer. The huge main shaft bored straight into the mountain, the air warming the further he'd explored.

Admittedly not far. The moss came to an end and the darkness beyond wasn't empty. Things rustled, disputing his presence with clicks and wet little smacks, vanishing by lamplight. Not gone. Airshafts pierced the ceiling and others the walls. Whatever clicked and smacked found those convenient.

Roche gladly kept to the apit, made comfortable by the olm's gift of warmth. Over time, he'd furnished a corner with what he could build from fallen branches and twine, or sneak from town. He'd flour sacks full of pine needles for bed and pillow, proudly adding a braided rug someone had discarded though barely worn, and later a blanket.

Roche kept a wistful eye out for eggs, those from birds horribly tasteless and the olm clearly magical, but there'd been none. He dutifully collected pebbles from the rushing mountain streams anyway, leaving them in reach around the well. When none of those disappeared, he tried a series of different little gifts, worried the olm's gift of warmth would end if not rewarded.

After months, it grew into a game.

"I've brought something new," he informed the creature cheerfully, reaching into his pack.

Barely a gulp. Unimpressed, that was.

Roche held out the little nodule of clear glass, tilting it until it filled with the olm's glow. "I made it for you." A drip of molten glass about to spill from his ladle, he'd delayed, charmed as the cooling drip caught the light. They were supposed to collect such waste for reuse; he'd let it fall and swept it under the table before anyone noticed, recovering it at day's end. "What do you—"

The olm's mouth opened wider than he'd imagined it could, revealing a row of sieve-like teeth. The depths of the mouth began to brighten, dauntingly like the shop's furnace, and Roche hesitated. Put his fingers near that?

The head gave an impatient flick, the quickest movement he'd seen it make. Give it to me, that said.

Sucking in a breath, Roche leaned as far as he dared over the now-steaming water, arm outstretched, nodule between his finger and thumb. The olm tilted its head back.

The young man took careful aim, blinking sweat, and dropped the bit of glass into the olm's mouth. Which snapped close.

The olm resumed its curl.

Roche waited.

Nothing happened.

Shaking his head at the ways of magical creatures, but pleased nonetheless, Roche went to unpack what he'd brought, lining up his provisions, including a handful of potatoes, a hunk of cheese, and a flask of water. They'd be safe. He'd found nary a trace of mice or their ilk in the mine, a lack he attributed to what rustled in the dark, not the sluggish olm. Pulling out his latest prize, a battered but sturdy pot, he set it on the rim of the well.

Roche sat on his bench, his well-wrapped bundle of precious letters on his lap, feeling the usual tingle of delight mixed with new apprehension. Why had they arrived now? "I don't know what to expect," he told the olm.

Untying the string, he wound it into a ball, tucking it in a pocket before unfolding the waxed paper. That he'd save as well. There were six envelopes and he'd give those to Noabi, who loved to collect what traveled. He didn't change the order or go through them to see who'd written, wanting to prolong the surprise.

The first was from Devins. Roche read it aloud, chuckling at his brother's meticulous listing of the fine qualities possessed by Palma's cousins and rather touched by his brother's woeful wish for his help deciding between their offers. They'd both seen the kind of joy the right match could bring, there having been four exceedingly happy weddings in Marrowdell last fall. Including Sennic Horst, now Sennic Nahamm, sharing his wife Riss' name.

The tone changed on the next page, the lettering growing smaller and cramped as Devins tried to include all he could of the terrible storm and lack of supplies, and Bannan moving in, then Bannan moving out because Tir Halfface had returned with two little boys, all to live with the truthseer.

His brother had known not to write their names or who they were. Roche sighed, nodding. "If he keeps it from me, they must be important," he assured the olm and began to read again.

Fell silent when he reached the last line. Frann Nall left us before the Midwinter Beholding, Ancestors Dear and Departed.

The loss of Frann changed Marrowdell, threatening his treasured memories of the place and people, and Roche threw the letter away.

Then hastily retrieved it, smoothing the paper and folding it with care.

"Ancestors Dear and Departed," he said huskily. "Frann— Frann put up with me, better than–" The words caught in his throat and Roche quickly opened the next letter, hoping for easier news.

From Master Dusom Uthtoff, of all people. A single page, in his elegant hand, wishing Roche well and, most startlingly, a request. Having heard from the dema of Roche's excellent work for the lensmaster, Dusom wished to commission a telescope or whatever Roche chose to make.

To hold such an object, the letter concluded, would give him great pride in his former student.

"He's being kind. I was a terrible student," Roche told the olm, feeling strange and confused. "I did my best to frustrate Master Duson so he'd tell me to leave."

There was a long letter from his mother. He held it to his heart, then put it aside to read alone.

One from Tadd Emms, full of details about the mill and how happy he and Hettie were, and that they'd travelled to see his twin Allin and Palma in Endshere, and how sad it was about Frann but Wen was pregnant with Wainn the father, this with several exclamation marks.

Roche lowered the letter to regard the olm. "The twins and me, if we got bored we'd pick on Wainn. Call him slow and stupid. Trick him, sometimes. Wainn knew I'd start it but he'd never get mad or tell."

The olm's plumes flattened to its sides.

"I know. Wainn's a finer person than I was or will ever be. I am glad he's happy." And it was true, he realized. Reading the passage again, then the next, Roche grinned wider and wider. Peggs and Kydd were expecting too. Marrowdell blossomed.

Jenn Nalynn's letter? Wasn't one at all. When Roche opened the envelope, out fell three perfect rose petals and a slip of paper with the words, "Keep Us Close."

The scent of roses filled the apit. He closed his eyes to savour it and suddenly felt Marrowdell's sun on his face, heard the river and the looing of Devins' cows, and almost believed he was home again. It was her magic, a gesture of forgiveness and care he didn't deserve.

Ancestors Blessed, how he wanted to.

Tears spilled down his cheeks when he opened his eyes. "'Keep Us Close,'" he echoed. "I'll keep trying, Jenn. I promise."

As he carefully tucked the petals and paper back in their envelope, the olm startled him by rising half out of the water, little mouth open.

Roche gave the creature a petal, smiling when it took on a pink hue and swam in quite dizzy circles, thinking for the first time that maybe, one day, he'd go back to Marrowdell.

Not to stay, for he'd a new home and future, but make a visit, like Jenn and Peggs' lady aunt. Bring gifts. Make something for Master Dusom.

Apologize to Wainn Uthtoff. To everyone. He could finally see it as possible. Finally believe they'd find it in their hearts to forgive him, as Jenn did.

One day.

The last letter was from Bannan Larmensu and Roche hesitated. The truthseer's advice had given him his new life. What he wrote would be profound and might change it again—

A quiet sound, neither rustle, click, nor snarl, lifted the hairs on his neck. An intruder!

Putting down the letter and grasping his pot by the handle, careful not to raise it, Roche slowly turned around.

Six: The Betrayed

Up! The path had been walked recently, meaning it was known to the locals, including those behind her and following, if Deter brought help and he would. She shouldn't be on it but Edis no longer cared. She stumbled forward more than walked, doubtless leaving a trail of her own.

Stars. She didn't care about that either, only to stay on her feet. If she fell, it would hurt.

If she fell, she no longer believed she'd stand again, and the mere thought of Deter searching her corpse had Edis fumbling at her pocket, ready to drop his precious pearl in the next hole in the ground.

Up! It wasn't the stones, despite being a gravelly growl of a voice. What stones rolled up a slope? And it refused to be ignored, insisted she hurry. If she hadn't left her faith in the marches, along with any and all fantasies, she'd believe she was being guided by the stars.

Or mad. Edis choked on a bitter laugh.

What she was? A mess. The bruises had yet to yellow from the beating they'd given her, let alone the pummelling she'd taken in the river. Edis hadn't waited to heal. She'd torn the string from her neck—Jon's drunken morality, she was sure, to leave it with her corpse—using the lugs to buy clothing and boots, a knife, and passage on an oxcart heading north, to Loudit.

Where Deter claimed someone would buy the pearl. Deter who'd murdered for it. Deter, who'd played the friend.

Jon, who'd been like a brother.

There'd been others who looked like them, like her, on the road. Others in ill-fitting clothes and new boots, others who looked away or down but never at you. They were heading to the great refuge to seek the heavens.

Why would the heavens care for forgotten soldiers now, when they hadn't before?

She'd kept apart, kept travelling, day and night, knowing her quarry. Deter and Jon would stop at an inn each night, take a leisurely breakfast, feel safe.

Edis had reached Loudit before them. Broke her silence to ask where she might find Lapec, and, a telling revelation about the town, no one asked her why.

Began her wait. Behind her, the forest sloped up to another mountain. To her left, beside the building, were rows of huts, each the same, with laundry hung to dry by some and stacks of wood by others.

A barracks–no, these wouldn't be for soldiers. Ansnan didn't want her soldiers anymore. The homes of workers or apprentices, some likely busy in what she recognized as some kind of workshop, by its abundant windows and chimneys. She'd settled in, like a quiet little spider in the dark. She'd been very good at that, in the marches–

Up!

"I'm coming," she muttered under her breath, her steps weaving or was the path?

–and would have had them, except Deter had come alone and she'd thought he'd disposed of Jon as well, and that broke the last piece of her heart so when he approached the door of the long building as if confident of welcome, Edis had leapt from the shadows, knife in hand, intent on murder of her own.

She was off her mark, or he wary. Whatever the reason, they went down together. In an instant, she was on top, knife ready to drink his traitor's blood, when he started begging for his life like the coward he was, offering her anything. The pearl.

Edis took it, planning to throw it aside. Deter went for her knife—she slashed his face, he threw her off, they both were on their feet and she'd the bloody knife in one hand, the pearl in the other—

The arrow thunked through her shoulder, spinning her around against a tree. She glimpsed Jon, saw him hesitate as he notched another, Deter swearing, urging him on.

In that second's grace, Edis ran.

She came back to the present to find herself facedown in moss and giggled. Wasn't running now, was she?

Up!

Rolling on her side, Edis pushed herself to sit, unsure why she made the effort.

Up!

She squinted up at a tree larger and uglier than any she'd seen before. It stood—or rather leaned—against a cliff like a drunk. "If you're what's been calling," she grumbled, "I've had better offers."

A branch shivered and pulled aside, revealing a shadowy cavity.

Stars. What if it led to the pits of hell?

Edis squashed the thought. Here was shelter. A hiding place. She got to her knees, supported on one hand, head hanging as she caught her breath, then made the push to stand. Staggered forward until she passed inside the branches of the tree, easier than she'd thought. Spotting the door, she found the strength to go to it.

What kind of door had no knob or latch? Or hinge in sight, for that matter. Feeling thoroughly offended—and by now light-headed—Edis raised her fist to knock.

Lowered it on a different impulse. She licked her lips then pressed her palm to the wood and whispered hoarsely, "My name is Edis Donovar, once of Mondir, now of no place. I seek refuge in this house."

The door opened.

Welcome.

It felt—it felt as if she were about to leave this world for another. As if one more step would change her.

She'd die if she didn't.

Edis took the step.

Then crumpled to the ground.

Seven: The Healer

The intruder lay prone in front of the now-closed door. Roche approached cautiously, keeping hold of his pot. In case of what, he'd no idea, but best be prepared than caught without, his mother would say, and he almost stopped, hearing her voice in his head for the first time since leaving.

Not important now. What was lay right in front of him, a dark stain spreading from underneath across the rock floor.

Blood.

"Whoever you are," he murmured, "you need help." He put aside the pot, going to his knees to investigate. Horst had taught him of soldiers and their weapons—like the arrow through her shoulder, made for one type of prey.

But it was his mother's knowledge Roche needed.

Edis

She wasn't cold. That discovery kept Edis quiet and still, relishing a warmth able to soothe her very bones, willing to accept comfort while listening to every sound. She'd passed out after entering—where?

Here. The same unheard voice, this time its gravel-growl smug.

"Where's here?" she snapped.

"You're in a mine," said a reassuringly real voice, deeper than Deter's. "It's abandoned. The door closed behind you. You're safe. Whoever hurt you, won't find you."

The first words were Rhothan—time in their prison had given Edis unwanted fluency and a fine set of curses–the remainder in accented but clear Ansnan. Who was this? Edis tried to open her eyes, to sit up.

"Shh. You need to sleep. Let me help."

She felt fingertips stroke her forehead then nothing at all.

Roche

"Passed out from pain," Roche informed the olm, who'd obligingly added more heat after he settled the wounded woman by its well.

He didn't have his mother's gift, to help those in her care fall into a healing sleep. Or did he? He stared at his fingers before bringing the tips together over his heart, "Hearts of our Ancestors, I'd be beholden if this poor soldier stays unconscious. However far we are apart, Keep Us Close."

He hadn't said a full and proper beholding since leaving Marrowdell. Not even at Midwinter, when all Rhothans told their ancestors of their mistakes the past year and their hopes for the next. The former was too daunting a list, the latter too fragile.

Why now?

The truth filled him. He feared for himself. Feared she'd harm him, if awake. Feared those who'd shot her would follow her here.

Guilt bowed his head. He hadn't had a dreadful dream. Roche chose that as comfort. Then another truth pushed forward, a better one. He did want to save her. He would do his best to try.

First, to see her wound.

She rested on the braided rug, his pack bracing her body. He removed the belt she'd used as a sling. After cutting off the tip and feathered ends of the arrow, Roche used his knife to remove her coat as if skinning a deer, leaving as much intact as he could. Next went the blood-soaked jerkin. He had to wet the shirt beneath before it came free of her skin. Once her arm and shoulder were exposed, he scooped warm water from the olm's well, washing clear the wounds on front and back, avoiding the arrow's ends.

Bruises, days-old. Older still were the scars on her muscular forearm. He'd seen their like before, on Horst's arms, the former soldier finally giving in to a boy's pleading to point out which were from practice swordplay—and which from battle.

Ancestors Troubled and Tormented, from this arm, her neck, even her face, she'd more of the latter. If he'd any sense, he'd search her for weapons, take them before she woke. Roche stretched out his hand.

Stopped, shaking his head. He'd have to hope she didn't rouse and attack him.

Roche retrieved the field kit from his pack—a gift of his mother's when he first went hunting on his own—and unrolled the pouch to find what he'd need. Gut and needle to close the wound—wounds, the arrow protruding from both sides of her shoulder. Bandages. The powder Wen Treff concocted from Marrowdell's plants to prevent infection. He put some in hot water, his pot's first use, washing his hands, then the needle and gut.

He glanced at the soldier. Unconscious, or feigning it. Took a deep breath. He'd sewed himself up more than once. Helped, reluctantly, with his younger brother, that time a prank of his left Devins impaled on a pitchfork tine, and he'd watched their mother, if never with the attention he should.

Do your best, she'd tell them.

Ancestors Witness. What he'd give to have her here.

Ready as he'd ever be, Roche pulled out the arrow.

Blood followed.

Edis

She was cold, so cold her bones were ice, and Edis was annoyed to hear someone speaking. No, murmuring in a soft deep voice. Like a prayer.

She was dead, then.

Except—Edis lost the thought, found it, grabbed it–the words were Rhothan.

If she wasn't dead…if she'd been captured, why was he praying?

Except—another blank moment—the war was over. She shivered and HURT.

You are safe. This is a healer. Words with that gravel-growl of ancient stone and Edis went back to believing she was dead, because stupid Rhothans put bodies in the ground—

The pits with that—her eyes flashed opened.

To find a stranger's face too close to hers. Edis heard a growl, this time hers and it hurt—everything hurt—and she cried out.

He didn't move away. "I need to put you in the well. I'm sorry. It's going to be painful."

Stars above—what wasn't! "W-why?"

"The olm will warm you," the stranger promised.

With the name, the warning tales burst forth–stories of the fell ones. Dragonspawn. The source of evil magic that would steal your soul and imprison it in the deepest pit of hell, cut off from the stars for eternity–

Calm yourself.

She hated that voice.

Edis felt herself being dragged across a floor. The Rhothan tried to be gentle, but the floor was of stone and her body a block of ice filled with agony.

She slipped into water. The river! She tried to struggle. To fight.

"Please don't kick the olm."

She'd most certainly try—

BE STILL.

The command hardened every nerve and fibre of her being until Edis feared she'd turned to stone herself.

Roche

The woman went stiff in his arms, her eyes rolling up until only the whites showed. Roche hesitated before continuing to lower her into the well. He let her sink, unsurprised the well had deepened, until she began to float. He stopped to keep her injured shoulder, with its now-sewn-shut and bandaged wounds, well above water.

The olm took an interest, aiming its blind eyes at her. "She's lost too much blood," Roche explained, as if it understood and why shouldn't it? "My mother—Covie—Covie Ropp—" He paused. How strange. He said the surname she'd taken from her new husband, Anton, with none of the bitter hurt he'd felt when she'd left his father's behind. A hurt he'd inflicted in turn all the years since, hadn't he? The shame of it brought tears to his eyes, but he kept talking to the olm. "My mother would keep her warm."

She'd likely also have something to say about clothing and the lack of, but there'd been no choice once he'd realized what had to be done.

He'd meant only to remove the soldier's coat and boots, but the rest of her clothes were filthy and most blood-soaked; Roche didn't think the olm would appreciate having those in its home, the soldier's body entirely sufficient trespass. He'd undressed her quickly but with care, as if she were a child, putting her clothing aside.

He'd brought out his extra shirt. His bed and blanket waited once she warmed. If she warmed.

Roche bent over the side of the well, his weight on his heels, supporting her braided head with one arm, the other around her waist. The water grew thick and turned silver. Threads of it rose with the steam.

Feeling her shiver, he lowered her as much as he dared.

Time past. The olm's sides wrinkled and its glow dimmed. Her shivers grew less.

Stopped. The warmth, or some virtue in the olm's water or the olm itself, Roche couldn't tell, slowly drew colour back under her skin. He watched in wonder as the flush flowed along her long, strong thigh and curved hip.

Sucked in a breath as he saw bruises fade to yellow on her ribs.

Averted his gaze before it reached her breast, slightly afloat and pale. Saw the bloom of life rise up her neck and warm her cheeks.

Then retreat, growing pale again, and the shrunken olm stirred, gills drifting back and forth. A warning.

Ancestors Lost and Languishing, they hadn't saved her, not yet. Despite his stitches and powder, the arrow's path must have done mortal damage.

And the wound remained above water.

Roche searched her face. Every line was etched in strength and resolve, her mouth grim and set. She'd unfinished business, he'd no doubt of it, likely with whomever owned the arrow. Someone he could pity. Even unconscious and dying, the soldier had an air of menace.

There was so much more to her. The braid crowning her head was intricately done and precise. Beautiful lashes caressed her scarred cheek and the lines framing her mouth and eyes were familiar. His mother had the same, lines of laughter and smiles.

"Hearts of our Ancestors—do what you can, friend olm."

Roche let her go, watching her sink beneath the surface and disappear.

Deter

"Didn't lose her." Jon pointed at the cliff with its timber wall. "The trail ends here. There, exactly." He pointed at a gnarled tree, its top leaning on rock.

Seeing disgust on the larger guard's face, Deter spoke up. "Jon's the best tracker we ever had."

"Found a tree, I grant him that."

The other of Lapec's men laughed unpleasantly. "Admit it. You lost the trail, if you even had it."

The pair nodded to one another and began walking around the flat pavement, searching for a trace of Edis they wouldn't find.

Jon was never wrong. Deter went to stand beside him.

"There," the other whispered. "Blood on that branch. Stars know a tree like that's hollow underneath."

Edis could be close. Could be watching them from the cover of branch and leaf.

Deter pushed Jon. "You go first."

Eight: The Soldier and the Truthteller

Wake…wake…wake…

Nothing was further from her wish but the voice, though not a command, insisted and Edis Donovar came back to life.

Underwater!

How she didn't gasp a lungful she couldn't later explain but mayhap the stars were watching after all. What did happen was she lunged upward, reaching for the side of wherever she was—not a river, that she could tell—to have her wrist taken in a firm grasp. She closed her hand around an arm and let the owner pull her up.

She found herself sitting against a rim of stone, accepting a blanket without question. He squatted on his heels a distance away, waiting.

No Ansnan, the stranger. Rhothan or Mellynne by his colouring, with thick brown hair loose to his shoulders and eyes as green as the first leaves of spring. He'd the compact build of someone strong and maybe quick; not trained or a threat. Deter's age or less, and as handsome, but this face held compassion and concern—

Unless it lied. There'd been a time she'd assess someone at a glance and trust her judgment. A time before she'd been utterly wrong. "Where am I?"

He knew what she meant, that this wasn't just a mine. "Where magic lives. You're safe."

Saying a thing didn't make it true and stars knew she wanted nothing to do with magic. "Are you real?"

She surprised him into a smile. "As real as you are. You should thank the olm." He made it sound important.

Edis turned her head, very slowly, to look behind her. Managed not to jump, finding a pale snout near her shoulder, framed in blood red plumes.

The vassal of evil and doom didn't look like much, up close. Wizened and slow–she could grab its neck and snap it—

Thank the guardian.

Gravel-growl was back. No hallucination, then. "Thank it for what?" Edis asked warily, eyes not leaving the creature.

"Does anything hurt?" the Rhothan asked.

Stars knew—Edis went still, listening to her body, a body that on any given day listed its complaints at her treatment of it, these years, let alone the more recent battering and—she rolled the shoulder pierced by Jon's arrow—nothing hurt.

She'd forgotten how it felt, to be free of pain. Even her knee—"You did this?" she asked the olm.

Its little mouth opened and closed as if gulping air.

Her voice hardened. "At what price? My soul?" She lunged for it in fury, the olm sank beneath what wasn't water—or was it?

And the stranger dared try to stop her.

Roche

Roche remained still, barely daring to breath, the safest option given the strength of the arms around his neck, one across the top of his spine as if ready to snap it. Ancestors Furious and Frustrated, he'd no doubt she could.

He'd been right to fear the soldier.

Who, like other Ansnans, had a superstitious dread of the poor olm, now curled around itself as if exhausted in the centre of its well, the water around it once more clear and hardly deep enough to cover his hand.

"Who are you?"

"My name is Roche Morrill, apprentice to the lensmaker in Loudit." He tried to stop there, not give her more, but the truth spewed forth as always it would. "I'm the son and heir of an Rhothan baron who died in exile, stripped of wealth and sent with his family by royal decree to the northern wastes of the world for being of Naalish descent. I was forced—I chose to leave home to seek a new future after someone of magic wished me to tell only the truth."

The pressure on his neck increased. "Why?"

"I deserved it. For most of my life, I'd been angry. Hurtful. Lied to everyone around me. And to myself."

"And now you don't," with disbelief.

"Now I can't. You mustn't tell me anything about yourself," he warned. "Not your name, not anything you want kept secret. I tell whatever I know, even when I don't want to." Especially then, it seemed to Roche, quite sure she'd snap his neck and he wouldn't blame her. "I'm sorry."

She released him with a push toward the bench. "Sit, Roche Morrill. I'm going to dress."

He obeyed, hands carefully in sight on his knees, gazing down. The olm slept, or whatever the olm did when it wanted to be unnoticed, but he thought it glowed, ever so slightly, as if paying attention.

Blanket around her, the soldier moved slowly, with care to her footing. Wary of him. Of everything. She surveyed her surroundings, looking everywhere but the well, pausing to stare into the great dark hole of the shaft. Again at the nearest patch of glowing moss.

By her frown, none of it met with approval.

When he indicated his spare shirt, she pulled it over her head, favouring the shoulder where his stitches pulled now-flawless skin.

"Those need to come out," he blurted.

A nod at his still-open field kit. "Yours?"

"Yes."

Her frown eased. She pulled on her trousers and belted them. Eyed her bloody jerkin and ruined coat, then shot him a sidelong look. "Forgive my discourtesy. Stars as my witness, I am grateful for your care, Roche."

"It's the olm you should thank."

Her head turned. She stared at the well and its occupant, the frown back and darker. "So you say. So says the voice in my head. A pox on you both. I'll not grovel to evil."

Were he the soldier, he'd not argue with a mysterious voice, not here. Roche tried reason. "The olm saved your life."

She spat a curse he'd never heard. "To damn my soul to the pits!"

He surged to his feet. "Ancestors Ungrateful and Uncouth, this generous creature risked itself to save you! Thank it properly or leave!"

Her eyebrow rose. He refused to back down.

With a growl, she spun on her heel to face the well, and gave a curt bow. "My thanks."

Without raising its head, the olm blew a rude little bubble.

She snorted. "See?"

"The olm deserves real gratitude. A gift," Roche told her, still angry. "What do you have?" When she opened her mouth, he went on impatiently, "Not your soul. It likes shiny objects best. I think. A button should do."

For an instant, she looked inclined to argue, then gave a strange half smile. "I've this." Going to her jerkin, she dug into a pocket, producing a dark ball. She rubbed it between her thumb and fingers, flakes falling away, then held it out. "Shiny enough?"

A pearl, half again the size of any Roche remembered from his mother's jewellery or that of relatives, and the Morrills had been among Avyo's wealthiest. It didn't shine. The pearl's smooth surface transmuted the light from the moss into a lustre as stark and cold as old ice and Ancestors Cursed and Confounded, he hated it on sight.

"Take that, dragonspawn. It suits you."

It mustn't touch the olm. "Don't—" he started to object.

Too late. She'd tossed it.

The olm vanished beneath the water's surface.

Its water drained from the well, leaving behind the pearl.

Roche

All Roche could think to do was jump in the well and pick up the pearl. It didn't help. The moss retreated into cracks, dimming the light in the apit, darkening shadows. There was an ominous rustling from the lightless shaft as those within sensed opportunity.

He flung the thing away. It bounced and rolled to a stop against a wall. Roche hurriedly wiped his hand on a pant leg to erase the taint. "You brought evil here," he accused, glaring at the soldier. "Not the olm. Why?"

Her face filled with abrupt, desperate grief. "Stars saw…" an anguished whisper. "I took it to save them. Stars know…" She sank to the floor, covering her eyes with her hands. "Taking it, I failed them. This is my doing."

Ancestors Bloody and Bent. His anger faded. The magic here welcomed her as powerfully as it rejected the pearl. "The pearl's to blame, not you."

With a sigh, she lowered her hands and looked at him, her face working. "You don't know what happened."

"I see what's here." He watched her take in the empty well, cringe at the grim change around them—

That, he'd try to amend. Still in the well, Roche crouched, laying his hands in the dry dust, brushing it aside to find a floor of blue tiles like those lining Marrowdell's well, with its gift of fresh and flowing water year round.

Heartened, he pleaded, "Forgive us, friend olm. We meant no harm. We need you. Please." Roche brought out a petal and let it fall. It landed on a tile, as fresh as if plucked from the flower that instant.

Filling the air with the scent of roses.

Edis

The Rhothan squatted where the creature had been, the water gone as if never there. Water once deep enough to drown her—

Hadn't, there was that.

Take it away.

The gravel-growl meant the pearl, though why rocks would care—Edis shivered suddenly.

Cold again. The light was almost gone—and what was that sound? She half rose, tense.

"I think we'll be all right." Roche stepped out of the well.

Before her eyes it filled with clear water, a single rose petal floating on top.

And then–

With a swirl of opalescence more beautiful than the pearl, being alive and yes, somehow she knew, good as the pearl was not, a figure swam up from a great depth, coming toward them. Edis saw a face with huge purple eyes, and a mouth shaped like hers, and a braid of stone to crown the head—

The olm broke the surface, swallowed the petal, and settled in its patient curl, a salamander once more. The glow from the moss increased.

Edis no longer felt the same welcome.

It can't stay here.

"The pearl can't stay here," she heard herself echo.

If he'd glimpsed the figure, Roche showed no sign. After bowing to the olm, he stared at the pearl, lying in shadow, making no move to touch it. "We should take it to the refuge," he said at last. "To Dema Qimirpik. He came to Marrowdell in search of magic–what he calls the gift of the Celestials," sounding as if he added that for her sake. "He'll know what to do with it."

Stars save them. A holy one who sought out magic—Edis took a breath, let it go. If a dema undertook such a study, it would be blessed, no question. "We have to get there first." She tipped her head at the door. "Won't be that way. Those after the pearl will follow my trail and wait outside in ambush. Unless the door opens for them. It won't, will it?"

"Not without an invitation. You had one," he elaborated. "It's how you found this place, how you knew what to say to open the door." Roche shut his mouth, pressing his lips together until they went white, then burst out. "You have magic. You must. That's why we're both welcome here."

Stars.

Wondering what to say, Edis sat on the bench. In truth, since they'd an uncanny amount of that going on, she needed to sit. He watched her, lip between his teeth.

Magic. Because of it, she'd survived a wound that should have killed her—felt no pain or discomfort other than the pinch of the stitches–and surely that was good, even if from a creature of the starless depths.

"I have a gift," she confessed. "The stars and my late mother are the only ones to know."

Roche held up his hand. "Then you mustn't tell me."

Do. Do. Do.

She resisted a moment, then grimaced. "Doesn't matter. It's nothing important. I hear stone." Tapped a toe on the floor. "What it remembers. Sometimes."

The rock below obliged. *Molten, flowing. Hard and long long long. Bite and bite and feet and wheels and…*

Edis blinked free of it. "Useless, mostly. Being a mountain, being a mine, rolling down a hill. Until today, it didn't talk or order me around." She flipped her hand at their surroundings. "It's this place."

Our place. Your place.

Stars. She glanced at the olm, relieved to see nothing but the olm. "What about you? Your magic. It's not being a truthteller, is it?"

"No. My mother, Covie, is a healer. I never thought I shared her gift—until today, when you needed it." The Rhothan sat cross-legged on the floor and unwrapped some cheese. He broke off a chunk for her, taking none. "I've my own," he said after a moment. "Some in my family dream dreadful things, warnings. I've had three such. None lately," this with a flash of green eyes.

Edis took the cheese, biting and chewing without tasting it. "Stars see. These mountains are full of those who work marvels— or claim so. What of my friends out there? I can't say. I thought I knew them, better than myself. Till they tried to murder me for that pearl. Twice." She took another bite, adding casually, "I'm sure it remains their intent."

The colour had drained from Roche's face and his eyes were round.

Would he take her word or assume, as almost anyone

would—as stars knew she would–the worst of her? That she was the thief and murderer, running from justice. Her word and, yes, the door and what he'd called an invitation.

Nothing said a person with magic couldn't be a villain. Didn't almost every tale told children claim them to be?

His hand reached out, as if to touch her; when she tensed, he let it drop to his side. "You fear I don't believe you," he said with quiet conviction. "I swear by my Ancestors I do." His head tilted, eyes now bright. "You fear the magic here is evil, a taint on your soul, but I swear it is not. Magic is simply part of the world. I grew up surrounded by it, heedless of it, without care or thought. Only after I left Marrowdell did I appreciate what I took for granted, that magic can live among us, peaceful–even helpful, like olm–or dangerous, as wild things are. We choose to see good or ill."

Compassion she hadn't expected. Wisdom even less–Edis bowed her head to acknowledge both. And to hide an unexpected confusion. How long had it been since someone offered her reassurance?

Roche coughed, then went on briskly, "If they haven't come through the door, they can't. Tea?"

The process required the cooperation of the olm, and Edis watched, fascinated and appalled in equal measure as water boiled around the creature, refusing to hesitate when Roche handed her a cup full of it, having added a sprinkle of leaves from a pouch.

It can't stay here. She made a face. "I'm told—again—to take the pearl away." Edis aimed the cup at the opening of the mine shaft. Level and flat, big enough for freight wagons to pass, there'd be side passages and airshafts. "That's our path. Have you explored it? Looks in good shape."

He shuddered. "It's not safe."

She grinned at him. "And we're safe here?"

"For now, with the olm back, yes. Though I must return on sevensday or be missed."

Nodding, Edis sipped the tea, letting it relax the tension of muscles that craved a fight; a reminder of how she'd wait with her seven before a patrol.

Take it away! With a *PUSH* and she sighed. "We can't wait that long."

Roche pointed to a pile of filled sacks. "Rest first." He'd a quirky smile. "As your healer, I insist."

Gravel-growl didn't argue and the sacks beckoned, an alluring promise of more comfort than she'd felt in—Edis couldn't remember. Every bone in her body wanted to melt at the thought of sleep.

Her fingers strayed to the necklace no longer around her neck and grief thickened her voice. "Take your bed. I won't sleep." All it took was closing her eyes and she'd feel the thud of boots and fists, remember smothering, tumbling in the river, the ultimate betrayal—

"Healer's touch, remember?" The Rhothan held up his hand, wiggling the fingers, his expression oddly hopeful.

—every time seeing Jon's cheery smile and Deter's cheeky grin, before imagining them limp and lifeless at her feet, her blade dripping with their blood. They'd vowed to carry one another so long as there was breath—now she had to take their last.

"We call it a soul stain," she heard herself say, harsh and rough. "When the stars see us commit an unforgiveable act. You can't know what that's like. The crush of it—"

"Lie down. Please."

Listen to him.

Edis did as he told her, as the gravel-growl urged, as if she'd no will left of her own. She stretched out on the sacks, the sharp aroma of pine rising about her, and suffered Roche putting a blanket over her.

He knelt nearby. Closing her eyes, she felt the warmth of his hand on her forehead, his fingertip pressing her skin, and didn't understand why she'd no urge to strike it away.

As sleep engulfed her in a warm darkness like the olm's well, the last thing Edis heard was the truthteller's soft voice.

"I know."

Nine: The Dreamer

He'd done it. Helped her sleep with a touch of his hand and, Ancestors Blessed and Bountiful, wasn't that something good to write to his mother?

Roche sighed. Insignificant, against the soldier's crushing burden, and while he understood carrying years of guilt and regret, he could—would–atone.

What she faced—people she'd called friends, who'd kill her, if she didn't kill them first—would darken her heart and future.

So he took the soldier's coat and scrubbed most of the blood from the leather, determined to do what he could for her.

Having cut along the seams, by habit unable to spoil so useful a garment, he set himself to sewing it back together. In Marrowdell, there was always mending and altering to be done. He and Devins would pull out the latest to stitch before the fire when a blizzard kept everyone indoors, or when a favourite garment or boots wore out.

Usually in silence; every so often his brother would feel in the mood for an argument and make one up. Or Roche would relate a juicy bit of gossip, whether true or not didn't matter, for the pair would wring all the salacious possibilities from it before switching to something else. At times they'd spin a story together, growing wilder and wilder until they couldn't stitch for laughing.

He'd write that memory to Devins.

Satisfied, Roche finished the collar edge and began reattaching the sleeve. His busy fingers paused. Then write what? That he'd helped a stranger who might break his neck before the letter arrived?

Not that she would. He trusted her. And couldn't lie on paper any more than aloud, so he mustn't write about the soldier at all.

Though the truth made a great story. Trapped together in a magical mine, those outside waiting to do her harm—for the pearl.

It was all, he guessed, about that. No wonder the olm fled the thing.

He'd wrapped the pearl in his piece of waxed paper, on impulse adding the last of Jenn's rose petals, tying up the small package with string from Marrowdell. If there was magic in objects, he'd done his best to counter the pearl with his.

Her jerkin was a quicker mend, though worse-stained. Roche put the affected portion in his pan and filled that with the olm's boiling water. Seeing how well that worked, he poured the water from the pan on his poor rug in hopes of saving it.

Wringing out the jerkin, he draped the garment over the bench to join her coat, then yawned.

Soldiers stood watch, Horst had said. Roche took his pack and settled against the well, choosing to read his mother's letter after all. The olm stirred a little, subsiding when it became clear he wasn't going to read aloud.

Roche Morrill had his next dreadful dream slouched over his arm and sound asleep by the olm's magic well.

He stood at the edge of the portal looking down at the waterfall and out over the valley and he was alone...but he wasn't. He was kneeling, both hands gripping that of someone about to drop...then he was the one hanging, looking up at his own face, trying to hold on...and the face he saw that was his own looked grim and sad...and the hands holding his let go...and he fell and fell and fell...plunging into the waterfall and down, unable to breathe–

Deter

Guane was the larger of Lapec's men, Sild the small one, and getting that much from them had been like pulling teeth. When not even Guane's axe marked the strange door they found beneath the tree, the two consulted in private, after which Sild sent Guane to town to "consult," churlishly refusing to elaborate.

Now, as the sun dropped and air gained a bite, Sild sat hunched at the edge, sword over his thighs, staring out over the treetops as if willpower would hasten his partner's return.

He should pray to the stars for brains instead, Deter thought with inward grin. The pair hadn't brought blankets or even food, blithely confident they'd catch their wounded prey within moments.

Trained by Edis, Deter and Jon bore full packs, lately replenished, and weren't about to share. They sat shoulder-to-shoulder on their bedrolls to eat, backs to the timbered seal of the mine, and didn't speak.

Jon hadn't said a word since going under the tree to find the door and appeared likely never to talk again. Uncanny stuff. Stars knew it shook them all, seeing her bloody handprint on the impassable door, her trail leading through it. Guane had made the old sign against evil but Deter managed to convince Sild to wait—

Not that Edis Donovar would give up any advantage she'd found, but come out to kill them? Stars knew she'd burn to do that.

He would.

When Sild got up and disappeared into the brush to take a

piss, Deter pulled out a flask of wine, offering it to Jon with a companionable bump on his shoulder, relieved when the man took it. Less when Jon looked to drain it at one go. He grabbed it back and glared.

Jon drew his arm slowly across his mouth, eyes meeting Deter's. "We shouldn't have done it. Stars as witness, we're doomed."

The younger man checked for Sild before responding. "Not if we're smart, Jon. Lapec's after the pearl—we get it first—"

"A pearl from the dark. Don't you see?" A hand clamped on his wrist. Jon leaned close, eyes wild, breath stinking of cheap wine. "A thing spat out of the pits of hell itself, the way it turned us against Edis, who's done us naught but good. I never want see it again."

Deter gave a quick nod as if he believed that nonsense. "Fine. I'll take care of it. But we can't trust these men."

"Think I'm an idiot?"

No, he thought Jon might become a serious problem, but Deter smiled his charming smile and held out the wine again. "I didn't want you to think they'd fooled me. Stars knows we're partners, Jon. Family."

After a more reasonable swig from the flask, the other gave a strange laugh. "Like Edis?" Before Deter could come up with an answer, Jon shook his head and passed him the wine. "I'd be on my way, stars as my witness, but we're in it now. We ever want to sleep at night or live in peace, we have to finish this."

"We finish this," Deter agreed, making it regretful.

When what he felt was triumph.

Edis

Wake. Wake. Wake.

Edis pretended not to hear, refusing to acknowledge the end of the most peaceful sleep she'd had since childhood. Maybe not even then, the bed crowded with her sisters and dogs–

A loud moan had her whip off the blanket, on her feet in a heartbeat, eyes scanning for Roche. And a weapon, that first, for the sound held agony—

Spotting him, she relaxed. Roche leaned against the well, head down, legs and arms splayed. Edis gave a little snort, recognizing the look of a someone fallen asleep on their watch, though by the scattered pages on the floor he'd tried to keep awake.

And been busy. He'd cleaned and repaired her coat and jerkin. Grateful, she donned the garments then did some slow stretches, pushing her muscles to assess the olm's work. Stars knew she'd get no second chances if—

Wake. Wake.

A second tortured moan! Gravel-growl hadn't been talking about her. Edis rushed to Roche. He'd thrown back his head, lips in a rictus of suffering. This was no natural slumber. She went on her heels beside him. The olm floated near, red plumes spread in agitation.

She poked his leg. "Roche. Wake up."

His eyes rolled back and forth beneath closed eyelids. He gasped as if unable to breathe, lost in a nightmare—and he'd told her, hadn't he, of dreadful dreams.

Making what afflicted him magic.

Stars. Edis shuddered, wanting no part of it. Having no choice, she took hold of his head in both hands, giving it a firm shake. "ROCHE!"

His eyes shot open. Before she could evade him, he wrapped both arms around her and pressed his face into her shoulder, his body wracked by sobs.

Giving the olm a don't-see-you-helping glare, Edis endured the embrace.

Roche

He gasped for breath. Another. Ancestors Ruined and Robbed, it seemed he couldn't fill his lungs after such a dream as if that part of it had been real, and Roche clung to what surely was, the soldier's leather coat.

Which had the soldier in it.

He stiffened and let go, hastily drawing away. A flush burned his face. "Ancestors—I'm sorry."

"Magic." She shrugged, balanced on her heels, head tilted to regard him. "A dreadful dream." It wasn't a question. "What did it tell you?"

"They don't—it warns of change." Drawing his arms tight around himself, he added miserably, "Something will happen, soon."

"We don't need a dream for that." Her teeth showed in what wasn't a smile. "Death, then."

"No. Not always. What happens affects me. At least–" The truth surged up in an irresistible wave, overturning everything, and he gasped again.

"What is it?"

"I've lied to myself. It's never been about me." Roche looked up to meet her eyes. "As a child I believed my dreams caused the bad things that followed. Later, I thought they warned of changes to my life, but the changes—every one of them affected those around me as much or more." His family. "There's change coming to the lives of those close to me now. The townsfolk. My friends. You."

She got to her feet with a muttered oath. Paced away from

him then turned to stare down at him, and Roche waited, sure of something else. What he'd said had struck a chord.

When she spoke, her voice was distant. "I'm not going out with only the stars as my witness."

He bit back a protest. Gave a reluctant nod and she sat on his bench, facing him.

"I'm Edis. Edis Donovar. I've been a soldier since younger than you, truthteller. I fought against the Rhothans till being caught and imprisoned for the last two years, with the sole survivors of my seven, Jon Palyenor and Deter Elenyas.

"After we were freed and given our walking papers, I found us work. It wasn't much but it was honest. Deter—hated it. He's always been one for the easy way, the wrong way. I did what I could but four nights ago he went to an inn alone." Her lips pressed into a grim line. "When he came back, I knew we were in trouble. Deter murdered for the pearl. Brought to us, boasting how he'd made our futures. Stars know, he'd done that. We'd be caught and hanged with the fool. I took the pearl, vowing to throw the thing in the river, and, trusting them, went to bed.

"Deter got Jon stupid drunk and they came for me—stars know I don't believe they intended harm, not at first, but that's not what happened." She drew a breath. Roche held his. "Deter's victim had a buyer in Loudit. I got here first to wait for them. I took the pearl but—Jon shot me."

"That's who's waiting outside," Roche said.

"Yes." Her hands curled into fists and a darkness filled her eyes. "The fools should have run." She collected herself. "No doubt they've reinforcements from the buyer. A woman named Lapec. Do you know her?"

The olm gulped, the moss dimmed, and Roche's new life shattered on a name.

This was the change forecast by his dreadful dream.

As always, Ancestors Dark and Dire, there was nothing he could do against it.

Deter

The crash and snap of brush—and an unexpected roar of voices–heralded Guane's return as three massive freight wagons laden with long timbers made their way up the slope, accompanied by what looked like everyone from Loudit able to carry a tool or basket. Teams lowed and snorted, their huge hooves scarring turf and knocking free stone; from his vantage point at the mine entrance, Deter could see the caravan followed an overgrown roadway.

And weren't coming here. He turned to Sild. "Where are they going?"

"To the rescue." A fat thumb gestured up the slope. "Everyone knows you can't break through a seal. Lapec's told the townsfolk someone's trapped inside. They'll set up a headframe wherever there's an open airshaft. Go down, make a racket." Sild licked his lips. "Flush our thief and the pearl right out her fancy door." A knife appeared in his other hand and he cut the air, chuckling.

Deter's fleeting hope the three of them would be the ones waiting in ambush faded as a small group broke away from the wagons, climbing straight for them.

Lapec among them.

Ten: The Explorers

Before entering the shaft, they shared more of the olm's tea, though Edis doubted Roche tasted it. After admitting he not only knew Lapec but was her apprentice, that he'd climbed the mountain every foursday to avoid her secret, the Rhothan had fallen silent.

How he'd succeeded this long was a marvel. And a conspiracy—the townsfolk, Roche told her, had deliberately kept it from him.

Did it speak well of Roche, that they'd made a concerted effort to protect him? Or damn the town as part of Lapec's illegal doings?

Stars knew—and weren't telling. Edis reserved judgement. It might even be both, that he'd won the loyalty of some, the rest wary of his gift or curse. Roche had managed until she'd blundered into his sanctuary with enough of the truth to make his former life in Loudit impossible.

Take it away.

Stars. "Time to move."

Roche took the cup to the nearest wall, holding it under a clump of moss. "If you please, we'll need light."

The moss let go and dropped into the cup. He repeated his request until he'd a cupful, glowing like a little lamp.

Not being moss. Edis nodded meaningfully at the olm, floating in its well. Roche had emptied his flask, refilling it with water from that source. Following her gaze, he shook his head. "Friend olm can't come with us. He needs water to live."

"As we are, then. Ready?"

"Almost." Roche wore his pack, producing a serviceable bow and quiver of arrows he slung across his chest. He put the tip and end from the one he'd cut from her shoulder in a pocket, then handed her the wrapped pearl.

AWAY!

Edis tucked the wretched thing in her jerkin, against her skin. It pressed hard over her heart and she scowled at the olm. "If you'd taken it, we'd be done."

The creature opened its mouth and closed it.

"Take this." Roche handed her his hunting knife in its leather sheath.

The blade was strong and well honed, with nasty serrations near the hilt. Edis tucked the sheath through her belt, against her spine, testing how quickly she could flip aside her coat to draw the knife.

By the look on Roche's face, it might be quickly enough.

Roche

Hearts of our Ancestors, Roche prayed to himself. I'd be beholden if my knife never tastes human blood.

Hardly a reasonable prayer, granted, and he'd left out the end, but nothing about this was reasonable. If things went badly, Edis would expect him to aim an arrow at someone as if they were a deer. Be ready to send it into a heart or eye, and what if it was someone he knew from town?

Horst had done such things. Bannan and Tir. Roche remembered being eager to hear tales of the glory of war, frustrated and peevish when none would speak of it.

He'd been a fool. There was no glory in battle or dealing death. If Edis killed her friends, she'd carry the guilt the rest of her life. If they killed her—they'd have killed him, too, Roche under no illusions.

To distract himself, he watched her. Edis walked ahead, her strides long and confident. She seemed unaffected by the shadows everywhere but around his cup, ignoring the clicks and wet little smacks from ahead and behind.

And above. He raised his eyes and cup. The sounds faded. "What is that?"

Edis looked surprised by the question. "Mine scamps. Harmless little things. Scavengers. Hard bodies and lots of tiny legs. They won't bother us."

"They don't sound small. Where we are—things can be different. In Marrowdell, what we called squirrels aren't like those outside it. They're dangerous." He paused, reminded of squirrel stew. He'd cooked his potatoes using olm water and his pot; and brought what remained of the cheese. It wasn't much for two. "Can we eat them? The scamps?"

Clicks erupted from every direction in clear protest, followed by an opinionated silence, and Roche gave a wry shrug. "Tell me your mine scamps do that."

She looked thoughtful. "No." Her lips twisted. "We can't eat them. Their flesh is poisonous. And their claws."

"Not so harmless," Roche concluded.

Edis snorted. "Walk faster."

Edis

Stars. She'd been lulled by the mundane nature of the shaft, like the ones she'd played in as a child. Forgot this wasn't a normal place, that magic pulsed through it, and Edis owed the truthteller for the reminder.

Realizing she'd another source of information, she began running her fingers along the rock wall.

Explosions! Excitement! Exposure!

Lonely, empty, dull dull dull…

She smiled to herself.

"Is it talking to you?"

Edis pulled her fingers away. "Not in words. I think—the stone misses the miners. The activity. It's been a long time." More briskly, "We want a side shaft heading at the right angle. Or an airshaft with a still-intact ladder."

"You know mines?"

She chuckled. "My family's worked our local mine for three generations. I was the rebel. I wanted excitement." Her good mood faded. If only the stars had warned her—she shook it off. Her choices were her own; she'd pay for them when the time came. "What about you?"

"I want to—" He stopped, going on slowly, "—I wanted to learn to build tunnels. My friends were helping me study—it's over now," with resignation. "I'll tell the truth about Lapec and be sent from town—unless we die first."

Stars. The truth shouldn't be a penalty and a young man lose his hope for it. "How about we don't die," she said lightly. "And you tell the truth to someone who can send Lapec to rot in prison."

Roche halted, the light from his cup waving over the walls before steadying. "Pardon?"

Edis pulled out the pearl. "Isn't our plan to take this to the dema? Tell him about Lapec."

The Rhothan raised both eyebrows. "But Dema Qimirpik an astronomer." He made it sound like being a plumber or miller. "What can he do?"

She smiled at him. "The study of the Blessed Celestials' dance is the highest calling in Ansnor. A dema may not seem to take an interest in local affairs but believe me, when one expresses an opinion, everyone jumps for the sake of their souls. Here." She gave him the pearl.

He tucked it away, his face working. "If the dema—then I could stay. I could–"

"Let's start with not dying," Edis interrupted, but rested a reassuring hand on his shoulder.

And didn't she know that shining look in his eyes?

Stars. Now she'd have to save him.

Roche

The main shaft took them into the mountain. They passed openings to the side, like black gaping mouths exhaling pulses of hotter air. Each time, Edis would walk into the darkness and disappear. Roche would wait, lifting his cup as a beacon, hearing the scamps crawl closer and closer, as if they feared the soldier more than his light.

Each time, just when he thought he could take it no longer, about to spin around to confront what stalked him, she'd reappear, shaking her head. Not this one.

He'd no idea how she judged it but, Ancestors Witness, if Edis didn't want to take a particular shaft, he wasn't about to argue.

So on they walked. Roche chose to think about the mine, the arch of the shaft and how it supported the mountain above them, and peppered Edis with questions. She answered with what she remembered, pointing out lines where miners had drilled holes for explosives, chipping away the rock one piece at a time, and showed him the faint rusty traces, all that remained of the ore they'd followed and taken.

After telling him the stones remembered the loss, she fell

silent.

Gradually his circle of light shrank until it barely showed their feet. When they stopped to eat and drink, half a potato and two tiny sips of water from his flask their ration, Roche dribbled a few drops on the moss, rewarded when the glow strengthened.

By that glow, he caught the flash of pain across Edis' face as she sat and how she favoured her arm. "What's wrong?"

"I don't—" Her lips pressed together and she reached under her clothes to her shoulder, bringing forth a bloody hand. "Stars."

The olm's magic was failing? "Let me take a look."

She wiped her hand on the other sleeve. "We left your stitches in. That'll do."

"Not if you're bleeding." He showed her the flask. "There's virtue in the olm's water."

She got to her feet, offering her good hand to help him up. "Then we save it till there's no other choice."

Deter

Lapec was a short wiry woman, with grey in the braid wrapping her head and the long-fingered hands of an artist. She'd fierce little eyes, bright as a squirrel's; their gaze flicked from Deter, crouched under the tree, to Edis' door, as if trying to decide which peeved her more.

She kicked the door with her boot, answering the question. "He'll be in there with her."

"Who will?"

"My comet's cursed apprentice, Roche Morrill." Lapec whirled around and strode back into the light. As he went to follow, she spun again, hand up to stop him. "The boy's a truthteller," she told him in a hard low voice. "A risk I bore because he's the dema's pet and because he's played smart, leaving town so he never saw what I did. When word spread someone was trapped in the mine, his friends jumped in, saying Roche spends his nights away in a mine." Her arm bent back, finger stabbing at the door. "My bet is this one.

"Meaning there's more than a chance he's met our quarry and heard what she has to say about you. About me. Maybe he's seen Arra's Last Tear. My buyer won't like that. He won't like that at all. He has plans for the pearl.

"The truthteller doesn't leave the mine alive. Understand me?"

Stars. Edis said a pearl like that would have a name and history. And those after it.

It was worth more than he'd dared imagine.

"That'll cost extra," Deter replied calmly.

Edis

Not far. Not far.

If gravel-growl would tell her what was "not far" Edis would stop cursing the voice in her head. Stars knew, she'd kiss the stone—or whatever it was—if it led them out.

Best be soon.

As Roche warned, these mine scamps were bolder than any she'd known or heard of, their clicks and smacks closing in behind, grudgingly making way ahead, as if they sensed her weakening. The shoulder was a sharp pain, the returning bruises—stars as witness, how was that fair?—a nagging throb around her midsection, and her knee–

Ignoring the pain, Edis made herself take normal strides, head up and shoulders back, knowing Roche watched her for any decline, ready to waste the last of their water on his belief it would restore the healing done by the olm's magic. Stars saw. Proof, wasn't it, that magic couldn't be trusted.

Nor, it seemed, could her senses. This deep should feel warmer, not colder, yet she fought a shiver and used a hand to close her coat.

"Edis—"

She glanced at Roche. He huffed a breath at her; it fogged in the air. "Is this normal?"

No more than these scamps, but Edis merely shrugged. "It's an old mine."

Her next step locked her bad knee, sending fire up her leg. Roche had her before she fell. Without asking, he put his shoulder under her good arm.

Without protest, Edis accepted his help, though it meant they moved slower now, too slow. Stars knew, there was a time to retreat and only good sense–

HERE! HERE!

She halted so quickly, Roche staggered and almost dropped his cup. "What is it?"

"I don't know." There wasn't a side shaft in sight. Limping on her own, Edis went to the wall, laying her palm against rock the same as all the rest.

Her hand kept going. She pulled it back hurriedly. "Try it."

Roche mirrored her actions, his hand also seeming to disappear inside solid rock. Bringing it out again, he wiggled his fingers in amazement. "This is wonderful."

Terrifying was more like it, Edis' imagination providing every possible danger beyond the rock—including the pits of hell.

Seeing his eager face, she swallowed her dread. "I'll go first."

"No." He took her hand. "I'm afraid when you leave me. Together."

"Together," she agreed. "Stars see. We'll likely break our noses."

"Or we'll find more magic," Roche said hopefully.

Edis grimaced. She'd rather break her nose.

They stepped forward into the wall.

Eleven: The Dancer

Roche squinted, shielding his eyes with his hand. After the faltering light of his cup, it was like stepping into sunshine and for an instant he believed they'd made it out of the mine.

Then the cold pierced his clothing and went straight to his bones. They weren't out, but they weren't where they'd been. Instead of a mine shaft, a cavern stretched in every direction, its centre filled with a mass of clear ice so tall Roche couldn't see the top, as if an enormous chunk of glacier had been swallowed by the rock. This ice glittered with its own pale light, as did icicles the size of giant tree trunks, hanging overhead like swords. Water, black as coal and crested with pure white froth, swirled and tossed around the base of the mass, and where they stood was a ledge high above that torrent and too narrow for comfort.

Ancestors Dazzled and Delirious, did something move inside the ice?

All at once, Roche spotted shapes he knew in the water, playing in the froth. Olms! Shivering with excitement as much as cold, he—

–was standing among icicles and each held an olm, but they weren't like friend olm for these had mouths full of teeth and they—

–he found himself turned sideways, his hands become feet, and he desperately shouted or maybe whispered, "I…Don't…Belong…Here."

And the words turned to shards of ice, cracking apart as they fell—

Somehow he looked—somehow he saw Edis.

She stood gazing outward, face set in a furious scowl, arms folded in disdain. As his words cracked she looked at him and her eyes were huge and purple, her braid of stone—she brought up her arms–

He felt a *PUSH*—

And like that, Roche was in the main shaft, clutching his cup of moss with the dark all around.

Alone.

Edis

Roche hadn't belonged.

Welcome, sister.

From deep within the iceberg came the dancer, her feet marking the delicate lines between crystals, her fingers trailing the colours of splintered light behind, and everywhere was music as the stones sang with joy.

"I don't belong," Edis Donovar said, the words floating from her lips as beautiful motes of blue light. Stars, that was annoying. She put her fists on her hips, failing utterly for she'd no hips.

Looking down, she saw she'd lost more than hips. Her arms were tiny stubs, ending in useless little fists. Her legs being a match, she rose up on a coil of—of—her body, a body shaped like—

She was an olm.

"No! No, I'm not!" More motes of light.

But she was heard, nonetheless.

The music stopped.

The dancer stepped free of the ice. Shrank in size and crossed the torrent on the backs of olms. Rose with a lift of her arms to the ledge, which at some unnoticed moment had become a sheet of limitless flat ice, and stood to regard Edis.

She had huge purple eyes and a crown of braided stone and a mouth like hers. Wisps of blue light wreathed a body of pearl and Edis recognized the figure from the well–or her twin. The sense of sheer power emanating from the dancer should have been overwhelming, but it came with gentle curiosity. *What would you be, sister?*

Free of the weight of her anger. Free of the world that betrayed her. If Edis were a truthteller she'd have said those words and be damned by them. Stars—however distant–knew. This being was magic incarnate and you didn't strike a bargain without paying a price.

"I would be as I was." Edis bowed, or rather curled, the best she could do as an olm. "Please. I must return to my friend and help him. We have a mission. To take away the pearl the olm refused—to tell the truth and save Roche's future–" Motes of blue floated up and away. She closed her mouth on the rest.

Killing those who'd betrayed her didn't sound noble or worthy.

It didn't feel right or good. It felt—her body spasmed and clenched, as if to vomit forth every foul thought and feeling festering inside, as if she'd this one chance to be rid of them–

Edis twisted around herself, tighter and tighter, as if it were possible to squeeze out the ache and the hurt—and did she imagine a cloud of dark specks spinning away, growing less and less?

Exhausted but exultant, her heart light as air, she untwisted.

"What—what just happened to me?"

The dancer bowed, light trailing the motion. *Only you know, sister.*

Stars. She did, didn't she? Revenge. Bitterness. Grief. She'd cast them out because they didn't belong here, or in her. "I change my request. To help Roche, I would be the shape I was before, not who."

Some of what you were has failed and gone. Some of what you are is of the Verge. Would you settle for a now and a promise, sister?

The Verge. With the naming the cavern unfolded and Edis found herself beneath an impossible sky, a sky with rivers of silver and mountains that were beneath as well above and were those dragons between?

If magic was part of the world, as Roche claimed, this was its true home. A home filled with more wonder and strangeness than her heart could hold and Edis wanted to laugh and dance with delight. Though she was somewhat embarrassed to have imagined this as the darkest pit of the Ansnan hell.

"If only there were stars…" she whispered.

It is never night and always light but there are stars, sister. Look for them.

As if to help her, a dragon's eye glinted, a pond twinkled, and there were sparkles from a net suspended in air. Together they shaped the constellation for which she was named, Edis, the harbinger of spring.

The more she looked for the faces of the Celestials, the more she found, as if here they were clearer and closer.

"I can't stay." The motes sank as she spoke. "I must help Roche. I must—I must get justice."

A hand made of ice—or was it stone?—cupped her jaw and Edis fell into those purple eyes. *Sister I call you and sister you are. Find your way here again, when that is your wish. Would you settle for a now and a promise?*

A momentous and daunting act, to agree to what she didn't understand, and yet a simple one, for Edis certainly didn't want to stay an olm. She gave a little nod. "Yes. I will."

As fingers of ice tore her asunder, she heard the stones sing.

Roche

"Edis! Edis!" Roche pounded the now-solid wall with his fist. All he achieved was to bloody his hand.

He bound it quickly, a hunter's caution if heeded too late. Already he heard the clicks and wet smacks closing in, drawn to the scent. Having dropped his cup, Roche scrambled to gather the scattered moss but the strands withered when he touched them, plunging him into the dark.

Ancestors Tested and Tried, was it the pearl he carried?

They'd promised to take it from here. He wouldn't give up. Roche drew the arrow piece from his pocket, with its deadly barbed tip that had done such damage to Edis, and gripped it like a knife as he stood, shoulders against the rock.

As his eyes grew accustomed to the absence of light, he spotted a faint moving streak of unwholesome green.

Another.

More and more below and to either side and in front of him.

Roche gritted his teeth. If each marked a scamp, in these numbers they'd eat him to death before he could scream.

Ancestors Witness, he'd not go so easy as that.

He roared his defiance, hearing echoes roll along the shaft. The streaks whisked away and he felt an instant's triumph.

Then, with a flurry of clicks and smacks the things rushed him! He tossed the useless arrow and grabbed the flask of olm water, sending a stream outward. Any moss it touched glowed anew, a relief so great he almost cried out again. Beyond the thin line of damp, claws moved restlessly, blind eyes searched for him, and he understood.

He'd die when the water dried up, the truth with him—

Suddenly the shaft filled with light, revealing an appalling jumble of jointed legs and claws. The scamps bit and fought in their urgent need to flee and Roche stood, shaking the flask at them before turning to see what had saved him. Or discover what new threat he faced.

It had Edis' face or he'd have bolted with the scamps, for the rest wasn't human.

Deter

Jon kept a worrying distance, brooding by the tiny fire he'd made near the misshapen tree. In a rare foul mood, was Jon; in the past, Deter'd be the one to cheer him up, with jokes and wine if they had it. Real joke was, if he failed, Edis would step in and insist they train—

Guane slouched over. "The master wants you." He jerked his big head at the tent.

There'd been more wagons, one bringing tents and gear. Seeing the number of people now on the mountain Deter had considered slipping away to pillage the empty town. Unfortunately, Lapec had someone keeping him in sight at all times, hardly bothering to hide it.

Take the score at hand, Deter reminded himself. He liked what he saw of Lapec's business. Most of her crew weren't thinkers. It'd be easy for someone with his talent to move up. Maybe all the way. He'd used the wait and busyness to ask a few careful questions. Most of Lapec's acquisitions were destined for Rhoth, easily moved under the guise of trade, or smuggled. Her activities wove in and through the town's honest dealings, making it nigh impossible for any to prove they hadn't been complicit all along.

Not that she'd give them time to try.

Deter could see room for improvement. He walked to the tent, choosing a pace to say he was no one's lackey but had the courtesy to respond, planning grander and grander schemes. Why, there was no end to the possibilities here.

There was a second tent nearby, one Deter swung wide to avoid, for it was marked with the sigils of the Celestials. The dema of the refuge had come to enlist the stars grace for those lost underground.

One of Lapec's best customers, word was, and not just for lenses.

"You there."

Deter sped up, pretending not to hear.

"You!" A hand caught at his sleeve.

He turned normally, fingers around the hilt of his hidden knife, letting go when he saw he'd been accosted by a servant— from the refuge, by her red robe and broad-brimmed hat. Aware of others nearby, he managed a gracious, "May I help you?"

"The dema offers his assistance."

"His prayers—"

She lowered her voice to a hoarse whisper. "With the magic door. He is concerned about–"

Deter took her elbow, steering her at a quick pace to Lapec's tent.

He'd start his move up today.

Twelve: The Changeling

As the scamps retreated, the light from her skin dimmed but didn't leave. Edis discovered she didn't need its glow to see Roche's face; she found it traced in warmth, sensed his presence through a new tingling along her arms.

Regardless how, there was no missing his expression. "Stars," she muttered, lifting her arms to see herself, relieved to have arms again. "That bad?" Everything felt the same, other the welcome lack of pain.

Other than the lightness of her spirit. She fought the impulse to dance.

"You sound like you." He closed his eyes and opened them again, his expression changing from shock to wonder. "Look like—a different you. What happened in there?"

"It's called the Verge." Curious herself, Edis took a look, easier since her body kept the olm's ability to twist around itself. "I'm told me part of me died. I think the olm tried to fix it with itself. Or how it fixed me did this." This being the pearl-like finish to her skin, with dots outside her arms that glowed or dimmed. She'd four fingers and thumbs on her normal-sized hands. Toes.

Had no clothes, which was a nuisance because she'd grown

fond of the coat and valued Roche's labour to repair it, not that she'd breasts either, or hips, her torso more olm than woman.

"Your eyes are bigger. Purple, with no other colour. But your hair—Edis, your hair!"

Alarmed, she reached with both hands to find her braid gone, a loss she'd grieve later, for in its place was—stone. She traced the shape with her fingers, puzzled to find it familiar.

"It looks like a soldier's helmet," Roche offered. "Not that I've seen one outside of books."

She was done with that life. Edis tried to take it off, but the stone was part of her. "Stars." She gasped. "I'm a monster."

"No. Nothing like that." Roche lifted his hand, waiting for her nod before gently touching her arm and the stone of her head. When she thought him done, he poked her where her ribs used to be, startling her into a laugh. "You're incredible."

The now of you will last, sister, as long as you wish. The promise of you awaits.

"What is it? You went dark for an instant."

Edis understood his note of panic. "Let's go."

"Wait." His head swung around. "Did you hear that?"

"Roche! Roche!!"

Voices shouting his name.

And they were coming closer.

Roche

Roche started forward with an eager smile, halting when he realized Edis hadn't moved. "What is it?" Instinct kept his voice low. "Those are people from town. I hear my friend Disel. They've come to rescue me—" He lost his smile. "There are other mines in this mountain. How did they know to come here? Why would they?" As he stared into the purple depths of her new eyes, reading compassion and sorrow, Roche worked it out for himself.

He'd been quite the schemer in Marrowdell, always devising clever traps no one saw coming.

Ancestors Betrayed and Beset, he'd never thought to be caught in one. "They aren't here for me," he said, his heart aching. "They're after you and the pearl. Lapec sent them. My friends— they were never friends. They're all in this."

"You don't know that." A hand of pearl took his, cool at first, then warmer. "But we're outnumbered. It's not worth the risk to stay and find out. Come on." She pulled gently, her voice compelling him to move, though he couldn't help a longing look back.

Had he heard Flam as well?

Edis

Stars knew she'd no words to heal him and only action offered any hope, so Edis kept them going at an almost run. Her light, or what she'd become, sent the scamps deep into their hiding places. If those behind them were honest folk, they'd come to no harm.

If they weren't—her glow dimmed and she made herself stop the thought before it became a—what—

A command. The little ones will do your bidding, sister, no matter the consequence.

Edis understood. An attack by what lived here would bring swift retribution and lasting fear. Explosives dropped down every airshaft, the apit destroyed. Even if the life down here survived it, there'd be no entrance for people like her to find. People who belonged.

Welcome.

Stars. The truth settled inside her with a strange wild satisfaction, as if she'd searched her entire life to find herself and had–as a part-olm pearl creature with a stone helmet head and purple eyes. Who saw with more than light and felt with more than touch and this was only the beginning. The dancer's promise meant more change to come and Edis found herself giddy with anticipation. She let out a deep, joyful laugh.

Running alongside, Roche gave her a startled look.

"I'll explain once we settle this. Meanwhile," Edis pointed ahead. "When we reach the apit, this is what we'll do."

And she told him.

Deter

Dema Qimirpik, leader of the Seventh Refuge of the Blessed Celestials, had forgotten his hat and looked to have donned his ornate pleated robes in his sleep or without servants.

Or in haste, Deter decided, reading the dema's haggard expression from his privileged vantage point, beside and behind where Calym Lapec sat at her table. The man appeared honestly distraught.

Changed things, if the dema cared this much about the truthteller. He should have asked more from Lapec to kill the boy. Deter dismissed the temptation to try for even more from the dema, to spare him. Lapec was admirably suspicious. No, he'd keep his word this time and make sure Jon took the blame. Let the dema curse his soul to the pits.

Lapec's tent wasn't a shelter. It was a throne room, plain and simple. Guane and Sild flanked the door flap, hands on the hilts of their swords. The town's five elders clustered like sheep to one side, muttering anxiously among themselves. Across from them were three more of Guane's ilk, Jon with them.

An unwelcome surprise—Deter hadn't planned on Jon knowing what was said and done here—but he'd manage.

The dema hurried to the table, giving perfunctory nods to acknowledge the respectful bows of those he passed. A thin young man and a servant with a sealed metal chest followed him.

"I've brought everything, Lensmaker Lapec," the dema announced hoarsely, stopping with his hands on the table. "We must try everything. Put it there, please."

There being the table. The dema made room. As the chest came down, Lapec half rose, then sank back. "Your grace," she protested.

Deter paid the chest greater attention.

The dema patted the lid. "We must try," he repeated. "The door that traps poor Roche—it may be we have the key." He opened the chest.

Having expected a display of gems or gold artifacts, Deter was disappointed to see an array of little leather bags, each with an inscribed metal tag. Soldier's luck. Why the dema had a collection of the worthless things he couldn't fathom. There'd be nothing worth stealing inside.

Selecting a bag at seeming random, the dema opened it and carefully shook the contents onto his palm.

A mummified fingertip, a sliver of ivory, and a crystal vial, its contents glinting silver. With a tiny curl of parchment that made it clear this was treasure after all.

These were spells–not the fakes peddled in markets across Ansnor but real magic.

Having spread the parchment with two fingers and scanning it, the dema made a disappointed tsk of tongue to teeth and stuffed the contents in their bag, tossing it carelessly aside. "Love spell. I've too many. But something here might do," he added, looking at Lapec as if she'd know.

The final piece of the puzzle snicked into place. Deter held in a smile. Lapec wasn't just a dealer in stolen property and smuggler. She acquired and sold magic tokens, the most lucrative business there was. If she'd sold these items to the dema, what might she have sold those with deeper pockets?

The pearl called Arra's Final Tear must be part of a spell. A priceless part, already with an eager buyer waiting. He'd get it back and—

"Who are you, sir?"

With a start, Deter realized he'd let greed distract him. He gave a quick bow. "Deter Elenyas, your grace. Once of the Ansnan border patrol."

As he'd hoped, the dema's face softened. "One of our very best, then. Welcome, Deter. It's good to have your help. Stars as my witness, this rescue may take all our efforts. This is Lenert, a friend of Roche." He drew forward the young man, who shot Lapec a hot glare before lowering his gaze to the table. The dema continued, "He tells me Roche has come up here every foursday since arriving last fall."

There was a question in that, a doubt. The dema might not be as guileless as he seemed.

"To hunt, yes. My apprentice wished to use his skills and, to my regret now, I encouraged him. I take full responsibility," Lapec said with admirable, if hardly believable contrition. "We suspect a cave-in." Her gesture included the elders. A second urged them to speak up and contribute.

When none did, her lips tightened.

A rebellion brewed. Was Lapec's hold on the town slipping? He'd find out–take the side offering the most advantage.

Lapec went on, "Our brave townsfolk have entered the mine through an airshaft, striving to reach the poor boy in time. I must warn you, dema, it's likely they'll find his corpse."

A message for him. Deter was to provide a corpse properly hammered by rock, to support her story. Two corpses, he decided cheerfully, to hide his own.

The dema looked shaken but resolute. "Then we must move with haste. Please, Calym. Which of these will open the door?"

Only Deter saw what happened next. Rising to her feet, Lapec made a show of choosing a bag from the chest, then palmed it, deftly switching it for one in her other hand. The bag from the chest disappeared on her person.

Untying the bag, she copied the dema and poured out the contents. The tokens were a claw from a mine scamp, a vial of purple sand, and a nugget of gold. "The spell requires two who have fought a bloody war," she announced, as if reading the strip of parchment. "How fortunate we have not only Deter Elenyas, but his partner, Jon Palyenor, with us. Jon, please come forward." She waved Deter to go and stand with Jon, who looked understandably dismayed and likely to ruin everything.

Deter put his hand on Jon's shoulder and said, with tears in his eyes and a husk to his voice, "Dema, we swear to find your young friend."

The elders rallied. The dema took their hands. Jon said something virtuous.

Deter caught Lapec's pursed little smile. Acknowledged it with loud and pious, "Stars willing," that was echoed by all.

Predictable, every one.

Thirteen: The Attackers

They ran and ran. Edis had him drink from the flask, refusing a share. Whether the olm's magic or hers, Roche found himself able to keep going.

Unless it was fear of a truth chasing him he couldn't bear–

There was a yell from behind. Someone had spotted Edis' light. The shout echoed down the now-inconvenient straightness of the main shaft, making it hard to judge distance. Did Disel wonder why the light moved away instead of toward them?

Or had Flam, always the quickest, realized Roche knew they weren't here to save him, that they'd come for the pearl—his friends, to betray him–

Edis stopped, beckoning Roche close. "We're almost there," she whispered, then said what chilled his blood. "I was right. We're being chased into an ambush. The door's been opened. Someone waits."

He didn't asked how she knew. Shrugging off his bow, he reached for an arrow.

Her hand shot out to prevent him. "I said you aren't to fight."

"Because you want to kill them."

Her lips curved up. "That Edis is gone. What I want is for you–truthteller, healer, and friend—to survive this. To have the future you dream."

It had the feel of a wish, like the magic of Jenn Nalynn, but Roche knew better than believe this time. They were trapped. About to die. As he obeyed, pulling the bow over his head, he couldn't help the bitterness in his voice. "How?"

Her smile widened and her skin glowed.

"With the olm's help."

Edis

Roche listened without comment to her plan, such as it was. Since much of it depended on what he couldn't see or hear, Edis was touched by his trust. "Is the pearl safe?" she finished.

He pressed his hand to his chest and nodded, looking miserable. "I don't want to leave you behind, Edis."

"You aren't. It's my choice to stay." Leaning forward, she pressed her lips to his forehead, then took his face in her hands. Their glow caught in his green eyes, the colour of verdant spring. The Verge had so many hues and colours, some she'd not even recognized. Edis vowed to find this green, to remind her of him. To remember who'd restored her trust in others. "What I am now and will be belongs here, not out there. I am more than content it be so."

Welcome.

"I'll tell them about you," Roche warned. "You know I will. I won't be able to help it."

She laughed gently. "Tell the whole truth, then. That Edis Donovar, a forgotten soldier, died from an arrow and a broken heart. That in this mine, you found strange and wondrous creatures who helped you and were kind, as well as those perilous. Never fear the truth, Roche Morrill. Stars know, it will set you free. Now.

Are you ready?"

He nodded, putting the moss from his cup inside his shirt, dosing its light.

Hers would betray them. She had to stop it, but how? This body hadn't come with lessons. Edis placed her palm on the rock wall and whispered, "How do I stop glowing?"

Don't breathe.

Gravel-growl being helpful? Before she could doubt, Edis held her breath, reassured when her light began to fade. First from her fingertips, then up her arms. Her torso dimmed and finally—

Take it away.

And back to giving orders. She found Roche's hand and caught it up in hers. Still here, that told him. While she didn't feel a need to breathe, best not waste what she had in her lungs on words.

After a moment, his hand tightened.

He'd seen it, too. A faint light from ahead.

The apit.

Roche

Roche had no idea what Edis thought the olm could do against armed assailants, if that's who awaited them. He'd no idea what he'd do, for that matter, but when she took his hand in the dark, his fear left him. Glimpsing a different, ominous light in the apit, his sanctuary, he discovered an anger inside him stronger than any he'd felt before.

They went together slowly, silently. Roche knew how to walk without sound, as did Edis, whatever her shape. When they reached the shaft opening, he realized the light wasn't from the moss, which had gone dark, or a lamp, but sunlight, streaming through where the door had been—

Ancestors Defiled and Despoiled, they'd cut down the tree!

He shook with rage. Would have rushed in and died if Edis hadn't restrained him.

And if the two waiting weren't arguing.

Deter

Lapec's spell had done its work, melting away the wood of the door and a good chunk of the stone supporting it, sending forth a smoke with a horrid cloying stench that had Deter cover his mouth with his arm, Jon doing the same, even as they ran through that cover, weapons drawn.

To find themselves in a cave of sorts, at least that's how it appeared, being dark, damp, and chill after the warmth of the day outside. Jon stood at his back, the pair turning in a long-practiced motion.

Deter halted, knife at the ready. "We're here first." There was a distant muttering. The people from town, the would-be rescuers, were closing in. They'd ruin everything if they arrived too soon. He took hold of Jon's sleeve. "Listen. It has to look like an accident."

Jon jerked back. "Stars. What are you talking about? We're here to save the boy."

Stars save him from idiots. "We're here, fool, to get the pearl and kill Edis. The boy can't be left as a witness."

"No. He's innocent. I won't touch him." The other took another step back, raising his bow and notching an arrow. "I won't let you."

Predictable. "You're right," Deter said, his expression full of regret. He lowered his blade. "It's wrong and we—" Whipping up his hand, he dove for the floor.

The knife buried itself in Jon's chest. With a gratifying look of surprise, he dropped his bow and fell to the ground.

Deter got to his feet, brushing dust from his coat. "If you want something—" A glint caught his eye and he whirled around.

A column of water rose from within a ring of stone, water that glowed brighter than the sun. He shielded his eyes, squinting to see. There was something in the water. Something that danced—with purple eyes and smiling lips, lips that pulled back to show teeth like daggers—

As Deter cried out, he felt a searing pain and looked down. An arrow's tip protruded from his gut, blood dripping from its tip, and it wasn't fair, it wasn't fair—

–and there was Edis, shaking her head in disappointment. She'd expected better of him.

She should have known better.

Predict–

Fourteen: The Friends

The well was dry as bone. The moss dark. Blood spread over his braided rug for the second time and Roche Morrill tended the one who lived, trying to ignore the one who didn't. "You heard him," he said, knowing Edis was close though he couldn't see her in the shadow. "You saw. He tried to protect me."

"Jon has a good heart," he heard her say. "A thick head, stars know, but a good heart. Give him the pearl. Tell him I forgave him before I died."

He didn't argue. Couldn't, after what he'd seen. How the olm had risen within a dazzling column of its water, how it had twisted and spun. A distraction allowing Jon to climb to his feet and stab his friend in the back.

There was no glory here. No happy tale of heroes. This was entirely different and Roche had no idea how it would end. Except for one thing. "He'll live." There was padding under the shirt. Jon hadn't trusted his so-called friend. Roche tucked the pearl in its wrap in one of Jon's pockets.

"To face his fate. Come back when you can, truthteller. I'd

like to know what happens next. And thank you." Her voice seemed to fade. "Be ready."

Startled, he looked up to find the shaft full of people. "Roche! Roche!" And all of them rushed toward him.

But Disel and Flam got there first, wrapping their arms around him, praising the stars he was safe and who were these men and what had happened and was he all right—

And as Roche gasped, the truth about to burst from him, Wibler the Great reached him and bent slowly to one knee, his eyes moist and mouth trembling. "Hush, hush. It's our turn, truthteller. We—" his gnarled hand swept around, encompassing the crowd filling the apit, their dusty faces serious and sure and several with tears "–will tell Dema Qimirpik the truth. We came fearing she meant to harm you, you who've done nothing but good. We came to end the lies."

And they shouted then, a loud and joyous noise that probably sent the mine scamps running and doubtless troubled the olm, who liked its quiet, but Roche had no heart to argue.

His arms being full of friends.

Fifteen: The Remembered

She waited. A week or a season, she wasn't sure, but time didn't weigh on her the way it had and Edis was content to listen to the olm tell her stories of the Verge. Stars knew she wasn't sure she believed them all, but she'd no where else to be.

Waiting, as she was.

The townsfolk rebuilt the door. Gravel-growl told her how to keep it closed, except to those with an invitation, and Roche Morrill came through it one day, because he did.

He had his pack and bow. Edis watched him prepare tea, the olm having refilled its well and willing, then sit to read letters.

Part way through the first, he paused and looked up. "Edis?"

She'd forgotten to breathe, while waiting. Stars. So she did, watching the light come from her fingers, her arms, and the rest.

"You're here!"

She hadn't left, but she understood. "As are you. I'm glad. What have I missed?" she asked him, as you did with friends, and curled beside him on the bench.

"Lapec and those who willingly took her orders were arrested and sent to prison in Mondir. You were right, the dema had an opinion, a very strong one." He grinned. "But it was decided by the people of the town. They'd looked the other way out of fear. They'd had enough."

Edis nodded. "And had a reason." She nudged him.

"And had a reason," he agreed, laughing, then turned serious. "Jon gave the dema the pearl. The olm was right to refuse it. The pearl was to be part of a spell to remove a person's will to live. The dema had it destroyed. Lapec refused to give up her buyer, but there are those searching. That magic was evil."

"As olms are not," she said, letting him know she understood at last. Edis stilled, but had to know. "What of Jon?"

"He confessed what he'd done to you. With no—no body—" When Roche hesitated, she waved him to continue. "I told how Jon saved me. The dema decreed he be brought to the refuge, to study and serve until the Celestials signal his penance is complete. Which really means earning the dema's good opinion," he added, Rhothan and truthful to a fault, but Edis didn't mind. "My friend Lenert says Jon seems at peace there, Edis. Even happy."

"I'm glad." And she was. "Jon earned that mercy. And you?"

"I've begun to study stoneworking but–I'll be leaving soon, to go to Mondir."

Edis wished she could blink. "Why?"

"To attend university. I'm going to be an engineer." He said the word with such pride, she hid a smile.

"What of your debt?"

Roche beamed. "That's the best part. The town gave Lapec's funds, what they could find of them, to her honest apprentices and staff to keep the workshop running. The rest went to scholarships. I got one. Disel too. I think Flam might." He turned to face her, her light sparkling in his green eyes. Or were those tears? "This is–I came to say goodbye. I'm afraid it will be forever. I'm afraid to go, thinking of you here. Unless—are you happy, here?"

"I am and will be happy, Roche."

And more. Being happy–having seen him again and learned what she needed to know, Edis was ready at last. Ready to join the dancer and claim her promise, whatever shape it gave her.

Roche nodded, then sighed. "I'll miss you." The olm rose, water glistening on its sides, then plunged like a fish, startling them both. "What's that about?"

Tell him, sister. With a hint of amusement.

Edis smiled. "Where I will be, the Verge, sits along the edge. Your Marrowdell is part of it. Where we are now, in this mine, is as well but these, the olm would remind me, are but tiny portions. The edge weaves throughout the world."

He sat straighter. "You mean—there might be a place like this in Mondir?"

"I'm sure of it," and she was. "Whenever you wish to see me, find the edge and call my name. You may," Edis added thoughtfully, "have to wait. I might be distracted." The Verge holding wonders beyond any dream.

Despite what she'd become, or perhaps because, Roche Morrill took her face in hands that to Edis felt oddly fragile. Pressed lips to her forehead she felt as overwarm, but the gesture was what counted and she smiled.

He smiled back, green eyes sparkling. "I will. I always tell the truth, you know."

Edis laughed, a song in her heart.

"I know."

Julie E. Czerneda - Fiction Publications 1997 to 2022

For detailed information on each title, visit www.czerneda.com.

Novels (published by DAW Books NY)

1997 *A Thousand Words for Stranger*

1998 *Beholder's Eye*

1999 *Ties of Power*

2000 *Changing Vision*

2001 *In the Company of Others*

2002 *To Trade the Stars*

2003 *Hidden in Sight*

2004 *Survival*

2005 *Migration*

2006 *Regeneration*

2007 *Reap the Wild Wind*

2008 *Riders of the Storm*

2009 *Rift in the Sky*

2013 *A Turn of Light*

2014 *A Play of Shadow*

2015 *This Gulf of Time and Stars*

2016 *The Gate to Futures Past*

2017 *To Guard Against the Dark*

2018 *Search Image*

2019 *The Gossamer Mage*

2020 *Mirage*

2021 *Spectrum*

2022 *To Each This World*

Short Fiction (*not in this collection)

1997 "First Contact, Inc." in *First Contact*, edited by Martin H. Greenberg and Larry Segriff, DAW Books NY

1998 "'Ware the Sleeper" in *Battle Magic*, edited by Martin H. Greenberg and Larry Segriff, DAW Books NY

1998 "Dear John" in *Odyssey Magazine*, Issue #6, edited by Liz Halliday, UK

1999 "Prospect Park" in *Packing Fraction*, edited by Julie E. Czerneda, Trifolium Books Toronto

2000* "The Passenger" in *Treachery & Treason*, edited by Laura Anne Gilman and Jennifer Heddle, ROC NY

2000* "Down on the Farm" in *Far Frontiers,* edited by Martin H. Greenberg and Larry Segriff, DAW Books NY

2000* "The Midas Spell" in *Spell Fantastic,* edited by Martin H. Greenberg and Larry Segriff, DAW Books NY

2001 "Left Foot on a Blind Man" in *Silicon Dreams*, edited by Martin H. Greenberg and Larry Segriff, DAW Books NY

2002* "Prism" in *30th Anniversary DAW Science Fiction,* edited by Betsy Wollheim and Sheila E. Gilbert, DAW Books NY

2003 "Bubbles and Boxes" in *New Voices in Science Fiction* edited by Mike Resnick, DAW Books NY

2004 "Birthday Jitters" in *Haunted Holidays*, edited by Martin H. Greenberg and Russell Davis, DAW Books NY

2004* "Brothers Bound" in *Sirius the Dog Star,* edited by Martin H. Greenberg and Alexander Potter, DAW Books NY

2004* "Out of China" in *ReVisions,* edited by Julie E. Czerneda and Isaac Szpindel, DAW Books NY

2004* "The Franchise" in *Space Stations*, edited by Martin H. Greenberg and John Helfers, DAW Books, NY

2005* "She's Such a Nasty Morsel" in *Women of War,* edited by Tanya Huff and Alexander Potter, DAW Books NY

2005 "Peel" in *In the Shadow of Evil*, edited by Martin H. Greenberg and John Helfers, DAW Books NY

2006* "What Lives in the Shallows Belongs to the Depths" in *Jim Baen's Universe,* edited by Eric Flint, Baen Books, NY

2006* "No Place Like Home" in *Forbidden Planets,* edited by Marvin Kaye, SFBC

2007* "A Touch of Blue" in *Heroes in Training,* edited by Martin H. Greenberg and Jim C. Hines, DAW Books NY

2007* "Ascent" in *Fate Fantastic,* edited by Martin H. Greenberg and Daniel M. Hoyt, DAW Books NY

2008* "Gossamer Mage: Intended Words" in *Jim Baen's Universe,* edited by Eric Flint, Baen Books, NY

2009* "The Forever Brotherhood" in *Campus Chills,* edited by Mark Leslie, Stark Publishing, Toronto

2012 "Water Remembers" in *Tales from the Emerald Serpent*, edited by R. Scott Taylor, Art of the Genre, California

2012* "Charity" in *When the Villain Comes Home,* edited by Gabrielle Harbowy and Ed Greenwood, Dragon Moon Press

2014* "Water Listens" in *A Knight in the Silk Purse,* Tales from the Emerald Serpent Volume 2, edited by R. Scott Taylor, Art of the Genre, California

2014 "A Taste for Murder" in *Solaris Rising 3*, edited by Ian Whates, Oxford, UK

2016* "Road Rage" in *all Hail Our Robot Conquerors,* edited by Patricia Bray and Joshua Palmatier, Zombies Need Brains, USA

2018* "Foster Earth" in *Amazing Stories,* Vol 76, Issue 1, Hillsboro, NH, USA

2018* "The Only Thing to Fear" DAW Books special epublication

2019* "A Dragon for William – a story of Night's Edge" DAW Books special epublication

2019 "Duck, Duck, Goose" in *Algorithmic Anxiety* NIXS Spring Issue #4, Amsterdam, Netherlands

2021* "Decay in Five Stages" in *Derelict,* edited by David B. Coe and Joshua Palmatier, Zombies Need Brains, USA

2022* "The Jade Jar of Slotch" in *Noir,* edited by David B. Coe and John Zakour, Zombies Need Brains, USA

2022* "Third Life" in *Life Beyond Us,* edited by Julie Nováková, European Astrobiology Institute and Laksa Media

2022 "A Pearl from the Dark" in Imaginings, curated and published by Julie E. Czerneda

Anthologies as Editor

1999 *Packing Fraction & Other Tales of Science and Imagination*,
    edited by Julie E. Czerneda, Trifolium Books, Toronto

1999 *No Limits: Developing Scientific Literacy Using Science
    Fiction*, with annotated stories from Packing Fraction, by
    Julie E. Czerneda, Trifolium Books, Toronto

2002 *Stardust*, Tales from the Wonder Zone, edited by Julie E.
    Czerneda, Trifolium Books, Toronto, with an introduction
    by Gregory Benford

2002 *Explorer*, Tales from the Wonder Zone, edited by Julie E.
    Czerneda, Trifolium Books, Toronto, with an introduction
    by C. J. Cherryh

2002 *Orbiter*, Tales from the Wonder Zone, edited by Julie E.
    Czerneda, Trifolium Books, Toronto, with an introduction
    by David Brin

2003 *Space Inc.*, edited by Julie E. Czerneda, DAW Books NY

2004 *ReVisions*, edited by Julie E. Czerneda and Isaac Szpindel,
    DAW Books NY

2004 *Odyssey*, Tales from the Wonder Zone, edited by Julie E.
    Czerneda, Trifolium Books, Toronto, with an introduction
    by Greg Bear

2004 *Summoned to Destiny*, Realms of Wonder, edited by Julie E.
    Czerneda, Fitzhenry & Whiteside, Toronto, with an
    introduction by Patricia McKillip

2005 *Fantastic Companions*, Realms of Wonder, edited by Julie E.
    Czerneda, Fitzhenry & Whiteside, Toronto, with an
    introduction by Kristen Britain

2006 *Mythspring*, Realms of Wonder, edited by Julie E. Czerneda
    and Genevieve Kierans, Red Deer Press (Fitzhenry &
    Whiteside), Toronto

2007 *Polaris - A Celebration of Polar Science*, Tales from the Wonder Zone, edited by Julie E. Czerneda, Fitzhenry & Whiteside, Toronto, with an introduction by International Polar Year Youth Steering Committee members, Amber Church and Tyler Kuhn

2007 *Under Cover of Darkness*, edited by Julie E. Czerneda and Jana Paniccia, DAW Books NY

2008 *Misspelled*, edited by Julie E. Czerneda, DAW Books NY

2009 *Ages of Wonder*, edited by Julie E. Czerneda and Rob St. Martin, DAW Books NY

2011 *Tesseracts Fifteen: A Case of Quite Curious Tales*, edited by Julie E. Czerneda and Susan MacGregor, Edge, Calgary

2017 *Nebula Awards Showcase 2017 The Year's Best Science Fiction and Fantasy Selected by the Science Fiction and Fantasy Writers of America*, edited by Julie E. Czerneda, PYR Amherst NY

2018 *The Clan Chronicles: Tales from Plexis*, edited by Julie E. Czerneda, DAW Books NY

About the Author

Canadian, biologist, award-winning author/editor, for the past 25 years Julie E. Czerneda has shared her curiosity about living things and optimism about life through her science fiction and fantasy, published by DAW Books, NY. In August, 2022, Julie was inducted into the CSFFA (Canadian Science Fiction and Fantasy) Hall of Fame for her achievements in the field.

The 20th anniversary edition of Julie's acclaimed SF novel, *In the Company of Others*, was released fall 2021 (Philip K. Dick Award finalist; winner 2002 Aurora for Best English Novel). Out now is Julie's 22nd novel, *Spectrum*, continuing Esen's misadventures in the Web Shifter's Library series, featuring all the weird biology one could ask. Her fantasy includes the Aurora winning novels, *The Gossamer Mage* and *A Turn of Light,* first in her Night's Edge series that continues in "Pearl". November 2022 sees the release of *To Each This World*, a standalone SF. Julie is represented by Sara Megibow, of KT Literary. Find more at www.czerneda.com

About the Artist/Designer

Roger Czerneda's love of photography began when he worked at his uncle's camera store. After obtaining a Bachelor of Science degree from the University of Waterloo, Roger worked as an environmental chemist and computer programmer, all the while continuing to develop his photographic and graphic design skills. By 1986, Roger grabbed his camera and computer and began life as a professional, first in film, and now totally digital. With Julie, he did contracts for several non-fiction publishers, including their company, Czerneda Publishing Inc. Roger's made the leap from commercial and industrial photography and design to also express himself as a visual artist, drawn to subjects in the real world that inspire the imagination or tell a story. Find more at www.photo.czerneda.com

About the Cover

The challenge of creating a cover to illustrate the wide variety of stories in Julie's collection took me deep into my own inventory. Over the years, I've amassed a wealth of photographs, many unique, and all of topics of special interest to me. I took the time to find images I felt worked together for this book, highlighting her themes of imagining and wonder. I used Photoshop to blend the images. Find me at a convention if you'd like to know more. I'll happily show you. – Roger Czerneda